mama dated Santa

A Novel By
AMY R. ANGUISH

Scrivenings
PRESS
Quench your thirst for story.
www.ScriveningsPress.com

Published by Scrivenings Press LLC
15 Lucky Lane
Morrilton, Arkansas 72110
https://ScriveningsPress.com

Printed in the United States of America

Paperback ISBN 978-1-64917-332-4

eBook ISBN 978-1-64917-333-1

Editors: Elena Hill and Linda Fulkerson

Cover by Linda Fulkerson, bookmarketinggraphics.com

All characters are fictional, and any resemblance to real people, either factual or historical, is purely coincidental.

For my mother-in-love, Carlynn. She loved all things Santa. And unknowingly dated a boy in college who grew up to BE Santa, inadvertently inspiring this story. We miss her every day.

Chapter One

"Aunt Tootie, aren't we going to go see Santa?"

Only Mark could make Trudy McNamara enter a toy store on Black Friday.

And he was barely enough force to bring her past the threshold. Maybe in a minute. After she swallowed the grief that practically drowned her around this time of year. It shouldn't be *her* bringing Mark.

"Of course, Mark. Sorry." Trudy forced a smile for the young boy.

But before she could take a step, the door bumped her from behind as other customers tried to come through. She'd stopped closer than she realized.

Any other day, she could've kept her equilibrium and the nudge at her back wouldn't have been a problem. Today she held the hand of her four-year-old nephew and wore new boots. On this slick linoleum floor, it was a rotten combination. Her widened step to keep from falling on Mark aimed her shoulder directly into the man walking toward them, his focus completely on the clipboard in his hands.

"*Oof!*"

"I'm so sorry." Trudy quickly straightened and stepped back, untangling her scarf from the pen that had been in the man's hand. "I seem to have caused a bit of a traffic hold-up."

"More like traffic accident." He jerked the pen from her fingers, pushed his glasses straight on his nose, and marched off without another word.

"Well, then. Bah humbug to him too." Trudy grinned at her nephew and motioned him on to the goal. Though, the idea of getting closer made her stomach curdle.

No. Truth be told, she wasn't in the Christmas spirit either. Hadn't been in five years. But she'd do anything for Mark. Even bring him to a toy store so he could talk to the man in the red suit.

A glance to the right showed Mr. Huffypants heading through a door marked *Office*. Must be a manager of some sort. Not very friendly. How could someone surrounded by toys and children all day be so grumpy? He proved it was possible. Or maybe he was having a rough day. One run-in with a man didn't show his full character, especially if he was as busy as he acted.

The glasses and stiff, button-down shirt gave a diligent and hard-working appearance. Nerds had a way of coming across as always doing something important, even if they weren't. She brushed that idea away too. That was just as judgmental as calling him Mr. Huffypants.

"Aunt Tootie, isn't that the most beautiful tree?" Mark tugged Trudy's hand, pulling her back to the reason they'd come.

She focused where he pointed ... and blinked.

The crooked artificial pine had branches angling in all directions. Three kinds of lights wound in and out of the greenery—two thirds of which flashed on and off in conflicting rhythms. Tinsel dripped in clumps. Old Styrofoam balls, whose silk thread had frayed, leaving gaps in the color covering the orbs, dangled from all the limbs that didn't already hold a plastic snowflake, and several flakes were missing points.

At the top, slightly leaning to the right, an old star with four of its five points still covered in silvery-blue garland, stood with as much state as possible. And from somewhere in the monstrosity, a tinny tune played, adding to the general cacophony of the toy store, yet conflicting with the "Jingle Bells" blaring from the speakers overhead.

None of this bothered Santa. He sat in a green wingback chair to the left of the tree, chuckling as he handed a squalling baby back to her mother. *This* was what everyone in town told her sister was a must-do? This was the best Temple, Texas, could offer?

"And who do we have here?" Santa's voice was jolly, full of the expected laughter. He motioned with his white-gloved hands for Mark to join him, and her nephew eagerly released her fingers to do so.

The line was non-existent. Not counting the pause in the doorway, they hadn't waited more than five minutes. Trudy had expected a snaking line across half the floor and then doubled back again. Maybe it was just early in the season. Although with today being Black Friday, most people were beginning their frenetic scurry to do all the Christmas things. For that matter, the store was relatively empty, considering it was Thanksgiving weekend.

Sale signs dotted the shelves, but no one had to push to reach the items. There were no mad scrambles for building sets, car tracks, video games, or the latest dolls to go with the movie releasing next week. Were the deals in this store pitiful compared to others, or was there a bigger problem?

Trudy shook her head and focused back on her nephew's conversation with the jolly elf. This shop wasn't her concern. When she returned to Austin in a few weeks, she could find businesses there who needed her services. For now, she was getting Mom settled in her new place and enjoying some time with family, including the precious boy in front of her.

"And I haven't been bad this year. Well, Mommy said sometimes I do bad things, but I don't mean to. Does that count?" Mark raised his eyebrows.

3

"That definitely counts." Santa nodded very seriously. "So, what's on your wish list this year?"

"I want my Nana and my Aunt Tootie to be happy again." Mark glanced her way.

Trudy swallowed a lump in her throat. Her suit of armor evidently had cracks. How had he seen through her smiles and laughter?

"Maybe Aunt Tootie needs to come tell me her wish list, huh?" Santa winked at her.

"Sure."

Santa returned his attention to Mark. "Anything else I can do for you?"

"I want a real firetruck that makes sirens and lights up and everything. Maybe even with a ladder and hose." Mark motioned with his hands to show how tall the toy should reach. "And a puppy."

"I can only bring puppies if your mommy and daddy sign the permission slip, okay? I'll talk to them about it between now and the big day. How's that sound?" Santa tickled Mark's side, sending a peal of giggles through the area, loud enough to drown out the awful music. "Want to take your picture now?"

They both grinned at the photographer, and then Mark gladly accepted the proffered candy cane. "Look Aunt Tootie!"

"Great, Mark." Trudy held her purse open. "Why don't you put it in here to save for after lunch, okay?"

"Don't you want to talk to Santa too?" Mark faced her, his head cocked to the side.

"I think he'd rather talk to the kids that are waiting right now, Mark-o. I can write him a letter, okay?"

Mark pointed behind her. "But Aunt Tootie, there aren't any other kids waiting."

Why couldn't this toy store be normal at this time of year? And Santa was no help, either, as his lips twitched with mirth behind that stupid beard of his.

"Come on. I'll go with you. He's really nice." Mark tugged her hand.

"Anything for Mark" was coming back to bite her. She followed him to the green chair, but there was no way she was sitting on some strange guy's knee. No way.

Santa held out a hand to shake. "Tootie?"

"Trudy McNamara, actually." She shrugged. "Mark couldn't pronounce *R*'s at first."

"Ah. Got it." Santa nodded. "McNamara, huh? You wouldn't happen to know a Connie, would you?"

"My mom's name is Connie. Do you know her?" Trudy frowned. Mom had only moved to town the week before.

"Well, I mean, Santa knows everyone, right?" Santa laughed. "But yes. Tell her ..." He glanced Mark's way and then back. "Tell her an old college friend, Paul Russo, says, 'Hi,' would you? He and I are ... *close*. I was real sad to hear about Derek."

Trudy swallowed again. These emotional boulders building in her throat were going to choke her before all was said and done. "Thanks. We all miss him."

"Miss him" was an understatement if ever she'd uttered one. But Santa didn't need to know how hard the last five years had been—especially around this time of year when the man who had made Christmas the best was no longer around.

"You be good, and maybe I'll find a way to fill your nephew's Christmas wish for you." Santa handed her a candy cane.

"Thanks."

Santa waved as Trudy tugged Mark to pull him away from the tree. "Merry Christmas!"

"Bye." Trudy couldn't wish anyone merry this time of year. Not when she didn't feel it herself. Would she ever be happy at Christmas again?

She stopped short as Mr. Huffypants stalked in front of them, heading the opposite way he'd come earlier. He didn't even glance up. Maybe the collision hadn't been completely her fault.

He paid so little attention, it was a wonder other customers weren't getting run into as well.

Something wasn't right. Had Nick dropped a page when he collided with that woman? He shook his head. No, she'd bumped into him. What had she been staring at before? The tree?

The Christmas area was definitely a ... sight. Last year the tree had been preserved in cling wrap for storage. Unfortunately, when Aunt Bett cleaned things out over the summer, the tree fell off the ledge, and chaos ensued. It lived on in the mess of the hastily-thrown-back-together monstrosity standing next to Uncle Paul. Nick made a mental note to have one of the teenage clerks work on that this afternoon before the season really picked up pace.

His eyes scanned the linoleum as he retraced his steps through the store. A jerky movement out of the corner of his eye alerted him to a second close call. By the scent of the perfume that wafted his way, it was the same woman. Go figure. Maybe if he avoided eye contact, she'd walk out of the store and not come back.

That was no way to bring in more money. And the store needed income. The fourth quarter was predicted to be the best fiscally, but his records weren't showing any evidence of it.

Ah. There. He leaned over and jerked the missing sheet out from under a rack of bikes. Maybe this would help his numbers match better.

He glanced out the door as he passed. The clumsy woman buckled her little boy in the back seat. Hopefully the straps on that booster seat were nice and tight. And she drove better than she walked.

Uncle Paul joined him at the window. "Know who that is?"

"No idea." Nick's fingers tightened around the paper in his hand. Inventory was supposed to have been completed an hour ago. Running behind made him antsy, but Paul was in Santa mode right now. That meant he was more concerned with keeping the children happy than worrying over deadlines or making sure records matched actual stock.

"Trudy McNamara. I dated her mom back in college."

"You dated someone besides Aunt Addie?" Nick frowned.

"Look, Buster." Uncle Paul poked Nick in the upper arm. "Just because you don't date doesn't mean the rest of us didn't go out with a few girls before we found the right one. And, honestly, I think Connie could've been the right one in another time. But we couldn't figure out how to make it work back then."

"Sounds romantic." Nick rolled his eyes. "And when would I have time to date? I'm too busy managing your store."

"You're working too hard. When your grandpa opened this store, he managed it by himself and still found time for family."

"Well, until the numbers look better, I'm going to have to keep working too hard." Nick waved the now-wrinkly paper in the air. "I've got to finish inventory so I can move on and get other things done this afternoon."

Paul followed him as he walked toward the office. "Why don't you hire someone to help you?"

"Do you know someone with skills who'd work for the pittance we could pay?" Nick shook his head. "I'm just hoping Christmas sales will pick up soon. This needs to be one of our best Christmases ever or we might not see another one here."

"Santa evidently has his work cut out for him this year." Paul turned a thoughtful expression back to the front door.

Nick shook his head and shut the office door behind him. His uncle might be taking this Santa thing too seriously. Either way, if these numbers didn't help the ones in the computer look better, the store might not make it through this holiday season, to say nothing of the next. He took a deep breath and slid down into his leather chair.

He input the last digit and hit enter. *Whew!* The numbers added up for one more week. Things were holding even today, but how long could they stay afloat? For this being the busiest shopping season, the store was practically empty. Did kids not want toys for Christmas anymore? What else could he do?

It might be time to call an owners' meeting. Getting knocked down by that woman earlier would've hurt less than letting his dad and uncles know they'd have to give up this business. Grandpa started it when they were just boys.

Uncle Paul better get busy on that Christmas miracle. Because that's what it was going to take.

Chapter Two

"Oh man. Look at this one." Trudy passed a crayon drawing to Mom across the piles in the floor.

Mom smiled as she studied the sketch. "You must've been about second grade or so when you drew this. Wasn't that the year you went ice skating?"

"I think so." Bitterness nudged at the edges of the memory's sweetness. Ice skating had been her idea. After that year Dad insisted it not make future lists. His ankles protested for three days.

"What's this?" Trudy's sister Katt waved a stack of envelopes from the room's other corner.

The paper crinkled as Mom accepted it and touched the writing on the front. "Letters."

"That's not Dad's handwriting, is it?" Katt leaned back against the wall.

"No." Mom smiled and pulled a note from one of the envelopes. "These are from Paul."

It'd been three days since Trudy took Mark to see Santa, and in that time, she'd forgotten the message she'd promised to pass on. "Paul? Paul Russo?"

Mom's head snapped up. "How did you know his last name?"

9

"I met him Friday." Trudy frowned. "He's playing Santa down at the toy store. When he heard my last name, he asked if I knew a Connie. He said you were in college together and was sad to hear about Dad."

Her mom laughed. "He *knew* me all right. We dated for a year and a half."

"Dated?" Trudy rocked back on her heels.

"Yes. Dated."

"You know—that thing where people go out, get to know each other, see if they're suitable for marriage?" Katt shook her head.

Trudy did the responsible thing and stuck her tongue out at her older sister. No need to be snarky.

"How are we just now finding out about Paul?" Katt pulled a photo from the same box. "Is this you and him?"

"Yes. That was at a banquet we attended together." Mom barked a short laugh and tapped the picture. "I'm glad those bangs are out of style. I worked so hard to get them looking just so back then."

"So, you're telling me you dated Santa?" Trudy still couldn't wrap her brain around this.

"He wasn't Santa back then." Mom passed the picture her way. "See?"

The early 80s styles were prominent in the snapshot. Paul was thinner in the photo than he was now, although no telling how thick he was in real life. Many Santas padded their bellies. And his hair had been a light brown instead of the white beard adorning his chin. A brown just a shade different from the chestnut color on Mr. Huffypants. Why was she thinking of *him* again?

"Wasn't Mark wanting a new toy the other day?" Mom's change in subject pulled Trudy back to the present.

"Doesn't Mark want a new toy *every* day?" Katt rolled her eyes. "I'm sure he does. But he doesn't need anything. Have you seen his room lately? I could start my own toy store."

"For Christmas. He mentioned wanting something when he was watching that show a few days ago. What was it?" Mom snapped her fingers.

"He was watching a show? What show?" Katt frowned. "You know he doesn't need that much screen time."

"Was it the fire truck?" Trudy passed the old picture back to her mom. "He asked Santa for one."

Mom nodded. "I wonder if they'd have one down at that toy store."

"Wanting to see what Paul looks like now?" Katt raised an eyebrow.

A shudder ran through Trudy, even though her sister joked. Mom couldn't possibly be interested in any other man than Dad, right? And definitely not one who liked to dress up as a fat guy in a red suit.

"He was a good friend. I'd love to say *hello* again."

"Please don't buy my child tons of toys just to have an excuse to check out your old flame." Katt tossed a wadded-up piece of paper at Mom.

"Would I do that?" Mom might feign innocence, but there was sure to be a stack of presents under the tree come Christmas, most with Mark's name on them.

"Mom, seriously."

"Okay, okay." Mom pushed off the floor and stretched. "I could use a break."

"We've only been at this for fifteen minutes." Trudy motioned to all the boxes. "If you hadn't moved all this junk, you wouldn't have to go through it now to figure out where to put it. This is what happens when you downsize your house but not your possessions."

When Mom left the house she'd been in for almost all of Trudy's twenty-three years, neither girl expected she would simply take everything to the new house without discarding some of it. Now they were stuck sorting boxes that could have been donated or purged beforehand.

11

"Yeah, yeah." Mom sat back down. "Who's the mom here anyway?"

Katt laughed. "So, should I be on the lookout for other old letters from boyfriends? Maybe one from the Easter bunny?"

"You're so funny." Mom tucked the letters into a *keep* box. "Just wait until you get a bit older. See how all your old boyfriends turn out."

"She had plenty. She could end up with one for every holiday." Trudy lobbed the tease across the room even though her heart wasn't completely in it. It was hard enough that Mom was moving past the life she'd built with Dad. Seeing her happy and thinking about other men was nigh on excruciating.

"Well, at least I was willing to go out and try to have a relationship. I'd much rather have lots of old boyfriends than never have any." Katt tossed something else toward Trudy, but Trudy ducked at the last second.

"Okay girls. Enough." The Mom voice was back. Even though they were both adults, the stern tone still came out every now and then when their mother thought they needed a reminder of how to behave.

They settled back into their rhythm, moving things from the boxes in front of them to either a *keep* stack, a trash bag, or a *donate* pile. No wonder her mom hadn't wanted to go through all these items before. There was a lot.

Containers were full of things their dad had stuck back at one time or another, most for an indiscernible reason. Computer parts, old CDs, pieces of paper with scribbles in a technical language no one in the house spoke anymore, and other paraphernalia from random jobs Dad had worked through the years would probably all be tossed.

The way Mom talked a little while ago, it was as if they were tossing Dad out too. Sure, he was gone. Nothing could change that or bring him back. The heart attack almost five years ago hadn't killed him, but the car accident it caused had. And the circumstances couldn't be reversed. But did they have to move on so completely?

"I'm sorry I can't give you better news. Especially this time of year. But there's no other way to say it. We can't afford another year like this." Nick leaned over the conference table and met the eyes of his dad and two uncles, trying to drive home the situation's gravity.

"We can't close." Dad pounded his fist lightly on the stack of figures before him. "We can't. I won't see Dad's hard work go down the drain like that."

"Nick's not saying he wants to close the store, James." Paul patted his brother's shoulder. "He simply wants us to know the truth of the situation. And the truth is, we need more customers."

"Have you tried putting out ads?" Uncle Andy flipped his paper's edges with one hand while stroking his beard with the other. "Newspaper ads used to help."

"We've run various ads, including one for Black Friday. We have notices up all over the place about our Santa, which usually brings more people." Nick shook his head. "But it's not working this year. If anything, we're getting less traffic."

"No offense to you, Paul." Dad chuckled. "I'm sure it's not your Santa."

"See if you make the nice list this year." Paul shook a finger at him, but mirth danced in his eyes. "We can turn things around. We only need some fresh ideas. Tons of other small businesses in town are being revitalized and brought back to life. This is a great era for Temple."

"I'm open to new ideas. But where are we going to find them?" Nick ran a hand through his hair. His mother would cringe, because it always left strands sticking up every which way, but he was past caring. His uncles and dad had hired him to run this store for them, and instead he was letting them down, losing all the hard work they and their dad had put into the Emporium over the last four decades.

"There's got to be a way." Paul tapped a pencil eraser against his stack. "I'm praying about it. It's too early to give up the fight. I mean, a herd of last-minute Christmas shoppers could turn things around, and this will all be a moot point."

"They'd have to buy almost all our inventory to make a dent in the numbers. We don't just need holiday shoppers. We need them all year long. Sure, that would help us stay in the black this year, but what about next year ... or the next?" Nick paced the length of the room. It wasn't long enough, only five steps each way.

"There aren't any other toy stores in town, right? We're the only one?" Andy scratched his head.

"The big box stores carry a bunch of everything. But no other places have *only* toys." Nick stopped and tapped his fingers against his thigh. "Our competition is probably online."

"So, how's our website doing?" Dad scribbled notes along the margins of the pages Nick had carefully prepared last night.

"I don't know. I hardly have time to look at it, to say nothing of updating things. I have something on there about Santa. And a list of our specials each week this month." Nick paced again.

"Someone to update the internet site would probably help more than anything, right? Aren't we supposed to be on all that social media now?" Paul leaned back and patted his belly, a bit slimmer out of his red suit.

"Yes, but I don't have time. I'm too busy trying to keep up with the brick-and-mortar part of our store."

"Our store isn't made of brick." Andy frowned. "Maybe that's your problem." Andy was the oldest of the three brothers and not always up on the current terminology.

"It's just a phrase. I meant the physical store itself instead of its online presence." Nick sighed. "Feel free to do some research

14

or try any ideas you might have as long as they're not outrageous or expensive. I know how much this place means to you all."

There was nothing else Nick had to say, so he gathered his things and headed back to his office, leaving the brothers discussing ... or at least talking in circles. He held little hope they'd come up with anything new.

They'd taken over when Grandpa Russo retired. When Nick graduated from college five years ago, he'd been granted the manager position. He'd discovered not much had changed since Grandpa started selling toys here forty years earlier. Nick updated things as much as he knew how, but his two marketing courses hadn't prepared him for a mess like this. He'd majored in accounting and business, thinking those subjects would be more helpful.

"How do you feel about this place?"

The question caught Nick off guard. He turned from his computer to face Dad, who leaned in the doorway. Nick shrugged.

"It doesn't seem like you really love this store the way your grandpa did." Dad moved a pile and slid into the chair in front of Nick's desk.

"I don't know that I *feel* anything more than loyalty to this place. Grandpa was passionate, but I never understood his zeal for toys. I do want to make it work to carry on his legacy."

"He wouldn't have wanted it to become a burden though." Dad leaned back and crossed one leg over the other. "And he wasn't passionate about the toys so much as he was about making children happy. There was nothing he loved more than God and your grandma, but seeing a child's face light up with joy came a close third. That's why he wanted to own a toy store."

What could Nick say to that? Sure, it was fun to make a kid happy, but he had also witnessed children throwing fits, screaming until they got whatever they wanted, or getting tugged around by their moms for walking too slow. Too often families had to tell their children, 'No.' Those weren't as much fun as the first part. How had his grandfather felt about that?

"Mom wants to know if you're bringing anyone to Christmas dinner." Dad glanced around the office instead of meeting Nick's eyes.

"Not planning on it." Nick tapped his pen against his desk. "Any reason?"

"She mentioned someone's daughter who wasn't married and ... short story is, the moms think you two would be just perfect for each other." Dad smirked. "I told her you're a grown man who can make decisions for yourself."

"Thanks. Can you also tell her to quit worrying about me?" Nick ran his fingers through his hair again. "I'm doing okay. Maybe I'll settle down someday, but I want to have a way to provide for a girl. And right now ..."

"I know. And I feel like this is partly my fault." Dad blew out a deep breath. "When you took over as manager, all of us stepped into semi-retirement as though it were the best thing ever. We forgot the part about it being *semi-* and left you to deal with a lot of this alone. That's not how it should've gone down."

"I'm the manager. I'm supposed to be able to manage the store so you don't have to worry about it."

"But you're also my son. And this store is still one third mine. So, I'm going to do all I can to help you pull it back into shape."

"Thanks, Dad."

"You bet." Dad stood and brushed off his pants. "I better get home and give your mom the bad news."

Nick frowned. "You're going to tell her the store is in the red?"

"No. I'm going to tell her you want her to butt out of your love life." Dad winked.

Nick shook his head. One more worry in his life. Just what he needed. Sure, it wasn't a huge problem to have a mom who wanted to set him up with a friend's daughter, but if he wanted a date, he could get his own. Couldn't he? It'd been a while since he'd even tried.

If he were going to look for someone, she'd have to be level-headed, understanding of his long hours, and maybe even a blonde. A memory of a brunette girl tugging a little boy through the store three days before ran through his head, the scent of her floral perfume clinging to his thoughts. Why had she popped up in these musings? She was nothing like what he wanted.

He blinked a few times before opening their website. Was there anything else he could do to make it bring in customers? Because unless they saved this store, he couldn't afford to date anyone. Not even absent-minded klutzes who wore flowery perfume.

Chapter Three

" I can't believe you're dragging me with you to see Santa." Trudy hiked her purse strap higher on her shoulder. "This is ridiculous."

"I just want to say, 'Hi.'" Mom pushed open the toy store doors.

Trudy peeked inside before stepping through, making sure no one with a clipboard was in collision range. The coast was clear, so she followed her mother. Her gaze landed on the tree, and she raised an eyebrow. It wasn't as pitiful today. Granted, it was still sad, but at least the branches seemed to be in the right slots now, so the shape was more natural.

In her decoration perusal, Trudy missed Mom pausing two steps ahead. For the second time in a week, she walked into someone. Trudy straightened and nudged Mom's shoulder. "What'd you stop for?"

"There's a line. I should have expected ..." Mom motioned toward the four families waiting to see Santa. "But somehow, I forgot. Now what? I can't stand in line. We didn't bring Mark as an excuse."

"He's already talked to Santa once." Trudy shook her head. Considering this was Mom's idea in the first place, she sure was flustered. "Let's go see if they have that toy for Mark while we wait. If it's like the other day, things will slow down in a bit."

"Good idea." Her mother spun and then froze again. "Which way do you think it'll be?"

Trudy glanced around more fully than she had the last time she'd been here. "*Hmm*. Not many signs, are there?"

"Okay. Let's just wander until we find what we're looking for." Mom meandered toward the back of the store, avoiding the Santa setup. Trudy followed, glancing down aisles. Games and puzzles. Baby toys. Dolls. Toys for playing house. Building sets. Surely, they were getting closer. Super heroes. *Ah. Vehicles.*

"Here, Mom. Let's try this aisle." Trudy motioned toward a rack of metal cars and the tracks to go with them.

"Goodness there are a lot of different firetrucks." Mom ran her finger down the shelves, checking prices and all the extras the boxes claimed each model had. Sirens. Working ladders. Squirted real water. Nothing without a bell or whistle.

"He mentioned a siren and ladder. But keep in mind that Katt has to live with whatever you buy. And she might not be as thrilled with all the noises and lights." Trudy leaned closer to try and see what made a style near the top shelf special. Were the lights not working? It wasn't very bright in here.

The bulbs glowed as hard as they could, but the shine didn't make it past the middle shelves, and the fixtures weren't sunny to begin with. This place would be happier and could sell more if they'd change those out.

Trudy took note of other things around her. No displays. Everything was packaged tightly away, no test runs allowed.

"I'm going to look around some more, Mom." Trudy wandered on, curious about the rest of this place.

"Sure, hon." Mom waved her off without even looking up from all the options.

This place didn't exude the happiness a person might expect in a toy store. Trudy studied each aisle, and each time came away wanting more. The shelves were almost sterile, boring, despite the fun encapsulated in the boxes. The music was Christmas-y, but the joy of the tunes couldn't penetrate the gloominess everywhere else. Nothing but grays and off-whites and blacks. Only the toys themselves had bright colors.

"*Oof!*" Trudy turned a corner and ran into someone—again.

"Seriously?" Mr. Huffypants himself straightened his glasses and stepped back. "Is it physically impossible for you to walk through here without running me over?"

"You think I did that on purpose?" Trudy crossed her arms. "If I wanted to run into a guy to catch his attention, it definitely wouldn't be someone like *you*."

His shirt was grey with light blue stripes today. His khakis had creases down the front that could only come from an iron. The only thing out of place on him was his hair, which stood up in all sorts of crazy ways, waving at her like the only friendly thing about him. What did he do? Run his fingers through it over and over again?

What would it feel like to run her fingers through his hair? Where had that rebellious notion come from? Didn't it negate exactly what she'd just said?

"Excuse me, then. Please, carry on with whatever you were doing that was so all-fired important that it kept your attention from such mundane details as noticing other people around." He held out his arm in a gesture to continue walking.

Trudy forced her jaw to relax ... at least a little. This guy must work here—he definitely fit the unwelcoming atmosphere. But that didn't mean she had to give in to the ugly retorts wanting to escape her own lips and tell him exactly what she thought of his store.

"I'm actually going this way." She turned on her heel to walk in the opposite direction she'd been wandering earlier.

"Which is why you ran into me when I was coming from that direction?" He hooked a thumb over his shoulder.

"I didn't mean to run into you." She huffed out a sigh. "Either time. And the other day, you were as much to blame as I was.

You had your eyes fixed on that clipboard instead of where you were headed."

"I wasn't expecting someone to go from a complete stop to moving at ninety miles an hour in a split second right as I passed her."

She brushed a strand of hair away from her cheek where it had escaped her braid. "Obviously, you've never had a nephew tugging you along then."

"No. I don't have nephews." He straightened. "Your nephew?"

"What? You thought he was my son?" She ran a hand down her denim skirt. "No. I'm not old enough—I mean, I *am* old enough, but ... He's my older sister's little boy. I'm not married. Not even seeing anyone."

And why on earth had she added in that last part? He didn't need to know—or probably even care—about the state of her love life.

What was that look that crossed his face? It was only there for a split second. Then his mask was back in place, frustration and stress settling into his features as if they were right at home.

"Trudy!" Mom's voice had her turning on her heel again.

Santa followed Mom at a clip faster than she expected from someone so large. He grinned from ear to ear and waved. Was the motion for her or the man behind her?

"We've just been talking and came up with the best plan." Mom grasped Trudy's arm and squeezed. "Paul here is one of the owners of the store and is looking to hire someone to help revamp it and give it new life. I told him you were perfect for the job."

"You *what?*"

Trudy glanced over her shoulder. Mr. Huffypants had said the exact same thing at the same time she had.

His look of incredulity must be mirrored in her own expression, but she couldn't think about that now. Other things were at stake. Like the fact that she wasn't planning to stay here that long.

"Mom, I'm not looking for a job in Temple. I live in Austin."

"It's just for a little while. And you mentioned staying here until after Christmas." Her mom flipped her hand back and forth in the air as if waving away a pesky mosquito.

"Because I was joking it would take us that long to go through all your boxes." Trudy pressed her fingers against her pounding forehead.

"Trudy, just hear Paul out. I really think you're exactly what he's looking for."

Nick needed to hear his uncle out too. He specifically remembered telling him they couldn't afford to hire anyone right now. Definitely not someone who couldn't even walk through a store without running into the manager ... and then acted like it was his fault instead of hers.

"Temple is really being revitalized right now. Stores left and right are updating and coming back to life after being in slumps for years—especially independently owned stores. My brothers and I are looking for someone who can introduce innovative ideas—bring new life to the Emporium. Your mom tells me you have the skills we need." His uncle sure trusted this lady Nick had never seen before.

"Uncle Paul, a word?" Nick motioned his head to the side. Maybe he could quickly talk some sense into his uncle before this situation worsened.

"Excuse us just one moment, won't you, Connie?" Paul squeezed the lady's hand and followed Nick down the dress-up clothes aisle. "What's wrong, Nick? You said yourself we needed fresh ideas."

"I told you we couldn't afford to pay someone what they'd deserve for such ideas." Nick thrust his fingers through his hair. *Ugh*. Every strand stuck straight up. How messy had it been earlier? So much for making any kind of good first impression. Or second impression. Not that he wanted to impress Trudy.

"I'll pay her salary from my own bank account. Don't worry about that." Paul turned.

"Uncle Paul." Nick caught his sleeve and waited until his uncle faced him once more. "Why are you so sure *she's* the one we need? How do you even know these people?"

"Remember what I told you the other day? I dated Connie for a year and a half in college. Even though I haven't seen her since then doesn't mean I don't know her anymore." Paul's smile reached all the way to his ears. "And if Trudy is anything like her mom, she's *exactly* what we need."

Something in Paul's statement sent Nick's heart into a staccato rhythm. Was there more than one meaning to those words? He didn't have time to find out, because Paul was already back to the women. Nick took a steadying breath and followed. No point in staying here and having no say in the matter. If he had to work with this klutz, he wanted to be sure the terms were clear.

"Okay. Let's get down to business and see if you're amenable to helping me." Paul rubbed his hands together.

"Shouldn't you be talking to little kids right now?" Nick pointed back toward the Santa station.

"I put up a sign that said I'd be back in fifteen minutes. So, let's talk fast." Paul turned to Trudy again.

"I'm sorry. I'm really not interested. I only came up here to help Mom get settled in her new house. I have a roommate in Austin, and several job leads there." Trudy shot a dirty look at her mom—again.

"You wouldn't be working fulltime." Her mom piped in. "Paul said it would be a 'when-you-could' basis. He knows it's the holidays. And that you're helping me. But he figured maybe you'd have a few spare hours each day to help them implement some new ideas. Maybe update their website. A few things like that."

"I can't exactly snap my fingers and update a website." Trudy snapped, adding emphasis to her words. "It takes time. Everything has to make sense and be easy to navigate. And I don't know what kind of ideas he's looking for in here either. I know it needs help, but why me?"

Paul pointed at Connie. "Your mom said you majored in design."

"Yes. But this is bigger than design, isn't it? Sounds like you need to change things to bring in more money." Trudy sent a glance Nick's way.

Had she heard his conversation with Uncle Paul?

"I'm not going to lie. The store needs help." Paul shook his head. "My brothers and I had no head for business, so we simply kept doing what our father had done. Since Nick started here, he's been fighting basically to keep things afloat. And done a good job. But we need more."

"How about you?" Trudy directed the question to Nick. "Thoughts? Feelings?"

"Me? I'm just the manager. I take orders from Uncle Paul, Uncle Andy, and Dad." Nick shrugged, caught off guard by her question. Why did she care how he felt?

"You said this place needs help too. What do you mean?" Paul leaned toward Trudy, as if ready to soak in whatever she might say.

"Everything is dark and dingy. The place doesn't come across as joyful. It's hard to find things. There are no signs to tell customers where dolls are versus blocks. Your Christmas display is awful. And your manager keeps running into me." Trudy ticked each point off on her fingers, a gleam in her eye as she spouted the last one.

Paul raised an eyebrow Nick's way. "Running into you?"

"My fault as much as his." Trudy held up her hands with a grin. "Neither of us was paying attention."

"Speak for yourself." Nick muttered.

"I usually do." Trudy winked at him.

The nerve!

"And I agree your website needs work. I tried to find out when I could bring Mark to see Santa and couldn't find anything. I finally asked the neighbors, who recommended this place."

"Will you at least help us with that, then?" Paul asked. "I promise to pay whatever you quote, even if it's double due to the holidays."

"I don't care about that." She waved her hand in the air.

She didn't? Nick would've pegged her as the type to soak up this time of year and relish every moment, considering she'd brought her nephew in to see Santa the day after Thanksgiving. Had something set her against Christmas? Surely not the stress of meeting financial deadlines that had hardened his own heart toward it.

"Let me think about it. If I can swing it, I'll stop by tomorrow to work out details."

"Great." Paul grabbed her hand and pumped it up and down. "See you tomorrow, then."

Trudy shook her head. "I said I'd think about it."

"I know. But I can tell a Christmas miracle when it walks in my store." Paul winked.

"I'm not a Christmas miracle or any other." Trudy shook her head. "If anything, I'm probably bad luck around the holidays."

"How can anyone who helped me find Connie again be bad luck?"

Trudy took a step back.

She looked warily from Uncle Paul to her mom and back. Were they thinking the same thing?

No way.

Chapter Four

"What am I doing?" For the third time in a week, Trudy stood outside Russos' Toy Emporium and readied herself to enter.

She hadn't wanted to accept Paul's job offer. Had no intention of doing so. But one thing kept running through her head, urging her to do it anyway. Mr. Huffypants didn't want her to either.

And that bothered her more than she cared to admit. After all, what had she ever done to him to provoke his animosity? Nothing but bump into him a few times—his fault as much as hers.

If she were honest, she should probably quit referring to him that way, even in her head. Now that they'd be working together, it was sure to slip out. But the name was so appropriate.

"No time like the present." She squared her shoulders and pulled the door handle. "Ready or not, Nick, here I come."

Over her shoulder hung a bag full of a projects already approved by Paul. She had a niggling suspicion Nick would protest, but that only motivated her more. Now, where to find the grumpy manager?

Paul waved from his Santa chair but was in the middle of

seeing some children and couldn't help her beard the dragon. She glanced over at the office door, but it stood wide and the room was dark. Nick must be on the floor somewhere. Paul motioned to her right, so she set off that way.

In the back corner of the store, past the coloring books and art supplies, she discovered a small, unexpected oasis. Hip-high bookshelves sectioned off the area, with a multi-hued rug and some beanbags and tables scattered throughout. Books were stacked or standing in every available space, just begging to be taken on an adventure. The outside wall sported a window, letting in more natural light, making this a perfect spot for reading and playing. Nick crouched, his back to her, rearranging some shelves of fantasy novels.

She paused for a moment, soaking it all in. If they could capture this atmosphere and carry it throughout the whole store, shoppers would come in hoards. *This* was what the Emporium needed. *This* was what she wanted to bring in. Would Nick agree? Who set up this space? Surely not him.

"Hi."

Her one-word greeting caused him to stumble, and he toppled over onto his bottom, taking four paperbacks with him.

"*Oops.*"

"What is it about you that makes me end up like this?" He dusted off his trousers as he stood, then neatly stacked the books back in place. "And why are you here again?"

"Your Uncle Paul talked me into helping after all." She purposely left out the part about her desire to prove herself to Nick, make him believe she was more than an airhead. "So, I came to scope out what needed to be done and what's available and talk to you about the website and social media."

He raised an eyebrow and folded his arms across his chest. "And if I tell you I don't have time to help you with all that?"

"Then I'll probably just assume I have free rein to do whatever I deem necessary and will start working immediately." Two could play this game. "Besides, if you were so busy, you wouldn't be straightening merchandise. You have other people who can do that."

"Oh. You know this store so well already, huh?"

"No. But I've worked in retail. I know how these places function." She shifted her bag straps to ease the weight on her shoulder. "This area is amazing, by the way. Why doesn't the rest of the store look like this?"

"Because Aunt Addie passed away before she could do more." Nick brushed past her, striding toward the front.

"Nick, wait." Trudy hurried to catch up to him. "I'm sorry." She tugged at his sleeve. "I meant it as a compliment to the book section. I didn't mean to tweak a sore spot."

He remained stiff but nodded. "What exactly do you need to see? If you want to look around the store, feel free. I obviously have no control over it."

"Your uncle wanted you to walk me through, show me all of it." Trudy shrugged. "He said you know this place better than anyone else. Maybe you can explain to me the reason behind things being where they are. Or just be there for me to bounce ideas off of as we walk so I can get a feel for what you want to happen versus what we can really do."

Nick released a long breath. "And how long is this going to take?"

"Depends. How long will you stand here trying to get out of it?" Trudy shifted her bag again. "Anywhere I can set this down? I'll use my tablet to take notes and pictures."

"Sure. Come on." He motioned her toward the office. "What's in that thing anyway?"

"Peel and stick tiles and lightbulbs."

He stopped so quickly she had no choice but to walk into him.

"Okay, that one really was your fault." She poked him in the shoulder.

"You already bought things to make changes? Without running it by me?" His voice drew the glance of several customers, and she sent them a smile she hoped was reassuring.

"Paul and I talked last night. He asked me what I would change. I told him we needed to brighten things up. It's too dull in here. You don't have front windows so no natural light, but they make these lightbulbs now that are really close. If we exchange all the installed ones with these, things will appear happier. Less dingy. And the floor is no longer white. So, my idea —at least on the main pathways—is to scatter multi-colored tiles in a pattern. It will make the store more cheerful."

"I suppose you also want to paint everything? How about we just go ahead and knock out part of the walls to put in more windows? Or we could just take everything off the shelves and pile it in the middle like a big ball pit. That would be much more fun than having things organized and readily available to grab." The sarcasm in his voice was nasty. And unnecessary. Did he want to save this store or not?

"Look, if you don't like these ideas, we can take it up with your Uncle Paul. But he's already paid for these supplies, so you might as well let me show you how it would look before you turn your nose up at them." Trudy pushed past him.

"Hang on. I need to rearrange a few things so you'll have room in there too." He stopped her as she reached the door.

He flipped the light on, illuminating the tiny space, barely large enough to hold the two desks, three filing cabinets, and a small coffee maker. His space, obvious by the name placard, was toward the back of the room, laptop open on its surface, neat stacks of papers in various piles, and a cup of pens and large calendar. No pictures or personalized touches were anywhere to be found.

The second spot was stacked with old ads, catalogs, receipts, and various other items that could probably be either tossed or filed. Nick wavered as he reached for the piles. Due to the cramped and crowded area, there was no other place they could go without being sorted into the home they belonged. He dashed a hand through his hair, sending the strands in all directions.

"It's okay. For now, I just need to set my bag down. We'll deal with that later. Or I can probably do a lot of work from my mom's house." She caught his arm before he mussed his tresses even more. "Let me grab my tablet, and we'll do a walkthrough."

How was she so calm? Why was she even here? She had sworn she didn't want to work here. And yet, here she was, barging through Nick's life again, jumbling everything up. He would have a long talk with Uncle Paul later. Especially about keeping secrets like the fact that Trudy had accepted the position Paul basically thrust upon her yesterday.

Nick took a deep breath and then motioned her ahead of him into what had formerly been his domain. Apparently, Uncle Paul had other ideas about that. Sure. The store needed help. There was no denying that. But did it need a complete overhaul? That's what it sounded like Trudy wanted.

"Something else I really think would help are signs to direct people where certain toys are located. You already have them grouped into sections like dolls or blocks or vehicles, etcetera, but people still have to walk around until they find the right aisle. Signs would make it easier to know which way they need to go and maybe lower some frustration for shoppers." She waved her hand in the air as if to conjure the signage into existence with her finger.

"But isn't it better if they have to walk around some? Then they might find something else they want to buy." He didn't mean to be so argumentative. It was a valid point. But he refused to agree to so many immediate changes. Maybe because even such simple ideas as what she'd already thrown out hadn't come from him.

"They'd probably still have to walk around some. But I know

when I was trying to help my mom find the firetruck for my nephew yesterday, it was totally annoying not to even know which way to start out." She lifted a shoulder. "Just a suggestion. When customers know they can find exactly what they're looking for as quickly as possible, they're more likely to come back."

"And remind me again why you're the be-all and end-all of knowledge on things like this?" Nick fisted his hands and then forced them to relax again.

"I'm not. But I do have a double major in design and marketing. And a minor in business." She flipped her brown hair over her shoulder. "So, I'm not the worst person to ask, either."

Oh, how he wished he could argue with that. But she was right. Her majors put her at an advantage over him in this situation. Might as well suck it up and make the best of this interim.

"You've already walked through the whole store." Nick pointed to all the shelves. "What exactly are you needing to see more than that?"

"I'm not completely sure. I just know we need more ... *something* in here. It's too boring."

"Boring?" Nick dashed his hand through his hair. "How can a toy store be boring?"

"I don't know. But can't you feel it? It's almost like there are signs saying, 'Don't touch!'" Trudy walked down an aisle and pulled a doll off the shelf. "Does she look like she's wanting to be played with?"

"Of course. She's a doll." He lifted the box from her hands and set it back where it belonged.

She waved her finger in his face. "Do you see what you just did there?"

"What?"

"You can't stand to have anything out of place, can you? Everything has to be lined up at perfect ninety-degree angles on the shelves, nothing out where it can be played with, no clutter, no jumbles. It's ... sterile."

He grabbed her finger to keep it from poking him in the nose. "It's not sterile. It's neat. Tidy."

"It's boring." She jerked her hand away and started walking again.

"You said that already. But I still don't believe you."

"I'm surprised you let them put that tree up in your store. It's not your style at all."

She had him there. "We've always had it. But I'm not in charge of the Christmas wonderland. Uncle Paul is."

They'd reached the back of the store, and she pointed down the hallway to the back door. "What's that?"

"There's bathrooms, a storage room, a room that's become a catchall, and a conference room." He dismissed it. "And a back door that leads to the employee parking."

"There's a room back here?" She headed toward the dim corridor.

"I just told you what rooms were back here." He huffed as she opened a door on the right. "What are you looking for?"

"This." She leaned against the doorframe and smiled.

"What? The catchall room?"

"Can't you see the possibilities?" She motioned around the area.

Boxes stood helter-skelter, stacked in various heights. Old holiday decorations, advertisements that were no longer valid, overflow from the storage area, and who knew what else covered every inch. All he saw was a mess.

"The lighting is great, with that window. We could paint the walls. Put in some tables. Ooh! What if we brought in a magician to do a show? Or a balloon artist? Or brought in authors to read their books?" She practically bounced on her toes.

"Where?" He couldn't picture anything but the disaster in front of him.

"Here, Silly. Sure, we'd need to clean it out, but that's doable."

"And how would we afford the magician and balloon artist and all these other people?" He crossed his arms.

"Well, first find out if they'd require payment, or you can look for someone who might need a place to do a few shows to get their name out and get some practice, some recognition. You can do a trial and see if you make more sales when they're here. It might turn out to be profitable for both of you."

"I'm still not sure."

"Well, keep thinking about it, but it's perfect. This space is being wasted as it is. You could be doing so much more." She flipped the light back off and closed the door again. "Come on. Let's go look at your website and see what we can do with it until closing. Then, we can start changing out light bulbs and sticking down tiles."

She was like a whirlwind, running rampage through his territory. He settled in his chair, pulled up the laptop and opened the website for her. She hovered, her light floral perfume wafting over him, her hair brushing against his arm every now and then. Would she end up wreaking havoc on more than the store? Surely her ideas could be implemented in less than a week. Then she could go back to whatever it was she did in Austin and he could return to his nice, safe, "boring" life, right? Isn't that what he wanted?

Chapter Five

W hy had Trudy considered this a good idea? She took shallow breaths through her mouth as she sponged off yet another square on the floor with her ammonia solution. The wax had to be removed before the new tiles could be stuck down. Nick was somewhere closer to the back of the store, changing lightbulbs. This left her working in half-light, hoping she got enough of the wax up to secure the new colored pieces.

She ran the back of her arm across her forehead and surveyed what she'd already accomplished. Half the main path now had red, blue, and yellow squares scattered amid the white. It broke up the monotony and added a playfulness to the floor. She nodded, took another breath, and moved to the next spot. Her goal was to finish this stretch tonight. She could work on more tomorrow. Assuming Nick let her come back. Did he approve of this change?

And why did it matter so much to her what Nick thought? Paul was the one who'd hired her and paid her salary. He was who she should be concerned with impressing. But after receiving so many disapproving glances from Nick through the last week, she wanted just one positive look.

A crash echoed. Several grumpy words followed from a couple aisles over. Trudy jumped up and rushed toward that area. She pulled up short when she came upon Nick with one foot hooked three rungs up on the ladder and the other jumping on the ground to try and keep himself from falling and knocking the whole contraption over with him. Pieces of glass were scattered all around him.

"What happened? Are you okay?" She moved to his side and offered her shoulder to give him a way to regain his balance and untangle his leg.

"I dropped the old lightbulb and then tried to climb down too quickly." He leaned over with his hands on his knees. "This better be worth it."

"It will be." She peered around. "Where's a broom, and I'll sweep up the mess."

"I'll get it. It's my fault." He limped toward the back of the store.

"It could have happened to anyone. Let me help." She caught herself right before she ran into his back. He'd stopped at the main path and was looking back where she'd been working. Her heart caught in her chest for a second before she could phrase a question. "What do you think?"

"It's different." He lifted a shoulder in a shrug. "The broom is in the storage room. Last door on the left."

She bit back the hurt. He didn't like it. She'd known that was a possibility going in, but she'd hoped. Swallowing down a lump of disappointment, she half-ran to the back of the store. The sooner they cleaned up the mess and she could get the last five feet of tiles down, the sooner she could go home and not have to face Nick Russo again. Until tomorrow.

She grabbed the broom and carried it like a weapon over her shoulder back toward the disaster. Nick was nowhere in sight— probably better for his safety. The pieces of broken bulb tinkled under the bristles as she moved them into a pile.

Brightness flooded her work area out of nowhere. She froze

and then turned her head toward the newly installed lights. Even without doing anything else, the difference was noticeable and lifted her spirits.

"Okay. I concede defeat." Nick appeared at the end of the row and pointed up. "It really is better."

"Yeah?" She leaned against the broom.

"Yeah. It really is." He reached down to hold the dustpan so she could sweep her pile into it. "Thanks for helping clean up. How can I help you with what you were doing? I'll wait to do the rest of the lights tomorrow. I can't reach above my head anymore tonight. It's putting a kink in my neck."

"You might not like what I was doing any more though." She pulled some gloves out of her pocket. "I was using ammonia to pull the wax off the tiles I'm putting new ones over. It's rather smelly."

He tapped the middle of his forehead. "That explains the headache developing right here."

"Sorry. The theory was good, but the actual doing of it, not so great." She slipped the latex over her fingers. "I'll continue with the stinky part if you want to stick tiles down where it's dry."

"*Um.*" He glanced over her work. "I'm not sure I'd know which color to put where. How did you decide?"

"It's sort of a random pattern. I wanted it to be whimsical."

"Give me the gloves and point to where you want the wax up. I trust myself much more with that part." He held out a hand.

"Sure?"

"Sure."

"Start there." She pointed to the next spot waiting to be scrubbed, then went back a few feet to where the tiles she'd rubbed down earlier were dry. "Just a few more feet and we can call it done for now."

"When you said we'd stay late to work on things after the store closed, I didn't realize you meant staying until it was almost time to open again." He cringed as he dipped the sponge in the solution and then wrung it out.

"I guess I didn't realize it would take this long." She shuffled through her stack of supplies until she found the color she wanted. "I hope from here on out it won't be as time consuming. After all, now we know how to do it, right?"

"Right." What was he doing? He paid people to put this wax down in the first place and here was pulling it back off again to put down something cheaper. And the odor was like a knife slicing through his head, adding to the pain already residing in his shoulders and neck from changing so many light bulbs.

Trudy carefully lined up a red tile several feet away, making sure it was straight before pressing it down with what little weight her small body had. Her wavy tresses dangled over her shoulders, almost brushing the floor every time she leaned over. His fingers itched to move it out of the way before it got caught in the sticky square. Instead, he ran them through his own hair and immediately groaned.

"Ugh!"

"What?" She glanced up and then giggled. "Forget about the gloves?"

"And what's on them." He tugged at a now-damp clump on his head. "What's this going to do to it?"

"It might lighten a bit." She shrugged. "But probably not."

"Just what I needed."

She crouched in front of him and picked at some strands. "It's not even that wet. I bet you'll be okay."

He stilled. Her touch was gentle and soft and sent shivers down his back.

"You done with this one?" Her question pulled him from his trance.

"Yes."

"That one's next."

The exhaustion of the day must be getting to him. Or the fumes. He gave himself a mental shake and moved back to his job. The sooner they finished, the quicker he could go to bed. He definitely needed sleep if he had to face this all again tomorrow.

"Just about five more, I think."

He hadn't even realized his back was only feet from the wall. He quickly knocked out the last three tiles she pointed to and then walked back down the finished part to pick up trash and make sure all the edges were stuck tight. The last thing they needed was for a customer to trip or slip on these. Everything looked good. In fact, he'd never admit it out loud, but the effect was growing on him.

"I had another idea." She hooked her thumb toward the room they'd discussed earlier. "And we might be able to pull this one off for free, depending on how things work."

"I do like free, but I'm still not sure how we'll get that space ready to use any time soon."

"It's tomorrow's main project." She stretched her back.

"Ha." He picked up the smelly bucket of ammonia water. "Tomorrow is delivery day."

"So, I'll get started without you." She loaded her leftover tiles into her bag.

"No way."

Trudy placed her hands on her hips, accentuating her slim waist. "You haven't even heard the idea yet."

"I was talking about you having free rein in that room. You wouldn't even know what to keep and what to toss." And he wasn't ready to trust her judgment.

"Then I'll help you unload the deliveries in the morning, and we'll be able to work in there in the afternoon."

"Has anyone ever told you you're an idealist?" He walked toward the kitchenette to dump his load in the sink.

"And an optimist, believe it or not, though not in the last few years." She followed him. "Can I tell you my idea now?"

Part of him wanted to delve more into why she'd lost her title of optimist, but she seemed unwilling to drop the other topic, so he might as well get it over with. "What is it?"

"Painting sessions. But for kids."

He hung up the empty bucket and faced her. "What are you talking about?"

"You know those places where you go with your friends and they provide all the supplies and show you how to do the picture of the week then let you do it however you want?" Her hands moved like crazy as she tried to describe the concept, but he remained clueless. "I saw a place not three blocks from here."

"Nope. Still no idea." He shook his head. "It sounds expensive."

"It's not that bad." She huffed a strand of hair out of her face. "And here, you could charge the cost of the art supplies plus a little and then they'd get to take the leftover supplies with them at the end. And if we got a college art student to be the instructor, that shouldn't cost much, if anything. You might even be able to work it out with the professor for class credit or something."

"That's a lot of *might*s and *if*s. I don't know about any of it."

"You didn't know about the lights, either, but you like them now." She poked him in the shoulder as he held the door open for her.

"It's late, Trudy." Nick pulled to make sure the old bolt had fallen into place and secured the door. "My mind can't process any more change tonight."

"Okay. But I really plan to convince you on this one." She tossed her hair over her shoulder and grinned. "I think it's perfect."

And if anyone could prove the plan perfect, it was probably her. *Wait.* Had he seriously just thought that? He needed sleep worse than he realized. He waved as she drove off and then slipped in his own car to do the same. Something told him the next few weeks were going to either save the store or drive him insane. Possibly both.

Chapter Six

"Good morning!" Trudy flopped her bag down on the extra chair in the office and turned to beam a smile at Nick. He glared back. "What?"

"Do you see this?" He pointed to his head.

"This?"

"My hair. Do you see what that stuff did to it?" He plucked at a few strands. "I look like I'm going gray. And I'm only twenty-seven."

Moving closer, she fingered his hair that had been so tempting the first time she saw him. He stiffened as she moved a few strands to try and find the lighter pieces he'd mentioned. She jerked back. He obviously didn't want her this close. And definitely not touching him.

"I didn't see anything. I think it must be a trick of your bathroom light or something." She pulled her laptop out and opened it up. "Want to see what all I've accomplished with the website so far?"

"When on earth did you have time to work on the website? We didn't leave here until almost midnight." He tossed a pencil down on his desk and glanced at his watch.

"I was rather wired when I got back to Mom's, so I tweaked a few things while I watched an old movie." She turned her screen to him. "What do you think?"

"I don't see anything different." He leaned closer as if that would make the differences more noticeable.

"Nothing huge. Some fonts, some colors. I moved a few links and pictures to make it more aesthetically pleasing and easier to navigate." She clicked on a tab she'd added. "We should upload your stock. I think you're missing out on not having an online shop as well as a brick and mortar one."

"Isn't that what you were talking about the other day, Nick?" Paul stuck his head in the office door.

"Yes." Nick huffed the reply out on a sigh.

"Perfect. We'll get that information squared away later today, and I can start working on it tonight." She turned to his uncle. "What did you think of the changes? Is it what you were expecting?"

"I love them." Paul glanced at his nephew. "I even got old fuddy-duddy there to admit the lights make everything look better and the tiles add a happy element we've been missing lately."

"Really?" Trudy turned to the fuddy-duddy himself, but his eyes were fixed intently on his computer screen with no evident desire to meet her gaze. "Interesting. Wait until you hear my latest idea."

"I can't wait." Paul rubbed his hands together.

"Painting sessions in the back room." Trudy held up some pictures of examples she'd printed off early this morning. "We sell the attendees the supplies at cost plus just a little to help pay the instructor. This brings people into the store who might not have normally come, offers a kid-friendly service that their moms will love, and might even give some college students teaching experience. And you have the cost of the supplies that might otherwise not be sold."

"Sounds perfect." Paul handed back the sheets. "What do we need to do to make this happen?"

"Clean out that room and freshen it up a bit. And line up an instructor." Trudy shrugged. Maybe if she made light of how much work was actually involved in those two sentences, no one would think about it.

No such luck.

"When she's going to accomplish all this, I have no idea." Nick tapped a pencil against the desk. "And I still don't understand these paint sessions. Why would anyone want to come paint what someone else tells them to?"

"It's fun." Trudy thrust the papers at him, but he wouldn't take them. "Maybe I'll drag you to a session at that place down the street."

"Great idea." Paul nodded enthusiastically. "That will give him a feel for how it could work here too."

"I don't paint." Nick stood. "The delivery truck is here. And she still wants to do more on the website and more tiles and more light bulbs and probably something else she hasn't dropped on my head yet."

"*She's* not expecting it to happen overnight." Paul clapped his nephew on the shoulder. "Work with her as much as you can. She knows you've still got other managerial tasks. Now, I've got kids lining up to see Santa. Better go."

"Where do you need me, boss?" Trudy stood in the doorway just enough he couldn't get past her without physically moving her body. "Put me to work so we can get busy on that room this afternoon."

"I'm really not sure this is such a good idea." Nick shook his head. "Those boxes can be heavy, and you don't know the protocol for getting things on the shelves."

"Either show me how, or let me get started on that room. Please."

He waved his finger in her face. "Do not go in that room without me."

She caught the offending appendage between her own hands and moved it back a couple inches. "Then give me something else so I can help you. The sooner we get your to-do list done, the sooner we can get to mine."

He slipped his finger from her grasp, an indiscernible look crossing his face. Was that disgust? "Come on. If you get hurt, it's not my fault."

"I told you. I've worked in retail before. I think I'll be okay."

"If you say so." He thrust a clipboard in her hands. "Here. Check things off as I pull them out."

"Yes, sir." She saluted him with the pencil. "Whatever you say, sir."

"And drop the sarcasm."

"Oh, the sarcasm is free of charge. It comes as a complementary service when you hire me." She winked as he scowled over his shoulder. She was saved from a snarky retort by the delivery guy greeting him.

For the next hour, Nick barked toy names at her. Then, she scrambled to find their line on the inventory sheet, marked off that the Emporium had received the right number, and wrote down their location in the storage room. Even though she'd worked in a store before, it had been nothing like this. She had worked the floor only and usually behind a cash register. But Mr. Huffy—er, Nick—didn't need to know that.

Trudy gained a new appreciation for why he said it would take forever to upload their inventory online. There was a lot of it.

But she was up for the challenge. This place was growing on her. It was humble and unassuming yet full of potential she itched to find and reveal. If Nick would let her. She was all for traditions and sticking to what a person knew, but if these changes could help save his family's beloved store, wasn't it worth going forward?

Nick glanced up from breaking down a box. "You daydreaming up new crazy plans for my store?"

"None of my plans have been crazy." She plopped down on an empty carton. "How much more do we need to do back here?"

"We're okay to leave it like this now." He tossed the cardboard onto a pile in the back. "My teenage clerks can handle distributing the rest this afternoon."

"You made it sound like we'd have much more to do." She sent him what she hoped was an accusatory look. "Were you hoping to scare me off? Because I don't scare easily."

"You haven't started going through everything in that room you're so stubborn about using either." He motioned her toward the door. "Let's go see what we can do about really scaring you off—I mean, about cleaning this room."

"*Ha, ha.*" How bad could it really be? She stepped into the room behind him and froze. Like Mom's house—times ten. How did she keep getting into situations where she had to help sort other people's junk?

The look on Trudy's face was worth it. Nick quickly swallowed a laugh. Yesterday Trudy had been all about the plan and how easy this would be. Now she had to face reality. And the truth was, this place was full of stuff.

"Okay. Let's get to it." He moved to the first box and lifted the flaps. "Old inventories from ... wow. From 1989. I'll talk to Paul and see how far back we're supposed to keep these, but I bet we can get rid of them."

"Sounds good. Maybe we should start piles? Definitely keep. Trash. And one for stuff we need to talk to Paul about?" She dug through another carton. "This looks like ... old Christmas decorations."

"Really? I thought we had that all together." He walked over to see what she was talking about.

"See? Almost exactly what's on that pitiful tree on the floor." She held up an ornament that had seen better days. "What's up with that tree anyway?"

"We've always had it." He tried to swallow the defensiveness bubbling up inside him, but it gurgled faster and faster the more she talked. "My grandma decided to have one back in the seventies when Grandpa started looking enough like Santa he could play the part. Back then, they only had Santa for a week or two. I think the first year, only one day. Not a big thing back then, I guess."

"It's neat that you've kept the tradition." She wrinkled her nose at some tinsel that had somehow become semi-melted together. "But it would look much nicer if you'd update the tree a bit. It's in people's pictures, you know. They'll want something really nice. Not some old falling apart, half-lit, artificial thing."

Of all the arrogance! Didn't she have anything that didn't look that great but was kept anyway? It was an heirloom. Okay, maybe *heirloom* stretched things a bit, but still ... His grandma had worked hard on that tree. And it was significantly better now that all the branches were in the correct slots.

Just because he griped about having to get the blasted thing out every year didn't give this chit the right to. She could just go back to Austin, where the stores probably had brand new trees every year. No traditions. No legacy. *Boring.* Wasn't that what she said about this place?

"Well, at least it's not boring. Isn't that what you said about my store?" The volcano inside him drew closer and closer to explosion level.

"Look, you talk about my ideas being crazy. And maybe you don't really like my tiles. But you've got to admit that neat and not shedding is a definite plus when it comes to decorations." She offered him several old ball ornaments that practically disintegrated in his hand.

"And I suppose you could find something nicer just like that?" He snapped his fingers, though he itched to snap something harder. Anything to release this anger she stirred up in him.

She sat back and blinked, her mouth a perfect *O.* And he had to work to draw his attention from her lips and back to what she was about to say. "What if I bring you mine?"

"Yours?" Not the comeback he expected. She struck him as the type of person who went all out decorating for Christmas. She probably even had a pair of holiday socks for every day of the week. How could she live without a tree for that long?

"I have to run back to Austin this weekend anyway. I'll bring it back with me. It's just sitting there, collecting dust. I haven't put it up since ..." She stood and brushed the dust from her jeans. "Anyway, I don't know if I'll ever use it. Someone might as well benefit from its existence. I think I have a few decorations too."

"You don't put up a tree?"

"No." She peeked in another box and then waved him over. "This looks like more for you and Paul to go through."

Why didn't she decorate for Christmas? What had she been going to say when she trailed off? Had something happened to ruin the holidays for her? He set the container she indicated with the other one and then dug into another. Just like that, the anger was replaced by curiosity and intrigue. Who was this girl, really?

"You two have made quite a dent." Paul's voice drew them out of their perusal of old advertisements an hour later. Trudy wanted to see if any could be reused before they discarded them all.

"And you get to work late tonight, too, Uncle Paul." Nick pointed to the pile by the door. "That stack needs your approval before we can dispose of it."

"Wow. So much for my plans." He lifted some papers and shook his head. "This should have been tossed long ago. Probably all of it."

"Will you look through it, just in case? I don't want to accidentally get rid of something we'll need later." Nick added another box to the discard pile. It was growing to the point that they'd need to make a run to the dump soon.

"Why is this here?" Paul fingered a piece of garland that draped from the box of old decorations.

Nick shot a look in Trudy's direction. "Ask her."

"This isn't the pile of things to throw away, is it?" Paul frowned like he couldn't believe anyone would be so callous.

"Paul, those are all falling apart. They can't be used anymore." Trudy waved a hand toward the stack, as if to sweep it all away. "I'm going to bring some newer ones in a couple days. When I run back to Austin tomorrow to grab a few things, I'll get my tree at the same time."

Paul's voice cracked. "These were my mother's."

"That's what I told her." Nick glanced between the two of them, unsure of what would happen. After all, he'd been told several times that Paul outranked him. Would Paul be able to pull rank on Trudy too? It wasn't even that Nick liked the tree they had now. It was more a matter of pride.

"Maybe you could take them home and use them there?" Trudy placed a gentle hand on his uncle's arm. "But I think it would look better if the store used ornaments and decorations that weren't ... disintegrating."

"I need to go see if there are kids waiting for me. Looked like there might be some coming in as I wandered back here." Paul blinked a few times.

"Now you've done it." Nick huffed as he shifted another box to the pile his uncle needed to look through. "He's the most sentimental of all of us."

"I'm not trying to break your hearts. I'm just trying to do my job. And my job is to make the store look better." She tossed her arms above her head. "I don't understand. Do you guys want to save this place or not? I'm going to grab a coffee. I'll be back in a little while."

She fled the scene, leaving only a faint scent of her perfume. Was he upset that she was angry? Not in the least. She brought this on herself, bulldozing through people's personal belongings and acting like they didn't matter. Right? And yet he understood too. They'd asked her to help and then stood in opposition as she tried to accomplish the task set before her.

He went to check his emails and answer any messages that had come in while they'd been sequestered in the room. Might as well take advantage of the break to his knees and back. He had just hit send on the last reply needed when the aroma of coffee wafted to him through the door.

"I brought you one too. I wasn't sure how you liked it, so I guessed." Trudy held out a paper cup. Her eyes sparkled again, as if she'd shed the earlier emotions when she left the building. "And I had the most brilliant idea yet."

"I'm not sure I want to hear this." He sniffed tentatively at the brew she handed him. The coffee he recognized as a rich, dark roast. But there was something else too. Peppermint? Not his go-to choice, but he'd at least take a sip to show he appreciated her trying. The flavors slid over his tongue and melded in a way that actually worked very nicely. He took a bigger drink and sent her a grin before remembering she was about to drop another bomb on him.

"Okay. Picture this." She spanned her hands in front of her, like she was rolling out a movie screen. "You know those murals people are painting on some of the buildings around town? What if we get them to do one on the front of the store?"

Nick barely caught himself from spewing his coffee. "What?"

"You don't have any front windows, so you can't do fun displays like some places, but you have this perfectly blank canvas. We could have them fill it up with toys or children playing or something else that would be fun and eye catching. It would draw people in."

"I don't want graffiti on the front of the store." He set the cup aside, the bitterness of the drink only adding to the sour taste in his mouth. "No."

"But Nick—"

"No." He splayed his hands out wide. "Tiles and lights are one thing. Painting a concrete wall is something else entirely.

And don't go to Uncle Paul about this either. I'm putting my foot down on this one."

"You're so stubborn." She actually stomped her boot.

"Takes one to know one." He tightened his jaw. "You've forced your way on things for two days now. You've gone far enough."

"Fine." She grabbed her bag with her computer and straightened. "I'm headed to Austin. I'll bring the tree just in case. I won't be in tomorrow. Enjoy the break from my pushy ways."

He had hurt her. Did he regret it? No. Not much anyway. She was trying to do too much too fast. And after the fiasco with the decorations earlier, he'd had it.

He wasn't going to miss her the rest of the day or tomorrow. Just to show her he could do quite well without her, he might even finish changing the lightbulbs tonight. He might even work some more on that stupid room.

The image of her face lighting up at all the junk gone ran through his head and left a glimmer of sunshine. He pushed it aside. He wasn't doing it for her. He was doing it because it needed to be done.

And he'd keep telling himself that until he believed it. No matter how many times it took.

Chapter Seven

"Are you not going to the store?" Trudy's mom stopped in the kitchen doorway.

"Not today."

"Can I ask why?"

"I told him I was running to Austin to grab a few things." Trudy shrugged. "He's not expecting me back." No need to say *his* name. That would only revive the memories of the day before.

"You went and came back last night." Her mom leveled her with a cool stare. "Now tell me the real reason."

"Some ... suggestions I made yesterday caused some ... contention. I didn't want to stir things up more than necessary." Trudy took a sip of coffee. "Besides, I'm supposed to be helping you too."

"Well, I can't say I won't take the help, but I don't like the idea of you hiding from problems." She motioned her toward the stuff still needing sorting. "Want to talk about it? I didn't even know you were having issues at the store. Paul never mentioned it."

"Paul?" Trudy stopped short. "You were talking to Paul about me?"

Her mom didn't meet her gaze. "I was talking to Paul. You were mentioned simply because you're a part of my life."

"When were you talking to Paul?" Trudy narrowed her eyes.

"We had dinner together last night." Her mom moved a stack from one pile to another, then picked it up and set it back where it had been originally.

"*You* were Paul's plans yesterday?" Trudy caught her mug before it slipped from her fingers.

"He wanted to catch up, more than we could between him seeing kids at the store. I agreed." She lifted a shoulder. "We met at a downtown restaurant for steaks. We both drove our own vehicles. End of story."

Why didn't it sound like the end of the story? Mom was almost acting like she wasn't saying something. But what could her mom be hiding?

"So, want to talk about whatever happened yesterday?" Her mom raised an eyebrow.

"Nope." Trudy set her mug on a table. Two could play at the "leaving out the rest of the details" game. "Where did we quit working in here the other day?"

"Over here, I think." Her mom lifted a flap. "Yes. Some of this looks familiar. The old letters."

"I still can't wrap my mind around you dating anyone but Dad." Trudy shook her head. "It just seems wrong."

Her mom paused a moment as if hesitant to answer.

"What?"

"Nothing." Her mom set the mementoes aside. "At least nothing you're ready to hear yet."

Trudy didn't like the sound of that one bit. What on earth could she mean? She was saved when her mom thrust a box her way.

"I think you're the one who needs to sort the rest of this one."

Confused, Trudy lifted out a stack of papers tied with a piece of red Christmas ribbon. A shadowbox decorated in jingle bells was buried underneath. It was filled with photo collages and ticket stubs. When she and Dad had ice skated. Gone to see the Nutcracker. Joined a group of carolers. Worked in the soup kitchen. Gone sledding.

Memories bombarded and washed over her in a wave of sorrow. The grief so thick she could hardly catch her breath. Would it ever get any easier?

She walloped herself with the papers as she reached up to wipe away tears. What was all this anyway? The edges were covered in childish drawings of Christmas trees, stick reindeer, presents, lights. As she skimmed the top page, her dad's even scrawl filtered through her brain and let her know what she'd found. The bucket lists. All of them.

Her dad had come up with the idea the Christmas she was five. "Let's make a bucket list of three things to do, just you and me. Anything Christmas-y. What do you want to do that we've never done before, Trudy girl?"

That was the year Katt had her tonsils removed and had been the center of attention. Dad had seen that Trudy was feeling left out. One of the activities she chose that first year was going to see the Rockettes. She'd wanted to see them in person ever since she saw *Annie*, and her dad had taken her.

The idea of a yearly Christmas bucket list caught on and became their thing until ... yes, at the back of the bundle was the last one, from five years ago. Of the three activities listed, one remained undone. The day Dad died.

Trudy drew in a shuddering breath. Her fingers traced the three letters at the bottom of the list: "TSO." They had both been looking forward to that concert. She'd begged to go for years. The timing and prices had finally lined up so they could make it happen. And then, his wreck ...

The doorbell chime drew her attention back to the present. Voices filtered down the hallway, but she couldn't make out anything in particular. She searched around for a tissue, but there was nothing so useful in this room. Her mom met her in the hallway.

"I hate to do this to you, but you have a visitor." She pressed one of Dad's old handkerchiefs into Trudy's hand.

"A visitor? Who?" Trudy mopped her eyes the best she could. "I don't know anyone else in town except—"

Her mom's eyes confirmed the truth before she turned around to see.

Nick shifted his weight from one foot to the other as he stood in the entryway. "Hi ..."

"What are you doing here? I didn't think you ever left the store during the day." She frowned. That had come out a bit harsher than she meant it. But she really did want to know.

"I came with a message from Uncle Paul. He insisted." Nick held out a red envelope.

"Paul?" Trudy reached to accept the missive, but then realized both her hands were full.

"Why don't you two sit on the couch for this?" Her mom steered them through that doorway. "Nick, would you like some coffee or anything?"

"No, thank you, Mrs. McNamara." Nick perched on the edge of the wingback chair perpendicular to the sofa.

Trudy set her bundles beside her and held her hand out for the envelope. "What on earth did Paul have to say that couldn't wait until I came in tomorrow?"

"I thought you were going to be in Austin until later today." Nick picked at an invisible spot on his pants but didn't pass the letter her way.

"I didn't feel like spending the night down there, so I came back after dinner with some friends. It's only an hour."

"I guess I just assumed you'd come in if you were back in town." He glanced up for a second and then back down again, seemingly interested in the stripes of the chair.

"I figured I'd help mom some more since I gave you a head's up I wouldn't be at the store today." She shrugged. Had he missed her? Or was something else going on? She couldn't fathom either of those things.

"I—" Nick shifted in his seat. "I can't help but notice that you were crying."

Now it was her turn to wiggle. "I came across some ... memories." Her hand unconsciously touched the stack of lists.

"Bad ones, I guess."

"No." She shook her head, swallowing back more tears. She would not cry in front of this man. "Good ones. So good they make me miss my dad more."

"He's been gone a while now?"

"Five years on the twenty-fourth." Her throat closed up on that last word. Five years of Christmases without her dad. Five years of no more bucket lists. Five years of empty, cheerless holidays.

When Trudy peered up at him with those soulful eyes, all Nick wanted to do was reach across and somehow make things better. And he didn't even really know what was wrong. Sure, he understood missing someone. He understood grief. But hers seemed to go deeper.

She hesitated as if trying to decide if he were worthy of hearing what she'd say next. He must have passed muster because she picked up that stack of papers she'd been carrying and held it up.

"My dad and I had a tradition every year." She fingered the edges of the colorful notes or whatever they were. "We made a bucket list for the Christmas season. Three or four things we wanted to do that were available only at the holidays. Usually, just the two of us. Sometimes the whole family."

"I don't understand. Things like what?" Nick frowned and leaned forward in his seat.

"One year we saw the Nutcracker. One year, the Rockettes. I

made him march in the Christmas parade with me and throw candy when I was ten. We sledded, had a neighborhood snowball fight on a rare year with snow, made cookies, caroled—you name it. If it had anything to do with the holidays, it would eventually end up on our list." She held out the bundle.

He clasped it between his hands in reverence, wondering at her trusting him with such precious mementoes. "Wow."

"I didn't realize Mom had saved them all. Although, knowing how much junk she's saved through the years, it doesn't surprise me." Trudy dabbed her cheeks with that piece of fabric she held.

He gingerly flipped through page after page. "You did all this?"

"We started when I was five. Ended when I was eighteen. So, there should be thirteen there."

"That's at least thirty-nine different holiday activities. How did you come up with that many?" He ran his fingers down the scribbles of their plans for each year. Sleigh rides—with an attached addendum that a wagon ride would work if it didn't snow ... which it probably hadn't since they lived in central Texas —plays, an opera the year she was fifteen, an attempt at making a yule log, and on and on.

"Some years were easier than others." She pointed to the opera. "That happened the year a singer came to my school and got me curious. Dad was game, so we went. The yule log we tried when we got hooked watching a holiday baking show and wanted to see if we could do one too. Mom wasn't too happy about the huge mess we made in the kitchen."

"This is amazing." He reached the last one. Three letters were at the bottom of the list but not checked off like everything else had been. "One isn't marked done."

She pressed her lips together and blinked. When she swallowed, it was so hard he could see it in her throat. "That concert was the evening of the day my dad ..."

"Oh." What a stupid thing to say. *Oh.* It made him look the fool he was. All he'd been supposed to do was deliver Uncle

Paul's letter. And here he sat, making her even more upset than she'd been when he arrived.

She dabbed her eyes. "Anyway, it will never happen. TSO was his idea. It just wouldn't be the same."

"What is it?"

She shot him a look of incredulity. "TSO? Trans-Siberian Orchestra? They do remixes on the traditional Christmas songs. Surely you've heard of them."

"Like the music synched to light shows on the fancy houses?"

"Yes." She laughed, and a weight lifted from his shoulders. "My dad loved them. We had saved and waited to go to one of their concerts for years. That was the first time it was going to work out. But it didn't."

"I'm sorry." Two words that he hoped encompassed how much he was apologizing for. It wasn't only that he was sorry her dad had passed away and she had missed the concert. He also apologized for yesterday. And for any additional pain he'd caused today.

She nodded as if she understood.

"Oh. This is from Uncle Paul." It was abrupt, but he needed something to lighten the mood ... at least, he hoped it would.

She pulled a piece of paper out and unfolded it.

"What is it?" Nick leaned forward.

"Your Uncle Paul has finagled us into the painting session tonight." Trudy waved the page at him.

"What?" Nick ripped it from her hands. It was a receipt for two people to attend the painting session that evening. Paul had scribbled that he'd liked her idea so much he went ahead and reserved a spot for both her and Nick.

"Seven o'clock." Trudy picked the handkerchief back up and twisted it between her fingers. "Guess we have plans."

"I told you guys I don't paint." Nick thrust the page back at her.

"It's not for professionals or anything. They have the picture outlined on the canvas and provide all the supplies, as well as

57

some instruction. All you have to do is fill in the lines." Trudy skimmed through the rest of what Paul had written. "Oh."

"What?"

"He's apologizing for yesterday, for not 'accepting my ideas with grace.'" She shook her head. "He says to bring the new decorations and he's already taken the old ones home for his daughter to go through."

"I suppose you and Paul are going to hold me to this painting thing?" Was he more scared of the artiness of this or that it resembled a date? He didn't want to fathom either option right now.

"It'll give you a better idea of what I'm talking about. And maybe a picture you can hang in your office." She grinned at him. "It's only one evening. What's the worst that could happen?"

Chapter Eight

T rudy glanced at her watch again. Nick was going to stand her up. Not that it was a date. Not really. But still. She'd anticipated showing him how perfect the painting idea would be.

A chilly wind whipped around the edge of the building, and she pulled her jacket tighter. She bounced on her toes as two more couples passed her, heading into the studio. Ten minutes until time to start. Where was he? The Emporium was only three blocks away.

A breath she hadn't realized she was holding whooshed out as he moseyed around a corner, hands full with two paper cups. A fleece vest covered his plaid flannel shirt, and tan corduroys hugged his legs in just the right way. Several strands of his hair whipped back and forth in the breeze.

She quickly swallowed her attraction and covered up her emotions with a chide. "You were almost late."

"I still have five minutes. And I thought you'd like something warm to drink." He didn't even look at his watch. "Shall we?"

Was this the same guy who had argued with her for the last three days? She entered and confirmed their reservations with the girl at the front desk. They followed the sound of laughter and chatter down a hallway and into a large studio, the walls covered with paintings. Canvases stood ready, grouped by twos, scattered around the room.

"Why are they all done together?" He pointed to the couplings.

"Um, Nick." Trudy raised a shaky finger to the sign by the door. "Either your uncle is trying to get back at me for all the changes he didn't like, or he has a wicked sense of humor."

"This is a couples' class?" Nick's voice raised in pitch at the end of the question.

"Apparently."

"Oh, no. It was bad enough you guys decided I need to come do this in the first place." Nick sliced his hand through the air. "I can't do this as a couple."

"Hi." A lady who appeared to be in her mid-forties came over and held out a hand. "I'm Genevieve, your instructor today. Is something wrong?"

Trudy accepted the handshake. "We weren't aware it was a couples' class. We wanted just a regular one."

"Every other Friday is for couples. Unfortunately, our schedule has been filling up fast. I'm not sure how many other sessions between now and Christmas have two open spots." She motioned behind her. "And tonight's paintings don't have to go together if you don't want them to. It's two reindeer with their noses touching, like in a kiss, but if you hang the paintings in different houses, no one would know they go together."

"Let's just do this session." Trudy tugged on Nick's sleeve. "You can get it over with, and then maybe we can get something set up for the store before Christmas to implement in the new year."

Nick narrowed his eyes, pressing his lips into a straight line.

"You're already here anyway." Trudy raised her eyebrows.

"Fine." He schlumped into the room, shoulders slightly in, weaving between the other people already seated until he found two unclaimed canvases in the back. He slid on a black apron and tied it with a jerk.

Trudy pulled her own cover on and wrapped the ties to the front before making a perfect bow. These things were never designed for people as short as her. She glanced up. Nick was staring at her.

"What?" She slid an elastic band off her wrist and pulled her hair back in a loose bun. "Did I get it on backward or something?"

"No." He cleared his throat. "So, we're just supposed to paint?"

"They'll give us the rundown in a minute about the techniques the various parts required. Although this one looks fairly straightforward. The paint is already here." She pointed to the globs on the paper plates between them. "And they've already penciled in the outline. I think they walk us through, step by step."

He traced the faint lines with his finger. "A reindeer. Of course it's a Christmas picture. On couples' night. Because why not make this as miserable as possible?"

"It doesn't have to be miserable. Just relax. I bet you'll enjoy it." She glanced around at the others nearby.

The two to her left sat with their stools practically on top of each other. No way would they have enough elbow room to actually wield a paint brush. But something told her they weren't as concerned with how well their final product turned out so much as spending time together.

The people on the other side of Nick laughed together as the woman reached over and pressed the man's arm or leg. He brushed her hair back or squeezed her shoulder. Seriously? Who needs to touch each other that often? All these happy couples, and here she and Nick sat, the only two in the room who didn't even like each other.

That wasn't completely true. Something about him had urged her to open up this morning, about her dad and the bucket lists.

Things she'd never told anyone. And she'd found herself missing him this afternoon as she sorted more stuff at her mom's house, wondering if he'd done any more work at the store on the projects they'd started or if he'd simply put it down until she came back. Probably the latter.

She took a sip of her drink and sighed with pleasure. Peppermint hot chocolate. How had he guessed one of her favorite drinks?

"Good evening!" Genevieve stood at one end of the room on a dais so everyone could see her. "I'm glad you all decided to spend your Friday night with us. I'm going to guide you through the steps of our kissing reindeer tonight. Feel free to ask if you have any questions while you work. Of course, you're welcome to use whatever colors you want, and if you don't see one, check with me, and I'll see what I can round up. The paint provided is what you need to make your paintings like this."

She held up two canvases together, the cartoonish reindeer's noses touching in the middle. Their antlers stretched up, and hanging from both was a tiny sprig of mistletoe. Trudy found herself smiling. Dad would have loved doing something like this. A knife of pain sliced through her happiness.

Nick leaned nearer, his hand touching her shoulder. "You okay?"

"Fine. Just a sad thought." She took a deep breath and tried to focus harder on what Genevieve said, but the spot where Nick had pressed was still warm and distracting. As was the fact that he was so attuned to her after only a few days that he could sense when she hurt. How had that happened?

"We're going to start with our background first. Don't worry if you go a little over some of the pencil marks. We can paint over that later. If you'll dip your brush just a bit in the darker red and then the lighter red, it will give us a deeper texture and color on the canvas." Genevieve's hands were enlarged on the TV screen behind her. "Now, go in an X pattern as neatly as you can all over the canvas around the reindeer."

"Here goes nothing." Nick grabbed a brush and hesitated.

"Dip here first." Trudy grabbed his hand to guide him to the maroon. She hadn't counted on how nice his skin would feel under her own. She swallowed and glanced up to see his eyes on hers. What was going on?

"Everyone good? Any questions?" Genevieve's question pulled Nick out of whatever trance Trudy had put him under.

He quickly jerked away and dipped his brush in the paint. Slapping the color on the blank canvas in a motion that somewhat resembled an X, he could see where this might look nice if someone else were doing it. Out of the corner of his eye, Trudy worked on her own background. Her strokes were much neater and closer together than his.

"Be a little more careful here." Trudy's hand neared his and then faltered as if afraid to touch him. "I know she said you could paint over the lines, but you'll wish you hadn't when we fill in the reindeer later."

"Right." He slowed down, easing the motions around the curves of his deer's head.

Laughter and conversations carried on around them, but Trudy remained quiet. Several times Nick considered saying something, but no words sounded right in his head. So, he focused on following the directions Genevieve delivered every few minutes, making sure his painting came out well enough to justify the money Uncle Paul spent on this.

"Okay, guys. Time for finishing touches." Genevieve's statement caught his attention. Were they close to being done already? A glance at the picture in front of him showed everything pretty much complete. That had gone faster than he expected.

"Are you going to do the mistletoe on yours?" Trudy leaned over to reach the green.

"I don't know." He tilted his head to try and picture their canvases pressed together. "Do you think I should?"

"Up to you." Her shoulder lifted. "I guess I'm a rule follower when it comes to these things, and I can't stand to leave a step undone."

"I don't think I would have called you a rule follower before now." He focused forward on what they were supposed to be doing. Genevieve dabbed little ovals of mistletoe onto the tops of her antlers. "You seem more like a girl who looks for a mold to break."

"In some ways I take that as a compliment." The corners of her eyes crinkled in a smile as she sipped her hot chocolate. Had she liked what he chose for her? She hadn't complained.

"But not in other ways?" He dabbed some green on his canvas too. Not that he wanted it, but he didn't know what else to do.

"I don't know. I guess it feels too close to being called a rule breaker. A troublemaker. Someone out to make change for change's sake instead of for the good of something." She shook her head. "That's not my goal."

"I can see that." He added one last white berry and then leaned back. That was as good as it was going to get. "But I don't think you come across that way ... at least not much."

"Only when I'm trying to get rid of old Christmas decorations?" Her eyes showed that her question was more teasing than serious.

"Right." He plunked the brush into the water cup. "Or running over the store manager every time you come around."

"I guess Paul decided he did want to use newer decorations after all, though, right?" She added one more swipe of color to hers. It was much neater than his.

"That's what it sounded like to me."

"So, when would you like me to bring my tree and the ornaments and stuff? I never actually took it out of my car."

Trudy shook her head. "No need to carry more junk into Mom's house. We'd never find it again."

"It didn't look so bad to me."

"You were in the already unpacked part." She brushed a strand of hair out of her face that had come loose from her bun. Her fingers left a streak of white paint at her temple. "The room I'm sleeping in only has enough space between the boxes for me to get to the bed and the closet. Not much else."

"Wow. I didn't realize she had so much stuff. Here." He picked up a cloth and reached for her forehead. "You have a little paint."

She froze as if afraid to move while he cleaned up the spot. Was she scared of him? Or something else? He gave a brief nod as he finished.

"Time to dry?" She scooted back and grabbed a hair dryer, turning it to blow on her canvas before he could react to her switch in subjects.

"Would you guys like to take your picture with your finished paintings?" Genevieve stood in front of them.

"I don't kn—"

"Yes." Trudy cut off his protests. "Just to prove to Paul that we didn't come in and buy these off someone else." Her laughter rang out and made the edges of his mouth tug up. "Come on."

He awkwardly held his canvas in front of him as she jumped up beside him on the dais. She leaned her head his way. Her shoulder brushed against his, and he barely caught his painting before it slipped from his fingers. Was he getting sick? His body was acting funny tonight.

"Say cheese!" Genevieve held Trudy's phone and snapped several photos.

"Thanks so much." Trudy swiped through the pictures. "This was fun. Maybe I'll come back with my mom and sister next year."

"I hope you do." Genevieve smiled. "Let me know if there's anything else I can help you with."

"Actually, you might be able to help us. We're looking for artists to lead painting sessions for kids down at the Toy Emporium. It wouldn't be as often as you do here. Or even as fancy. Maybe an art student?" Trudy's words rolled out in a wave, the excitement behind her idea obvious.

"Oh. I didn't know the Emporium offered sessions like this."

"They don't yet. But we're trying to offer more things like story times and activities like this to revamp the store and give it some new life." Trudy pulled a business card out of her back pocket. "If you think of anyone, please let us know."

"Sure."

"I don't think she liked that one bit." Nick glanced over his shoulder as they walked back to their station to gather their things. "It's competition."

"Not really. They don't do kids' classes here." Trudy tipped back her paper cup and slurped the rest of her drink. "And thanks for this. It was exactly what I needed."

"We can get you another if you need one." Where had those words come from? Wasn't this the same woman he couldn't get away from fast enough a few days before?

"Thanks, but if we do anything else tonight, I think it better be putting up a tree." She led the way back out of the studio. "What time is it anyway?"

"A little after nine." He shook his head. "You're not seriously thinking we need to go back and work tonight?"

"How long will it take to put up a tree?" She shifted her canvas to her other hand. "And it would get it out of my car."

"I've worked late every night this week. Don't I deserve one night to be home before ten?" He hated how whiny his voice sounded, but he didn't want to do anything else that even resembled Christmas tonight.

She frowned. "Fine. Tomorrow then. But we can't do it while there are customers."

"You're not going to let this go, are you?"

She widened her eyes. "What? I'm just trying to figure out

66

the best time to do things. It's only two and a half weeks until Christmas. If we wait much longer, we might as well not do it."

"*Mm-hmm*." He motioned with his head. "Where are you parked? Let's get this over with so I can go home."

"You know you're secretly glad you get to spend more time with me." She turned on her heel and walked toward the parking lot.

He was. But he wasn't anywhere near ready to admit it.

Chapter Nine

"Something's different." Trudy halted in her tracks at the end of the hallway.

"You have a bad habit of stopping in the middle of a pathway." Nick grasped her upper arms and steered her out of the way.

"Wait." She grabbed his sleeve. "The lights."

"What about them?" He raised an eyebrow.

"You finished them." She gaped from the ceiling to his face.

"You didn't expect me to?" He crossed his arms. "I thought that was the plan. I'd finish the lights and you'd work on tiles some more. You know, before you stormed off to Austin."

Her mouth formed an *O*. Yes, she had originally planned on just that. But she had left him, figuring he wouldn't do any more work until she returned. Instead, he'd forged ahead with the plan. Her plan. The one he hadn't even liked.

"I also did this." He moved back down the hallway, his scent wafting over her in his wake. Something clean and masculine she couldn't quite put her finger on. He opened the door to the room that had caused so much strife the day before.

Her breath whooshed out. "It's empty."

"Except for the two tables and a few chairs we found. I

wasn't sure what all you wanted for the setup." He pointed to the various pieces of furniture.

"Wow. You must have stayed really late last night. I still think it needs a new coat of paint." She ran her fingers over the wall as she walked farther into the room. "Something bright and friendly."

"How can paint be friendly?" He leaned against the doorframe.

"Colors can spark emotion. Haven't you walked into a room with dark walls and felt melancholy or some other brooding emotion sort of take up residence inside you? Then you leave that room for something with a lighter color and your mood lifts?" She spun in a circle. "I'm thinking yellow."

"I'm sure Uncle Paul will be pleased to let you do whatever you want in here. He seems to go along with all your plans." Nick flipped the light switch, leaving the room in moonglow. "And roping me into helping you pull them off."

"Don't be so dour." She playfully bumped his arm on the way back out. "You know you're having fun."

"Right." He shook his head, but a grin played at the corners of his lips.

"Okay, first things first. Let's move this old tree out of the way. Got some boxes to put the decorations in for your Uncle Paul to go through? Like he did with the ones from the conference room?" She stood the closest she'd let herself come to Santa's station and studied the mess. "I don't even know where to start."

"It wasn't always this ..." Nick's voice trailed off as he plucked a piece of tinsel from a branch. "My grandma used to pride herself on the decorations, but as the years went by, I guess they took a back burner to everything else, and we just pulled the same things out over and over again, not paying attention."

"It's easy to do that, isn't it? To see things without really seeing them?"

"Yes." He studied the artificial pine in silence for a few moments, then snapped his fingers. "I have an idea."

She stared at him as he dashed back the way they had come. "Your idea better not be leaving me to do this by myself."

"Ha!" He stood in front of her a few moments later, pushing his glasses up on his nose. Then held out a box of cling wrap. "This should help."

She raised an eyebrow. "How?"

"We wrap it around the whole thing and then move it all at once back to the storeroom." He pulled out a length and frowned. "Assuming we have enough left in this pack of course."

"Of course." She took the plastic he handed her and held it as high up on the tree as she could reach. "Why not?"

"Here we go." He started wrapping, passing the end to her as he moved around so she could reach it back to the other side again. They fell into a rhythm and had it mostly covered before they ran out with five branches to go. "Close enough."

"I never would have thought of doing something like this." She admired the wrapped column. It wasn't quite so gaudy covered in the clear plastic.

"A few years ago, an employee had the idea. We've been doing it ever since. But this last year the tree got jostled quite a bit during some storage room changes. That's why it was a mess last week." He bent his knees and hugged the decoration. "I'll carry this. Walk behind and pick up anything that drops."

She laughed. "Got it."

As if to prove the need for it, a half-covered ball bounced to the floor and rolled in several circles before stopping a few feet away. She snatched it up and then followed the trail of tiny pieces of tinsel, garland, artificial pine needles, and glitter Nick left behind on his way to the storeroom.

"We might need to sweep when we're done." She dumped her stack of discarded confetti on the floor next to the tree. "But I don't want to think how long that would've taken if we'd taken it apart piece-by-piece."

"Anything else need to go?" He motioned his head back toward the Santa area.

"I don't think so. The tree was the main thing." She started toward her car. "Mine might be half a foot shorter. Do you think Paul will mind?"

"I don't think he even knows how tall that one is."

She popped the back hatch of her SUV and picked up a box of lights and ornaments. Spinning around, she walloped Nick in the stomach, not realizing he was right behind her. "I'm so sorry."

"You do make a habit of that move." He stepped back. "Where's the tree? I can carry it in while you grab this other stuff."

"There." She nodded to the box.

"Okay." He huffed a bit as he lifted the box containing the pieces to a six-foot-tall tree, but then he got his arms around it better and walked it back into the store as if it weighed nothing. For such a skinny nerd, he must be hiding some nice muscles under that plaid.

Trudy set three boxes on Paul's green chair. "Just a couple more things, and that should be it."

"I'll walk back out with you."

"You don't have to. It's not much to carry."

"That alleyway isn't bright. I'd feel better if you didn't go out there alone." His hand hovered at her lower back, and she glanced back at him, unsure what to do with his chivalry.

"Thank you."

"You're welcome."

She quickly grabbed the last few bags and shut her vehicle. "This is it."

"Okay. Let's get this put up and get home. They're calling for rain later tonight."

"Ugh." She wrinkled her nose. "I'm getting tired of rain."

"We've got to take it while we can." He set the tree box up

and ran his fingers over the seams. "This thing isn't even opened."

"No." She avoided his gaze. Here it came. Twenty questions about why she had a Christmas tree she'd never used. Was she strong enough to get through this?

"Trudy." Nick didn't say anything else.

She peered up. Curiosity shone in his eyes, but so did something else. Worry, maybe?

"Are you sure you want to open this?"

Was she?

Nick shouldn't have brought it up. The emotions flitting across her face were raw and deep. And yet after learning so much about her in the last few days, he couldn't deny wondering why someone who had obviously enjoyed Christmas so much in the past would have a Christmas tree that had never been used.

"We don't have to do this. We could bring Grandma's tree back out." Nick started to walk that way.

"No!" She shook her head so hard her bun flopped sideways. "No. We've got to have a tree out here, and it needs to look nice enough to appear in people's pictures. Do we need a knife or something to open the box?"

He lifted the cardboard once more. "I might be able to pull here and ... yes. Got it."

"I haven't touched it since—" She busied herself studying the instructions on how each branch connected to the rest.

He dug around until he discovered the base and main pole. "I've discovered it helps to lay out all the pieces and then assemble them bottom to top."

"Sounds good to me. I'll see if I can put them in order." She pulled branches from the box and stacked them around the area.

Much quicker than he ever got his mom's tree up, Trudy's stood, stately and proud. They really did work well together.

"Lights?" She held up a couple packages, also unopened.

"Great." He wouldn't ask this time. If she wanted to tell him, she would. He hadn't known her long enough to deserve an answer to such personal queries. "Want to do like we did the cling wrap? You stand on one side and pass it back and forth instead of making ourselves dizzy walking in circles?"

"Sure." She quickly hid herself behind the branches.

The glow filled the space with a light even warmer than the new bulbs above, casting multi-hued sparkles in her eyes every time she met his gaze. He'd forgotten how magical Christmas lights could be. His fingers lingered a few moments longer each time he handed the strand to her, brushing against her hand with more purpose than accident. She reached up on tiptoes to loop the end around the top, and then this task was done.

He drew a deep breath and glanced around at the other bags and boxes she'd carried in. "What's left? Tinsel? Garland?"

"Ugh. No tinsel. That stuff gets everywhere." She lifted the lid from a plastic tub and tilted it to show rows of peppermint-striped ornaments. "One year my mom agreed to let us all do theme trees in our rooms. Mine was obviously candy. I thought these might be fun here."

He knelt down and reached to get a glass ball the same time she did. This time, his fingers caught hers and didn't let go. "Trudy, why aren't you using all these for yourself?"

She pressed her lips together and slowly raised her gaze to meet his. Would she answer, or just blow it off and move the conversation somewhere else like she had been doing? She took a deep breath that ended almost in a shudder.

"My dad died on Christmas Eve, Nick. My dad, who made Christmas so magical, so ... vibrant. He's the one who got me the tree and lights. He caught them on sale after the holidays when I was seventeen and added them to the cart, telling me I'd need them when I moved out on my own."

"You haven't celebrated Christmas in five years, have you?" Nick squeezed her hand.

73

"We put out just enough to make Mark happy. I couldn't let him down. But I don't do anything myself. It's not the same."

"I'm sorry." The words hung in the air as if time had stilled in this bubble of Santaland in the middle of the store.

She tugged her fingers from his and straightened her back. "You wanted to go home over an hour ago, and here we are dawdling. Let's get these hung already."

Just like that, the connection was broken, the moment past. But it had been there.

"What about you?" She handed him some candy canes to dangle from the branches. "Do you put up a tree?"

"No. With having one here and doing my real celebration at my mom's house, I guess I never saw the need." He rolled his eyes as she came behind him and repositioned an ornament he'd just hung. "I mean, what's the point? I spend most of my time here anyway.

"I dread Christmas, to be honest. In the retail world, it means more work than anything. Trying to get numbers up for the end of the year, dealing with impatient customers, listening to the same songs over and over, watching kids throw fits to get what they think they want."

"That's so sad." She handed him a box of garland made of candy-shaped beads.

"That's managing a toy store." He shrugged. "The season is more about moving merchandise than anything."

She shot him a look, but he couldn't make out what it meant. The wheels in her mind were spinning. Was she going to try and fix Christmas for him as well as his store? That would be ironic.

After the tree had been adorned in red, white, and silvery balls and shapes, they stood back and admired their work. She tilted her head and moved to the left, then the right. What was she looking for?

"It's missing something."

"Looks fine to me." He held his arm stiff, refusing to glance at his watch. If he didn't know what time it was, maybe it wouldn't be as late as he feared.

"The topper." She knelt and rummaged through the bags on the floor. "I know I put it here somewhere. I just found it in Austin. When I saw it last night, I couldn't resist."

"You bought a tree topper last night for a tree you weren't going to use?"

"I bought it because it was perfect for here." She leaned back on her heels. "Where did it get to?"

He pointed to the packages on the chair. "Is it in one of these?"

"Yes!" She leaped to her feet and dashed over to start hunting again. "Here!"

She lifted a red star, garland lining its five sides, lights in the middle. Almost an exact replica of the one that had sat on his grandmother's tree—but new instead of falling apart. He swallowed a lump forming in his throat. She had gone to a lot of trouble to find something so similar to the one from the seventies.

"You want the honors?" She held it out to him.

"We can do it together." He grasped a corner and walked with her over to the tree. She had to lift up on her tiptoes to match his reach, but they made it to the top and set the star in place. He attached the end to the lights already there, and it lit up brilliantly, not a broken bulb in sight.

He simply stood and stared for a moment, in awe of their work. She was right again. This was the tree that should have been here the whole time. Why had he fought her on it? Maybe he should reconsider some of her other suggestions too. But not tonight.

"We did good work." She rearranged a bulb and stepped back, only to get her foot tangled in the extension cord.

Her arms windmilled as she tilted. He caught her forearms and pulled her to him with more force than necessary. A soft *oof* escaped her as her torso collided with his. Her eyes grew wider as she stared up at him, her hands pressed against his chest. Even through his thick vest, the heat of them left a mark on his skin that wouldn't disappear for a while. She took a step back long before he was ready to release her.

She brushed a loose strand of hair behind her ear. "It's getting late. We should probably get all this cleaned up. I'm sure you need to be back here early in the morning."

"Right." He cleared his throat and scanned the area. "I'll go grab the broom."

What was going on? He couldn't possibly like Trudy, could he? He shook his head to try and clear it. A girl he'd practically despised three days before. But more than *like*, he was attracted to her. These late nights were getting to him.

It must be the magic glow of all those Christmas lights. And since when had he last wanted to do anything in the holiday spirit? Most of this time of year was ruined for him thanks to the business aspect. This was the busiest shopping season, and it had become all about the money.

He needed sleep. And a dose of reality. Because nothing about this—whatever *this* was between him and Trudy—could go further. She was moving back to Austin, and he wasn't about to leave the store ... especially after all this work. This work she'd inspired and pushed for. And if he kept reminding himself that they couldn't possibly have anything come of this, maybe he'd start believing it.

And maybe he'd start believing in Uncle Paul's Christmas miracles too. Yeah, right.

Chapter Ten

T rudy let out a frustrated grunt.

"That's the third time you've made that noise in the last half hour." Nick stacked several papers on his desk and then filed them away. "What's going on?"

"This website isn't cooperating." She tossed her pencil down and leaned back in her chair. "I thought I'd figured out a way to make a page for inventory, but I can't get my link to work."

"Didn't we agree there's not enough time right now to load all our inventory on the website?" Nick came around and leaned against the front of his desk.

"I know." She shook her head. "But I had asked another friend for advice on the best way to make it work, and it seemed like we'd come up with a reasonable solution. Now I'm not so sure."

"Maybe you need a break. You can come back with fresh eyes." He straightened and grabbed their jackets off the hooks by the door, tossing hers at her.

"Who are you, and what have you done with the man who doesn't have a moment to spare?" Trudy slipped her arms in her sleeves and then faced him. "Are you seriously suggesting leaving the store during working hours for the second time in as many days?"

"Just come on." He tugged her sleeve and led her toward the door.

"Where are we going?" She gave him just enough resistance to let him know she wasn't completely impressed with his kidnapping skills.

Paul's eyes widened with surprise, if not a bit of skepticism.

"There's a place down the block you need to try." Nick tucked her hand through the crook of his arm and led the way through the blustery wind. At least it wasn't raining. Clouds hung low overhead, though, promising it could start again at any moment and add to the puddles she skirted around.

"You know Temple isn't the only city in Texas with fun places to go, right?" She flipped her hair over her shoulder. "I mean, I'm from Austin. There are tons of great places to eat down there."

"I never said we were the only city with fun places. I said this one was worth trying out." He motioned toward a brick building in front of them. The masonry was painted white and decorated with a large mural of all sorts of yummy treats. Near the bottom a large fork and spoon stood sentinel, and a little girl stood between them, having her picture taken.

"So fun." Trudy breathed the words out. "Is it a bakery?"

"A confectionary." He pulled the door open and motioned her through.

The scent of sugar permeated the air. The walls were a light pink and covered in elongated ovals that resembled giant sprinkles. Three glass cases made a *U* of confections and treats that would make a diabetic go into a shock just by looking. Her mouth watered as she took it all in.

"It's a great day to have some fudge." He led her toward the left side of the options.

Her heart skipped a beat. Fudge. Of all the sweets he could have offered, he had to pick fudge. She mashed her lips together, willing her body to act normal. Nick was simply trying to do something nice. He couldn't know. She hadn't told him this story yet.

Nick plucked at her sleeve and she realized her feet had stopped moving. "What's wrong?"

"Sorry." She swallowed hard. "I guess I got sidetracked."

"Something is going on in that head of yours." He narrowed his eyes. "And I'd bet it's not the website issues. What did I do wrong this time?"

"It's not you." She ducked her head. "It's—"

He stood there as if frozen in anticipation of whatever she was going to say.

She pointed to the case of treats.

"The fudge?" He leaned down to meet her gaze. "Are you allergic or something?"

"No." She shook her head and stared at the display. "I—" Her lips pressed together again. Anything to control the tremors that came with the memory.

"Your dad?" He almost whispered the words. "Fudge was something you did with him?"

She accomplished a barely perceptible nod, but it was enough.

"I'm sorry." He reached like he might hug her and then awkwardly squeezed her upper arms instead. "If I'd known it would trigger a memory like that ... I never would have—"

"I know." She shifted her weight. "I know it's ridiculous. I mean, it's just sugar."

"We need a few minutes to think about what we want." Nick informed the girl watching them from behind the counter. Then he led Trudy over to an iron table and sat across from her.

What was it about this man that brought out stories she hadn't let herself relive in years? Regardless she wanted him to understand. "It was maybe the third or fourth year of the lists. I was around eight or nine."

"The perfect age to soak up Christmas, if I remember

correctly." One side of his lips turned up. "That was around the time I got my dirt bike."

"Yes." She clasped her hands together. "I suggested we make fudge. I must have seen someone making it on a movie or something. Dad was game and researched several different recipes until he found one that should have been easy enough. We actually had to buy a candy thermometer because Mom never wanted to make something that had to be so precise."

She met his gaze and let herself smile at the next part. "There we stood, in matching aprons Mom had whipped up. This was going to be the best batch of fudge anyone in our family had ever tasted."

He sat there for several moments in silence, but when she didn't say more, he leaned forward. "Was it?"

"It was a disaster. Neither one of us could figure out what went wrong. It was a bit scorched. And didn't set right, so it was crumbly and dry. My sister Katt turned her nose up at the first piece we offered. Mom ate the obligatory first bite. Dad went over the recipe time and again, trying to figure out what we had missed. I was afraid he was upset that no one else would eat it. So, I ate as many pieces as I could to show him it wasn't as bad as the others said."

"Oh, no." Nick wrinkled his nose.

"I don't think I've ever felt so sick in my life as I did that night." She pressed a hand to her tummy, the memory inciting phantom queasiness. "Since then, even the mention of fudge makes me a bit squeamish."

"Got it." He pushed to his feet. "No fudge. But I think I know something you'll like even more. One of their specialties. Stay here."

The glare of the lights from this angle made it hard to discern exactly what was displayed in the middle section of cases. He pointed and then motioned with his hands to the girl helping him. She scooped several of whatever he'd asked for into a white paper bag and handed it to him before accepting his money. He came back to their table with a huge grin on his face.

The mystery of it had her antsy. "What did you get?"

"Do you trust me?"

"What kind of question is that?" She crossed her arms. "We barely know each other. And it's not like you've shown a lot of trust in me either."

"Fair point." He tilted his head. "But you seemed to approve of the hot chocolate I brought you last night."

"Okay. Yes. I did like the hot chocolate. How did you know peppermint is my favorite?"

"Lucky guess." He smirked. "You brought me a peppermint mocha earlier this week. And all your tree decorations are red and white."

"I guess I gave myself away." She studied him a second, debating a proposition. Finally, she continued, "I will trust you on one condition."

He raised an eyebrow. "What's that?"

"I will try whatever it is you bought if you will seriously talk to me about hiring whoever did the mural on this building to come do one on yours too."

His breath came out in a whoosh. "That's not even on the same level. I'm talking food and you're talking ... well, something more permanent."

"Hey. Coming here was your idea. I don't have to stay. I could walk back right now and try to fix the problem on that website ... for *your* store." She started to stand.

"Okay, okay." He waved his hand for her to sit again. "We can *talk* about it. I make no promises beyond that."

She bounced a bit as she regained her seat. "Really?"

"Talk about it. Nothing more."

"Still, that's more than you would have given me several days ago." She held out a hand. "Fine. Deal. What did you get?"

"Close your eyes."

"What?"

He rattled the bag. "Close your eyes and open your mouth. I don't want you to go into this with preconceived notions about what it's supposed to taste like."

"Now you've got me nervous."

"No need to be nervous. I really think you're going to love this." He ran a hand through his hair. "But I want to surprise you."

Trudy's heart rate picked up speed. This was a little crazy. "And you can't surprise me by putting it in my hand?"

"Just trust me, please." The look of sincerity in his eyes and the *please* had her eyelids fluttering shut.

"Fine." She leaned forward and opened her mouth.

Nick's fingers brushed the edge of her lips as he set something on her tongue. Thrills ran through her from more than just the tastiness of the confection. Her breath hitched. Her eyes opened once more, and she held her breath for a second as he backed away. Maybe she was allergic to him, going into anaphylactic shock. But no. As he regained a bit more distance, her tongue told her to pay more attention to what he had given her than to the man himself.

"It's a peppermint hot chocolate truffle. The center's chocolate marshmallow fluff." Nick's words came out breathier than he wanted, but he hadn't expected the reaction from her or his own body when he placed the goodie in her mouth. When she had let out that little gasp, his heartbeat accelerated and all he could focus on was the shape of her lips, how her skin glowed, the blue in her eyes as they shot back open.

She backed up, too, and then let herself chew. Her cheeks were pinker than earlier, but he wasn't about to point it out. Instead, he removed a truffle for himself.

"This is amazing." She wiped the corner of her mouth with

her fingers, drawing his attention right back to where he'd been admiring before. Why was this a good idea again?

He held out the bag so she could get another.

"Thank you." She studied the way the ball in her hand appeared, with the mini chocolate chips and crushed peppermint pieces all over it. "You're right. It's worth coming for."

"Maybe almost as good as something you could find in Austin?" He couldn't resist the tease.

"Maybe." She drew out the word with a smile before enjoying her second treat. "Now, let's talk murals."

He wrinkled his nose. "I was really hoping you'd forget that."

"In three minutes?" She shot him a skeptical look.

Was that all it had been? Time was becoming surreal to him this morning. He popped his other truffle in his mouth and wadded up the bag.

"Let's walk."

She pulled him to a stop right outside the store. "Look. This is exactly what I was talking about for your store."

"You want sweets on the front of a toy store?"

"You know what I mean." She swatted at him. "Something interactive and playful. Eye-catching."

"Everyone is getting murals now. Wouldn't that simply make us blend in?" He steered her down the sidewalk and back toward the Emporium.

"Not if it's done right. And not everyone has murals. Temple is pretty big. But why not embrace the mural movement going on in the downtown area, which you're a part of?" Her steps were more of a skip than a normal walk as they made their way back down the block. "I was doing some research—"

"When on earth did you have time to do more research?" He dashed a hand through his hair and then cringed as he imagined how askew it must be now. He'd run his fingers through it at least four times this morning. It was a trait he needed to get a grip on if he was ever going to impress a girl. Not that he was trying to do anything of the sort with Trudy. Right?

"I was messaging back and forth with my computer friend for a while last night about the website issue and decided to look a few things up while waiting for him to respond." She shrugged.

Him? His heart skipped a beat, wondering how close she was to this *computer friend*. He didn't want to analyze why. She had guy friends. Of course, she did. Just like he had friends who were girls. Or would, if he had time for friends.

He pulled open the door of the store for her and waved at Uncle Paul. He was sure to get grilled over leaving during working hours later, but he'd deal with that then. He was more concerned with what Trudy had just said.

"We didn't leave here until after eleven."

"Yes." She plopped down in her chair and opened her laptop once more.

"Are you sleeping at all? Every day, you mention everything you accomplish after leaving the store hours after we close." He leaned against the front of his desk instead of sliding behind it. For reasons he couldn't fathom, he wanted to be closer to her for this answer.

"I think too much if I go to bed early this time of year. Staying up late helps keep me distracted, and then once I do give up and lay down, I'm so exhausted I fall asleep right away." She wouldn't meet his eyes.

He lifted a brow. "Eleven-thirty is not early. You know that, right?"

"I was still wired from everything earlier in the evening." She clicked a few times on her mouse pad. "Look at this."

He didn't want to end the conversation they'd been having, but something told him she wouldn't give another inch. Instead, he leaned forward to look at her screen. A big mural was in the middle of it. Back to this topic, then.

"'Artégés'?" He read the title.

"It's a group Creative Temple started to coordinate a bunch

of high school art students to work up and paint this mural. Isn't it cool?" She waved her hand in front of it like a game show hostess.

"Sure. But what does it have to do with us?"

"I think you should offer your wall for them to do next summer." She ticked off points on her fingers. "It would be great publicity for your store. It would get the mural done. It's giving these kids an opportunity like no other."

"Even if I agree to this—and I'm not agreeing to anything yet —what if they don't want to use my wall or go with your suggestions on what to paint?" He crossed his arms over his chest.

"Then we'll come up with a Plan B." She leaned back as if she hadn't a care in the world.

"We?" His rebellious heart leaped at the word. "Aren't you moving back to Austin?"

She shrugged and spun her chair around. "Doesn't mean I can't help collaborate."

"Right." He stood. "I better do a walkthrough of the store, make sure all is going well."

"Sure. You up for helping do more tiles tonight?"

"Probably not." He leaned against the door frame for a moment. "I want one night this week where I can get home early and rest, especially since tomorrow is our day off."

"Oh." She slapped herself in the forehead. "I didn't even think about the store being closed tomorrow."

"Sundays are for church services." He gave a quick nod and moved out to do his job ... and maybe get his head on straight again. A day away from the store and Trudy McNamara would do him good in more ways than one. He didn't even recognize who he was becoming lately. Whether or not he liked the changes, that was debatable.

Chapter Eleven

"Why are we here? This isn't where Katt normally worships." Trudy pointed to the church building in front of them.

"Katt hasn't been particularly happy where they are lately." Her mom gathered a Pashmina shawl closer around her shoulders and then headed up the steps. "And Paul recommended this one."

"Of course he did." Trudy muttered under her breath. Paul was becoming more and more of an influence in her mom's life, and Trudy wasn't sure what to think about it. Sure, her mom was still alive and deserved companionship as much as any other person, but did she want more than that?

The last few days, it seemed like every other conversation she had with her mom included something Paul had said or done or mentioned. Surely, they hadn't crammed that much into one dinner a few nights before. When had they found the time to create this much conversational fodder?

Mom hummed softly as she scanned the auditorium. Who was she looking for right now? Knots tangled in Trudy's stomach. Sure enough, not two minutes later, Paul appeared before them, a welcoming grin on his face.

"Glad you could make it." He clasped her mom's hand in his for much longer than Trudy felt necessary. She stuck hers out so he'd be obligated to let go of the one he held and greet her too. It might be slightly childish, but she had to do something.

"I hear you're the be-all and end-all of knowledge about Temple." Trudy let a bit more sarcasm slip through her voice than usual. "Mom has been telling me all the places you've recommended."

"Come now." Paul winked. "I know Nick has shown you at least one or two places this week too."

Trudy pressed her lips together. Were her cheeks as pink as they were hot? Because her thoughts automatically went back to the day before when Nick had fed her that delicious truffle. And the physical turmoil he'd stirred up with his slightest touch. No fair of Paul to bring up such a memory on a Sunday morning.

Her mom followed Paul down the aisle to where his family sat. Nick peeked up from his phone and blinked when he noticed her standing there. His hair was slicked down more than normal today, and Trudy had the itch to reach over and give it its usual tousle. He stood and pulled his vest straighter before nodding a greeting. The bowtie was the perfect accessory to set off her preconceived opinion of his nerdish ways. It was a nice touch.

"I wasn't expecting to see you here."

"That makes two of us." Trudy scanned the space. "Evidently your Uncle Paul convinced my mom that this is the place to be. Katt usually worships with a smaller congregation on the other side of town but isn't happy with some things happening there. So, Mom took Paul's advice to gather us all here today."

"I didn't realize your mom and Uncle Paul were such good friends." Nick glanced down the row where they stood talking to some others.

"I'm beginning to wonder just exactly how good of friends they are." Trudy clutched her Bible so tightly she wouldn't be surprised to find fingerprints in the leather cover later.

"Huh." Nick motioned to the seat beside him. "Well, you're welcome to join us, if you want. That's my dad and mom Uncle Paul's introducing your mom to right now. And Uncle Andy is on the row behind us with Aunt Bett."

"Bett?" Trudy glanced over his shoulder.

"Short for Elizabeth. None of us could pronounce it correctly when we were younger, so it got shortened."

"*Ah.*" She nodded. "How many cousins do you have?"

"Six and a brother." Nick crammed his hands in his pockets and rocked up on his heels. "But they've mostly moved to other places now."

She tucked a strand of hair behind her ear. "Which explains why you're the only one working at the store."

"I was the only one really interested at the time. Although I'm sure several others will inherit some of the ownership eventually, since it's split between the three brothers." Nick shrugged.

"Aunt Tootie!" Mark collided with her leg and wrapped himself around it.

"Hi Mark-o." Trudy ruffled Mark's hair the way she'd wanted to muss Nick's a moment before. "You look nice today."

Mark wrinkled his nose. "Mommy said I had to wear these clothes so we could make a good impression."

"Well, you're making an impression on me." Trudy squeezed his shoulders and wondered if her leg would ever regain its proper blood flow after his tight tackle.

"Mark, come on. Let's go find your Sunday school class." Katt appeared and dislodged her son from Trudy's lower half. "Save me a seat, Trudy?"

She was gone before Trudy could reply. The people in the auditorium slowly sat down and grew quiet. Trudy noticed her mom slid in next to Paul at the end of the row. She eyeballed the space next to Nick and decided at least three people could fit.

Taking a deep breath, she tried to relax her shoulders as she sat next to this man she'd known for almost a full week now.

They'd gone from arguing over everything to something else in the last few days, but she wasn't sure exactly what that something was. Or what she wanted it to grow into. She'd never turn down another friend, but was that all this was?

"Tootie, huh?" Nick's whisper startled her, his breath moving a tendril of her hair against her cheek.

"I guess that's right up there with Bett, right?" She was rather proud of how steady her voice sounded.

"Right."

Katt slid in next to her with Brian right behind. The space suddenly seemed much smaller than her original estimation. Katt wiggled over until Trudy had no choice but to scoot a few inches closer to Nick. The heat of his body penetrated her sleeve. His arm brushed against her as he moved to open the Bible app on his phone. Trudy held herself very stiff, trying to keep from bumping into him more than necessary. So much for relaxing.

Standing for hymns during the worship service didn't bring much relief because they were still crammed tightly. Even more so now with Mark wiggling among all his loved ones. Katt had no idea what she was forcing Trudy to go through by leaving her such a small area. Why, oh why, had Mom insisted they come here this morning?

As they sat once more, Trudy glanced down the row just as Paul slid his arm around her mom's shoulders. Trudy's heart skipped a beat, and she collapsed onto the pew much harder than she intended. Katt and Nick both shot her a frown, but she didn't care. She just wanted this service over as soon as possible.

The rigid woman sitting next to Nick today was not the same girl who bounced down the sidewalk from the confectionary yesterday. On Saturday he'd tucked her hand through his arm, and they'd walked amicably together. Now she was stiff as a board and distracted, as if she'd rather be anywhere but next to him. What had changed?

Nick would have draped his arm across the back of the pew, but something told him it would be unwelcome even if it gave her more wiggle room. Each time their sleeves brushed, memories from the previous week ran through his head. Had he ever grown to know someone so quickly? To change his preconceived notions so fast?

Was their proximity doing the same for her? If it was, it obviously wasn't as pleasant on her end. Had he forgotten something that had passed between them? Was she upset he knew her nickname? Nothing made sense.

Despite how taut she'd sat all through the worship service, she didn't move after the final amen. She remained with her head bowed, her hands gripping her Bible so tightly her knuckles were white. Was she sick? Praying?

"Trudy?" Her mom stood before them.

Trudy stared up, a wariness in her eyes that Nick had never seen before.

"You okay, honey? Paul asked us to join him for lunch." The sparkle in her mom's eyes seemed even brighter compared to the dull expression in Trudy's.

"I can't today." Trudy clutched her Bible into her chest like a shield. "Maybe you can drop me off at the house?"

"You sure you're okay?" Her mom leaned forward and pressed her fingers against Trudy's forehead.

Trudy brushed them away angrily. "I'm fine."

"Okay." Her mom peered down where Mark tugged at her skirt. "Hey, big boy. What's going on?"

"Nana, did you find the cookie cutters? You said when you found the cutters, we could decorate cookies."

"You know what?" Trudy's mom nodded. "I found them, and your Aunt Trudy used to love making cookies. Do you think she'd like to do that this afternoon?"

"Mom." Trudy finally stood, gripping the pew in front of them as if afraid to trust her legs. "Seriously."

If Nick had to place a bet on it, he'd guess her dad had baked cookies with Trudy as one of their bucket list items. A visible war waged inside her. But he had no idea how to help her fight this battle.

Katt jumped in the conversation. "Oh, if you guys could watch Mark this afternoon, that would be great. Brian and I have a few more things we need to get without certain eyes seeing."

"I really need to do some more on the website this afternoon." Trudy shook her head.

"It's Sunday." Nick and his uncle said at the same time.

"No work on Sundays." Nick poked Trudy in the shoulder. "Not even on the website."

"I actually already had plans for this afternoon." Connie glanced between his uncle and her daughter.

Trudy physically stiffened. She was losing this fight. Nick had to do something.

"I'd be willing to help." He wouldn't know how to make a cookie if the recipe slapped him in the face, but it was the first thing that came to his mind. He'd longed for time away from her yesterday, and yet here he was, offering to spend more. How would she take it? She hadn't exactly shown a friendly front this morning.

Trudy's head slowly turned to him, a frown creasing her brow. "You want to make cookies?"

"I don't remember ever making Christmas cookies before." Nick leaned toward Mark. "Think you could teach me all your tricks?"

Mark nodded with solemn eyes. "You have to let them cool off before you can put on the icing and sprinkles."

"Got it." Nick nodded.

"Sounds like you all are going to have fun this afternoon." Connie raised an eyebrow as she glanced from Trudy to Nick.

"Should be interesting, at least." Trudy shot a dirty look at his uncle again.

"I'll bring Mark by after lunch. And maybe a quick nap." Katt grabbed the boy's hand. "That work for you?"

"Doesn't sound like I have a choice." Trudy muttered low enough Mark couldn't hear and then pinched her lips together. She was either biting back sharp remarks or fighting tears. Possibly both.

"Can I give you a ride home?" Nick studied the intriguing girl before him. Her answer would probably determine the way the rest of the day went. "I know a little sandwich shop on the way, if you want to grab a bite."

Uncle Paul chuckled.

Trudy's cheeks pinkened. "Can we just go? I don't even care anymore."

The words were obviously untrue, but he gladly escorted her back up the aisle and away from his family and her mom. "Are you sure you're okay?"

"I wish people would quit asking me that." She slapped her palm on one of her legs so hard that he winced, imagining how it had hurt.

"Got it. No more asking about your welfare." He opened the car door and motioned her inside. "How about lunch? Does a sandwich sound good?"

"Fine." She stared straight ahead.

"Do you want me to order for you, or would you like to have a say in what you eat?"

She shot him a glare.

"Right. I have no idea what that look means, so you're going to have to give me a little more to go on." He pulled into a parking place at the eatery.

"Sorry. My mind is a bit ... unsettled right now." She looked down where her fingers twisted her Bible's ribbon bookmark around and around her thumb. "I wasn't expecting a lot of things that happened this morning, including babysitting Mark and having to make cookies. I haven't done it ... in a while."

"Babysit or make cookies?"

She shot him another look, and this time he easily determined its meaning. She wasn't impressed by his attempt at lightening the mood.

"Right. I'm guessing it's been at least five years since you decorated Christmas cookies?" He cut the ignition and waited in the silence that followed.

Her shaky breath confirmed his suspicions.

"Sandwich preferences? Want to trust my judgment on that too?" He opened his door.

"Nothing with gross stuff like horseradish." Her voice only trembled slightly.

"Be back in a few minutes." Maybe by the time he got their food, she'd be able to give him more to work with than what he'd gathered so far. Because if this was the way the afternoon would be, he already regretted offering to come help. And yet could he really regret it? He'd imagined time apart would be good for them—help him clear his head and figure out exactly what had been developing this week. Yet he'd also thrilled when he saw her in front of him in the auditorium.

There was a great possibility that nothing would come from this whatever-it-was besides an improved store, but he couldn't help hoping something might. And if something might, he definitely wanted to be around to see what it was. He shook his head free of the jumbled thoughts and ordered potato soup in bread bowls—comfort food. He had an inkling she needed it.

And by the end of making cookies with a four-year-old, he'd probably need some comfort too. What had he gotten himself into? Besides more time with Trudy.

93

Chapter Twelve

What first? Trudy scanned the kitchen, trying to remember where they'd stashed things while unpacking it. The layout in here was much different from the house in Austin.

"Sit. Eat first." Nick motioned with one of the containers that had his car smelling so divine on the way over here.

She didn't want to follow orders right now, but her stomach took control of her body and pushed her toward a chair. She'd eat just enough to satisfy him and then get organized before Mark arrived. Nick lifted the lid with a flourish and a bread bowl appeared. Next, he pulled the lid from another container and revealed potato soup.

Comfort food. Her tummy gurgled with appreciation. Fine. She savored a few bites and appreciated that he stayed silent.

"Do you believe in heaven?" So much for him not talking.

"Of course I do." She spooned another bite.

He pinched off a piece of bread and chewed slowly. What was he insinuating? The longer he went without talking, the more she wanted to know.

"Why did you ask?" She finally broke the silence herself.

"I'm just thinking back over all the conversations we've had over the last week."

There were so many options there, from chocolate to painting to lightbulbs.

"O-kay." She stretched the word out, hoping it would remind him she needed more information.

"Your dad ..." He trailed off. "One of the reasons you haven't made cookies in a while is because you did it with him, right?"

She nodded.

"But you believe he's in heaven, right?"

Her heart jerked in her chest. "Of course." She swallowed several times, blinking against moisture in her eyes. "I know it's supposed to make things easier. But it doesn't help with the missing. He should be here. And he's not."

"But you wouldn't want him to give up paradise and come back to this world, right?"

"Nick, please. It's not that easy. I know as a Christian I'm supposed to be able to just pick up and move on, but it's not that easy."

He grabbed her hand. "I wasn't trying to say it was easy. I'm sorry you thought that. I'm just trying to understand."

She pulled away again and shook her head. "I need to get ready for when Mark gets here. He won't have the patience to wait while I round up ingredients."

"Sure." He rose too. "Give me just a few minutes and I'll help."

"Don't worry about it. I've got to remember where we put things." And she needed a few minutes away from Nick too.

Back in the kitchen, she drew a shuddering breath. Time to push that conversation aside and focus on what she needed for her nephew. How had she gotten suckered into this?

What a rotten morning. She slammed the flour cannister on the counter, grateful at the last minute that it was plastic and not ceramic. If it had broken, the mess would've been more than she could handle today.

Sure, she would do just about anything for Mark. She had to maintain her title of favorite aunt after all. But the shock of Nick offering to come help had made it impossible to turn Katt and Mom down.

Mom. There was a whole other issue. She had an inkling of what was going on between her and Paul, and she didn't like it one bit. Her mom couldn't possibly be interested in Santa, of all people! Could she? Not after twenty-nine years of being married to Dad, a man who would have bled wassail if cut, he loved Christmas so much. To go from someone who exuded the very spirit of the season to one who acted like a caricature of it? No.

She set the sugar next to the flour with slightly less force. If she kept this clatter up, Nick would be sure to come investigate. It would be safer to have Nick around when Mark was here to run interference.

Now to round up the parts Mark would be most interested in —sprinkles. Just her luck, all the way on the top shelf. She dragged a chair over from the table and climbed up to find the right colors.

"Can I help?"

Nick's voice startled Trudy, and she lost her balance. What was wrong with her? She wasn't normally this clumsy, but how many times had she tripped or dropped or bumped the last week? Nick's hands grasped her waist and steadied her ... or at least her balance. The rest of her still felt very off-center as the warmth of his fingers seeped through her sweater and permeated her skin, finding emotional places she hadn't even realized were waiting to be awakened.

"You okay?" Nick removed one hand and held it out to help her down. "You should've told me there was something you needed help reaching."

"You promised not to ask me that." She pressed her fingertips to her eyes for a moment.

"I apologize. I will strive to do better for the rest of the day."

"I'm rather used to fending for myself. We haven't had a guy around in years. And this kitchen's cabinets aren't nearly as tall as the ones we had in Austin." After a moment's hesitation, she accepted his help and stepped down. "Thanks."

"Did you get everything you needed from up there?" He wasn't relinquishing his grip. Did he realize it?

It took her a minute to remember he'd asked a question. "Oh, yes. I think this should be enough, don't you?" She laid out the bottles of green and red sanding sugar, red, green, and white jimmies, and chocolate chips for extra details.

He finally released his hold, and she instantly missed the warmth of his fingers. "I'd hope so."

"Do you really not remember ever decorating cookies as a kid?" She opened a drawer and rummaged for measuring spoons to have something else to do.

"I'm sure we did it at least once." He leaned against the counter. "But my mom was never big on sweets. She makes an amazing dressing to go with the turkey." Nick shook his head. "Baking just wasn't her forte. That was more in line with my aunts and Grandma. They would always bring the desserts, Mom was in charge of the main course."

"Probably why you're on such familiar terms with the menu at the confectionary, huh? I can't imagine growing up not making sweets at least every few weeks. We always had cookies or something around to snack on after school." A laugh burst from her lips. "Maybe that's why I had such bad acne as a teen. All that sugar."

"Really? But your skin is perfect." He ran a finger down her cheek and then jerked his hand back as if he'd only realized what he was doing.

She cleared her throat and turned the other way. Surely there was something on the other side of the kitchen she needed. Cooling racks. She marched over to the pantry and opened the door. Of course Mom had put them on the top shelf. Why not?

"Can you get these down for me?" She spit the question out

and then stepped back so there'd be no chance of them bumping as he came closer.

"Which?"

"The cooling racks, all the way over on the right side."

"Aunt Tootie!" Mark's voice rang down the hallway as the front door slammed. Saved by the nephew.

"He wouldn't lay down for a nap, so good luck." Katt set a bag on the table and then caught her son to remove his jacket before he could get into anything. "You listen to Aunt Tootie, okay? Do what she says. Mommy and Daddy will come get you in a little while."

"Okay, Mommy. We're going to make lots of yummy cookies." He bounced over to the stepladder Trudy's mom kept in the kitchen for when he visited. It had been the girls' when they were little. "Ready, Aunt Tootie?"

"Call if you need help." Katt dropped an air kiss next to Trudy's cheek and was gone as quickly as she'd appeared.

Nick rubbed his hands together. "So, what first?"

"Butter and sugar and eggs."

They put the mixer in front of Mark, with each of them flanking him. Once the wet ingredients were combined, it was time to add the dry. Trudy funneled a bit of the flour mixture into the mixer and set the rest aside.

"Okay, Mark-o. See this button?" Trudy indicated somewhere around the second or third speed level. "We need to start very slowly so the flour doesn't go everywhere. Can you—"

"Sure." Mark's little fingers shot out and pushed hard. The lever flew over to the highest speed. A white cloud of dust covered them all.

"Mark!" Trudy fumbled to kill the power.

"I'm sorry, Aunt Tootie! I didn't mean to." The four-year-old melted into a puddle of contrition.

"I know." Trudy brushed the front of her shirt and wondered if there were any way to salvage what was left. "It's a big mess, though. Can you just ... can you just step over there for me?"

"Hey, bud. Let's go see what we can find in here." Nick was there helping the boy down. Trudy had forgotten he was even there. Tears welled up in her throat as she surveyed the disaster left behind. Hadn't she been thinking earlier this afternoon that spilling flour would be more than she could handle? Yet here she was.

"I've got him occupied for now." Nick appeared at her elbow.

She glanced through the doorway but couldn't see far enough around the corner. "What's he doing?"

"There was an old Christmas special on television."

"Katt will love that." Trudy rolled her eyes. "She barely lets him have any screen time."

"What she doesn't know won't hurt her." He used the edge of his hand to ease the piles of flour off the counter and into his other palm. He added the scoop back into the mixer. "I bet we can save most of this."

"How?" She flopped her hands at her sides. "How can you be so calm? After this?"

"Well, I wasn't quite as wound up as you were to begin with." He turned to her, already having most of the counter swept up again. "So, that probably helped."

"Wound up?" Her fists automatically went to her hips.

"You've been on edge all day." He wet a washcloth and came toward her. "Having something you didn't want to do pushed on you without a chance to turn it down, I'm sure didn't help. And then Mark's excitement. Something like this was sure to happen." He dabbed at her forehead. "You have a little flour here."

So much for her keeping her frustration and stress under wraps. She must be an open book. His touch was gentle as he wiped the mess from her face. He had been nothing but kind the whole day despite her lousy attitude.

He stood so close, only a breath away. Not even that far—she could feel each of his exhales as he worked to remove every particle. She studied his eyes as they focused on their task. They met her gaze and locked on.

Everything froze around them.

The mess.

The sounds of the show in the other room.

Her heart.

What was going on? His hands framed her face while his eyes sought hers, glanced to her lips and then back up. Was he going to kiss her?

Did Trudy have any idea of the crazy thoughts running through his head right now? Nick swallowed, afraid to move, to break the moment, to ruin ... anything. And yet he wanted to move, to get closer to her, to see if she wanted the same thing he did the more he spent time with her. Was this ridiculous? They were so different, but ...

He inched closer, just enough to see if she'd move back, stay still, or even, maybe, meet him halfway. Her breath hitched a little, her eyelids lowered to half-mast. And she didn't retreat. That had to be a good sign.

Here went nothing. He eased forward, closing the gap a tenth of an inch at a time.

"Aunt Tootie?"

Trudy jerked out of his arms so fast he wondered if he'd dreamed her there in the first place. She drew a shaky breath and then squared her shoulders as her nephew barreled back into the room. Mark ran straight at Trudy's legs and wrapped himself around her, as tightly as Nick had hoped to be only moments before.

"Hey, Mark. Good news. Nick thinks he's saved enough of the flour that we can still use this batch." She lifted him onto the step stool once more. "How about we get this ready to bake?"

"Yuh-huh." Mark nodded.

This time Trudy guided Mark's fingers on the switch. The process went much smoother. She helped him roll out the dough and press the cookie cutters into it, making Santas, gingerbread men, candy canes, and reindeer. The last ones reminded Nick of their paintings. What had she done with hers? His was stored behind the filing cabinet in his office, but he wasn't about to offer up that info.

They fell into a rhythm, with him using a spatula to place each shape onto the baking sheets. Soon the house filled with the sweet smell of sugar. Mark peeked into the oven at least twenty times in the short minutes it took to bake them to golden brown. The hardest part was convincing him to wait for them to cool before decorating.

Watching a four-year-old squeeze icing onto a cookie was a mess like nothing Nick had ever prepared for. He didn't have any nieces and nephews of his own yet, so this was a new experience. Trudy caught Nick's eye above Mark's head as the preschooler dumped half a bottle of sprinkles onto Santa. The crinkles at the corners of her own baby blues showed she enjoyed Nick's reaction more than the chaos her nephew inflicted.

They all looked up half an hour later when Katt walked in. "Goodness! How many cookies did you make?"

"A normal batch. I think it makes three dozen or so." Trudy shrugged. "Mark's only eaten half of them."

Katt pressed fingers to her forehead and squeezed her eyes closed. "Please tell me you're kidding."

"He's had one. And I even helped him pick one without a million sprinkles. Only a hundred thousand or so." Trudy winked at Nick. She obviously got a thrill from ribbing her sister.

"Looks like it was a productive afternoon." Katt glanced around at the still-slightly-white kitchen where the flour had exploded earlier. "Glad it was you and not me. You always deal with things like this better than I do."

Trudy pinched her lips together and took a rag to the counter.

Nick decided a change of subject was in order. "Did you finish your shopping?"

"Yes, thank goodness. It always gets so crazy the closer to Christmas you wait." Katt pointed at her sister. "Oh. And Mom wants to put up her tree tonight when she gets back."

Nick had no idea a spine could go as stiff as Trudy's did. She had decorated a tree only two days before. What was so different about this one?

"Trudy, can you show me somewhere I can clean up a little?" Nick held out his shirt to show the flour remaining on his front.

"Oh." Trudy dropped her rag and started toward the hallway. "Yes. Sorry I didn't think to offer something earlier. I'm sure we have a T-shirt you could borrow."

"You don't have to do that." Nick had to pick up his pace to keep up as she practically ran from the kitchen. "I just wanted to make sure there wasn't any left on my face."

Her skin grew pinker at that. Was she remembering earlier? She flipped a light switch to a room that he would never have known was actually being used by a person if she hadn't warned him before about all the boxes. A bed hid in the back corner, a dresser next to it, and a path through the boxes wove to the furniture and the closet. No wonder she wanted her mom to get rid of some stuff.

"Hang on." She opened the bottom drawer of the dresser and pushed a stack of shirts aside before pulling a dark blue one out. "Try this. I can even wash your other shirt if you want. It's sort of my fault it looks like that."

"It's not your fault. It was an accident." He squeezed her upper arm.

"Well, I'll just let you change now." She started to sidestep around him through the narrow path the cardboard left.

"Trudy." He caught her hand. "Can I help? With tonight?"

She swallowed so hard he could see her throat move. Her hair draped like a curtain in front of her face as she shook her head. Then she straightened once more.

"I have to face it eventually. Life goes on, right?" The words were spoken well, but he could hear the hurt behind them.

"But not all at once."

"I guess my family disagrees." She shrugged and pulled away, closing the door behind her.

He let out a sigh and unbuttoned his shirt. Might as well change since he was in here anyway. And while he agreed it was good for her to face some of the memories she had with her dad, he couldn't understand anyone who would force it. In setting his soiled top on the dresser, his hand brushed a pile of papers, knocking them off the edge.

As he gathered the pieces up, he realized what they were. The lists she and her dad had created. He glanced over his shoulder, ensuring the door remained shut. On a whim, he pulled his phone from his pocket and laid the lists out side-by-side on the bed. Three at a time he snapped photos, making sure he could read them afterward. Then he stacked them in the order he assumed they had been and quickly pulled the T-shirt over his head. He snickered at the "Keep Austin Weird" on the front. Weird was definitely how this day had turned out.

But he wouldn't have changed it for anything. Unless it was to keep Mark distracted for just a bit longer this afternoon when he and Trudy were in the kitchen. *Hmm.* Something told him that almost kiss would haunt him for a while. That moment and the one where she'd put on her mask of being all right with what her family was forcing her to do. Maybe these photos could help him think of something to make this Christmas easier for her.

Chapter Thirteen

"Let me guess. Uncle Paul approved it?" Nick's voice in the doorway had Trudy spinning around. Her paintbrush flew across the room. It landed on Nick's shoes, leaving a swath of yellow on the brown leather.

"Oh, Nick. I'm so sorry." She grabbed a wet cloth and started swiping at the spots.

"Trudy." His hands covered hers and pulled them back. "It's my fault. I should know by now not to startle you."

She searched his face. Was he teasing? The crinkles at the edges of his eyes gave away the laughter hiding just below the surface. She leaned back on her heels.

"Still, I now owe you a new pair of shoes." She motioned to the half-yellow walls. "And yes, Paul approved it last week and even bought the paint and supplies."

"I thought maybe you weren't coming in today. I might not have found you if I hadn't needed to come to the storage room for something else." He motioned with his thumb over his shoulder. "The suspicious plastic curtain in the doorway gave you away."

She laughed. "It was the best I could manage to keep the smell from taking over the store. Is it working?"

"As far as I can tell. I couldn't smell anything until I got to this side of the tarp." He plucked at his plaid shirt. "I'm not really dressed to help."

"I wasn't going to ask you to." She dipped her brush into more paint and filled in some spots near a corner. All things told, she had intentionally slipped in while he'd been tucked in the office. She didn't want Nick to notice her walking through the store. It was too hard to face him after everything that happened the day before. She honestly couldn't even define exactly what had happened. Or almost happened.

"You're going to climb a ladder by yourself with no one back here to spot you or anything?" His eyebrows lifted, and he dashed a hand through his hair.

"Believe it or not, I'm usually not a klutz." Before she could stop herself, out popped more words. "Only when you're around."

"Oh, really?" She didn't have to look at him to know he was smirking.

"Obviously you're a bad influence or something." She directed all her focus to making smooth, even strokes on the wall. "And I've already got most of the edges done. The rolling won't take too long, especially since I have an extension for the roller. I'll let it dry and see how it looks this afternoon."

"So what event are we getting ready for?" He crossed his arms and leaned against the door frame. "Have you already lined up an artist to lead the art class of your dreams?"

"No. But it would be fun to offer a story time with Santa. We can have cookies and let Paul read a classic Christmas book. I'll talk to several flooring stores in town to see if they have any carpet remnants they'd be willing to donate. Those would be fun to scatter around for story times or magic shows or whatever."

He shook his head. "Do you ever stop?"

"Not often." She glanced at him over her shoulder. "Why? Am I moving too fast for you? I mean, I have several other ideas I wanted to run by you this afternoon."

"Of course, you do." He straightened. "You're a bottomless pit of ideas."

"And none of them have been good?" She turned to fully face him.

One corner of his mouth turned up. "I didn't say that. You wanna go over them now?"

She glanced at the drying walls. "Let me get the first coat up, and then I'll bring my tablet to show you what I've come up with."

"I'll brace myself." He saluted her and walked on down the hallway.

Was he flirting or returning to the grumpy attitude from last week? She couldn't tell. But he didn't seem as set against her ideas now, so maybe she was making progress. Trudy hoped so because some of the suggestions she'd come up with last night were going to take some work ... and willingness on his part.

She screwed the pole to the bottom of the roller and got busy covering the walls. A cool breeze came through the window she'd cracked for fresh air, sending shivers down her back. This might be central Texas, but it was also December, and the weather was acting like it for once.

Painting didn't take much mental effort, leaving her brain too much time to think about other things. Like how often her mom and Paul had actually gotten together last week. Had it only been the one dinner and lunch yesterday ... or more? With Trudy spending so much time at the store, she'd never know if her mom went out every night.

What was up with Nick? He was going to kiss her yesterday before Mark interrupted. She was sure of it. But where had all that come from? One day they were forced to work together, barely being cordial, and the next day they were laughing and flirting and almost kissing? Sure, they'd spent hours together last week, but when had it switched from obligation to wanting to be together?

And once the holidays were over and she'd done everything

for the store that she could, then what? Would he still be interested in seeing her? Or was this only happening due to forced proximity?

She pressed the middle of her forehead trying to stop the pounding. Circles. Her thoughts ran round and round and got nowhere. Where did she want them to go? She had no idea.

Trudy covered her painting utensils with cling wrap and grabbed her bag to go talk to the man who confused her more than anyone else she'd ever known. Maybe if he turned his nose up at her ideas, she'd know better where she stood. But something told her he wasn't nearly as averse to her suggestions as he had been. Was it because he knew her better or because he genuinely liked the ideas? Here she went again, thinking in circles.

Her quick rap on the office doorframe brought his head up and revealed a frown.

"What's wrong?" She dropped her things in the seat across from his desk and glanced at what he'd been studying. "Inventory?"

He pushed the papers aside. "No. Year-end numbers. They're not adding up right."

"Well, it's not actually the end of the year yet, so maybe that's why."

"Maybe." He folded his hands on his desk and raised an eyebrow. "Okay. Lay it on me. What are you wanting to do now?"

"First, I wanted to show you what I came up with last night." She grabbed her tablet and pulled up the store's web page. "What do you think?"

He glanced at the pictures and promotions she'd added. "Looks good." Then he focused directly on her. "I take it last night didn't go well?"

"What do you mean?" She glanced down and noticed a paper cup in front of him. "Is this coffee?"

"I actually got that one for you. Though it's probably cold

now." He caught her hand as she reached for it. "Trudy, how did it go putting up the tree?"

She lifted a shoulder. How to tell him enough to placate him and not have to relive each agonizing moment? Maybe she could distract him with needing to warm up her coffee? A glance into his brown eyes told her that would never work.

"It could have been worse. I mean, it wasn't the same ..." She swallowed, trying to push emotion back. "Different house. Actually, a different tree. Mom had bought a skinny one, claiming it fit the room better. Mark had a great time. He's so short, most of the ornaments were hung on the bottom half. And Brian took care of the lights, so I mostly just sat and watched."

"So, you're saying your nephew gets his height from you?" Nick winked.

Some of the grief choking her broke as the laughter bubbled up. "I'm going to go heat up my coffee now."

Paul waved at her as she walked to the kitchenette, but she couldn't bring herself to offer more than a nod. He was nice enough. And once they got past the sadness of purging old decorations, Paul had been a bigger advocate of her changes than anyone. But she couldn't like him. Not even as Santa.

The woman had an eye for detail. Nick scrolled through Trudy's newest pictures on the website once more. She'd added photos of the new decorations and Santa talking to Mark to help advertise that promotion. He'd already seen where she had shared those on the various social media pages too. On the right side of the page, a big *Coming Soon* flashed with the promise of activities, story times, and more. Nothing like railroading your idea through to fruition.

What if it didn't work? That would show her what happened when you didn't listen to the man behind the numbers. He shook his head. No. He wanted her idea to succeed, not only because she deserved it but also because the store needed something to bring the bottom line back up. And soon.

"Okay." She flopped down in the chair across from him once more. He rather missed the way she had pulled the chair around to this side of the desk last week. "Ready to go over some more improvements?"

"You make it sound like the store wasn't good enough to begin with." He leaned back and crossed his arms.

"There's the rotten attitude I've been missing the last few days." She smirked and then laid a large sheaf of paper in front of him. "You're going to love all of this."

"Such faith." He accepted several drawings she passed his way. "What are these?"

"Know how I said I wanted to make the store more fun? These are little animals I could paint in various places on shelves and walls, etcetera. If I do it over a weekend, we could reveal them the next week by holding a scavenger hunt. Everyone who participates the first week gets entered into a drawing for a fifty percent off coupon or something."

"You want to paint lizards on the shelves?" He frowned at her and then glanced out at the metal units holding most of their merchandise. "Where?"

"Lizards, birds, maybe even a cat or mouse—anything, everything." She bounced a bit in her seat, the way she always did when an idea got her excited. "Oh! We could have the mouse driving a toy car."

"Where?" He asked again.

"Come here." She grabbed his hand and tugged him around the desk and out onto the floor. "Look."

He followed her to the back walls, where the shelves Grandpa had built himself stood sentinel over everything else. They were wooden, with thicker edges than the metal ones that filled the center of the store. Her idea started to make more sense.

"See? I could totally fit a little mouse right down here." She pointed to a corner. "And maybe something holding an umbrella right here behind the water fountain? And another creature reading a novel at the edge of the book area. The metal ones were harder to think of, but these end caps have space here above the top shelf, assuming you don't move the shelves much. I could fit a bird there for sure. And then, of course, I could squeeze a few in on the walls or the doors or even maybe the floor if I needed to."

"Okay, okay." He waved his hands. "You're right. There are spaces."

"So, what do you think?" She watched him as if daring him to hate it. But he couldn't. Her enthusiasm was rubbing off on him.

"When are you wanting to do this?"

"We're two weeks from Christmas." She ticked it off on her fingers. "If I can advertise it this week, paint Saturday evening, touch up on Sunday afternoon—yes, yes, I know. No working on Sundays. I'll do my best to finish it Saturday. Then we can have the scavenger hunt cards printed out ready to go Monday with the cutoff maybe Wednesday or Thursday. Christmas is on a Saturday this year. Will you guys be open on the twenty-fourth?"

"We're usually open half a day on Christmas Eve."

"Okay. So, *hmm*. Do you think this will work?" Sudden doubt filled her features.

"Yes. But what if we stay late one night this week and start it before next week? Would that give you enough time to advertise?"

"If I start today." She grinned at him.

"Okay, what else? You said there was more."

"I'm wanting to work on some more tiles this evening." She pointed to the floor. "And it hit me, even though we can't put up inventory on the website right now, we could still put more … charming pictures of the store."

"We have pictures of the store on there." He frowned as he followed her back to the office.

"No. Like this." She pushed some sketches over. "Showing people actually doing things *in* the store. Shopping, reading books in the corner, checking out, trying out a bike, something that shows how fun it is here."

"You can't just photograph the customers. Especially without their permission."

"That's why I'm going to stage them with people you're going to help me round up."

"Me?" He leaned back to study her, but she was serious.

"You and Katt and anyone else we can think of who might be able to gather some friends with kids to come shoot a few photos." She glanced up at him. "You do have friends, right?"

"Of course I do." He just couldn't think of any off the top of his head.

"Fine. I'll get Katt working on it and see how many she can come up with." It hurt a little that she didn't believe him. Not that he sounded very believable, but still.

"What else, oh mighty change guru?"

She rolled her eyes. "Besides the mural?"

"Still hung up on that one, huh?"

"I *will* win you over."

Thankfully she was shuffling her papers and not looking at him. It took him far too long to school his face. Did she realize how close she was to winning over his heart? Who cared about the stupid mural? More was at stake than the store.

"I looked up contact information for several professors at the university. Want to reach out, or is finding students for art sessions something you want me to head up? I just figured since I'm done after ..." Her voice trailed off as she handed him the list.

"Sure." He swallowed the disappointment inside him at her not sticking around. "I'll see what I can line up. Although with it being so close to the holidays, we might not reach anyone until next year."

"So, we'll have the Santa story time to get us started." She straightened her stack. "And another activity might be a building club. You could sell building sets or pieces and then have time with people to help put them together."

"Maybe."

"Or even model cars or something." She shrugged, staring off. "Might be fun."

Was she sad at the idea of leaving too? Is that why she seemed so melancholy all of a sudden? He needed to change the subject, get her back to her happy, excited self.

"So, you're finishing up painting and reaching out to flooring places *and* advertising for the scavenger hunt all this afternoon?" He raised an eyebrow.

She crossed her arms, her spitfire attitude back in place. "I can do it."

"And still have energy to put down colored tiles tonight?"

"Of course." She smirked. "Why? Can't you keep up?"

"Ha." He slid back into his chair. "I was just thinking we'd need sustenance to get everything done on your to-do list. And it's half-price night at my favorite taco truck."

"You have a favorite taco truck?" She plopped down in her chair and opened her laptop on her desk.

"Don't you?"

"Nope. Obviously, you need to teach me your ways."

"I'll do my best." He hid his grin behind his computer screen. A week ago, he'd never have believed he'd be looking forward to more time with her.

He scrolled through his emails, deleting junk. Right before he discarded one, he took a second glance at the heading and froze. What was the name of that concert she'd wanted to attend with her dad? Wasn't it ... And they were coming to Austin next week.

Chapter Fourteen

"You're a lifesaver, Katt." Trudy ushered her sister and several other families into the store Tuesday evening.

"What flavor?" Katt spouted off the next line of their childhood joke without hesitating.

"Lemon."

Katt looked askance at her. "Lemon? You used to say pineapple or cherry."

"That was before you started having so many sour moments." Trudy wiggled her eyebrows. "Would you prefer grape?"

"I didn't have to help you round up all these people, you know."

"You're right." Trudy held up her hands in surrender. "Thank you."

"The floor looks good." Katt turned in a circle. "I haven't been in here in a while."

"Thanks. I like the way it turned out." Trudy smiled at the colorful tiles breaking up the monotony of all the main aisles. It had taken her and Nick until midnight last night to finish, but it was worth it.

"What else are you doing?"

"We're hanging signs on all the aisles to make it easier to find things." Trudy pointed to the five colorful boards they'd installed that afternoon. "And I updated the Christmas tree."

Katt glanced that direction and did a doubletake. "Wait. Isn't that the one Dad got you?"

"Wow." Nick approached at that moment and rescued Trudy from having to finish the conversation, although her sister shot her a look that said it would continue another time. "You really did round up a lot of people."

"This is what it looks like to have a life outside of work." Trudy sent the tease his way, then stuck her finger and thumb into her mouth to whistle for everyone's attention.

"Show off." Katt muttered.

"Thank you all for coming to help on such short notice." She waved her hands to encompass the store. "Here's what I need. Go explore to your heart's desire. Check out toys, test ride a bike." She ignored Nick's grimace. "Read a book. Whatever—just don't take anything out of its package. I'll walk around and snap candid photos for our website and future ads."

Nick spoke up behind her. "Everyone gets a ten-percent-off coupon for willingly giving of your time and sharing your beautiful children."

Who was this guy? Surely not the same man who had been concerned about losing money by bringing in a magician.

"We'd appreciate if you could stay for about an hour before leaving. Any questions?" Trudy took their lack of response as a *no*. "Okay. Go check things out."

"How can I help?" Nick ran his hand through his hair, setting several strands on end.

She reached up and patted them back into place, something she'd been itching to do for days. He exhaled shakily, and she met his gaze as reality crashed down on her. She needed to focus … on the store. Not on Nick's hair.

"I might need you in a picture or two, helping people, checking someone out, etcetera. So, we've got to keep you looking nice." Maybe that would explain her slip a moment before. "But for now, you can walk with me and carry this. It helps the pictures have a more natural light."

He took an umbrella shade from her hands. "Isn't that what all those light bulbs I installed were supposed to do?"

"Yeah, yeah." She swatted his shoulder. "Just come on."

"I look nice, huh?" His whisper tickled her ear as he leaned close beside her.

Her heart skipped a beat. Had she said that? Heat crept up her neck as she noticed Katt giving her a curious look from two aisles over.

"It's a figure of speech." Trudy pointed toward the back. "Let's start back there."

"Yes, ma'am."

She paused near the book corner, taking in the various activities going on. A dad read to his daughter in one of the tiny chairs. Several boys studied a pirate series. She grabbed Nick's sleeve and tugged him to her other side, then indicated he needed to lift her umbrella. After another slight adjustment, she figured it was as good as it could get. She positioned her camera at her eye and peered through the lens, focusing in on the magic of adventures unfolding.

Someone took up her suggestion of the bicycle trials. She snapped several shots of a little boy figuring out the pedals as his mom held onto the back. Two aisles over a girl tested a hula hoop. Dolls were cuddled. Cars raced.

Every time she turned a corner, she discovered more joy. Including when Trudy caught her nephew showing her sister the exact fire truck her mom had secretly bought him last week. Christmas magic at its finest.

A mom came up as they neared the front again. "Are we allowed to use the ten percent off coupon tonight?"

"Of course. I can check you out now if you're ready." Nick handed the umbrella to Katt and led the other lady to a register.

Katt took Nick's place to help keep the light diffused while Trudy captured several shots of him checking the family out.

The little girl turned and gave her mom a look of pure bliss, and Trudy hit her shutter as quickly as possible.

"Did you get what you needed?" Katt lowered the umbrella once more.

"I think so." Trudy scanned back through her viewscreen and showed several shots to Katt. "What do you think?"

"I think your artistic eye hasn't faded. Those are beautiful." Her sister's tone was sincere, and warmth spread through Trudy at the compliment.

"Thanks, sis."

"This should help. Along with everything else." Katt motioned toward the tiles.

"I hope so. This and the painting sessions and story times and other activities should bring in more people even after the new year." Trudy nodded. Was Nick's wariness rubbing off on her? Suddenly she wasn't sure she was doing enough.

"If you really do get a magician and some of those building time activities going, I'll bring Mark, for sure." Katt shook her head. "He loves stuff like that. He'd probably beg to do something like that for his birthday in March."

"Oh. That's a great idea. Birthday parties!" Trudy pulled her phone out and added it to a list of other ideas in a shared document both she and Nick could access.

"Okay. It's Mark's bedtime, so we're off. You about done for today?"

"I don't know. I might see if I can get some of these pics edited and uploaded tonight before I crash. You know me. I don't stop." Trudy clicked her camera off.

"Don't go too long. After all, you've got to get your beauty sleep." Katt patted Trudy's shoulder and grabbed Mark before he could knock over a display of dinosaurs.

"I don't think you need beauty sleep." Nick's voice made Trudy jump as she watched her sister leave. When had he come up? Good thing her sister hadn't tried to bring up any of the other conversations Trudy had avoided this evening.

"Um. Thanks."

"I'm going to do one more sweep, round up anyone left and get all the purchases complete." He hooked a thumb over his shoulder. "Did you need anything else, or did you get what you wanted?"

"I think I caught a lot of good shots." She leaned her head toward the office. "If you don't mind, I'm going to go upload some of them now and see what you think."

"Sure."

Nick clicked the bolt into place on the front door. It had been a good evening for sales. Several of the families had even mentioned coming back during the day to see Santa and telling their friends about the scavenger hunt. Maybe Uncle Paul really could pull off a Christmas miracle. Or Trudy.

He paused in the doorway of the office to take in the picture she made. Trudy leaned forward in the chair, so close to the edge of the seat he wondered how she didn't fall out. Her hair hung over her shoulders in soft waves. Her finger clicked quickly as she moved the mouse around, editing a photo on her screen. She was so focused she hadn't even realized he was there.

"Well?"

She jerked around at his question, lost her balance, and wound up on the floor. "Ugh. I wish you'd quit startling me."

"Sorry." He reached down and gave her a hand up. "It honestly isn't my intention. You're just so intense when you're working that you lose track of the real world."

"My art professors used to have to shake me at the end of class to let me know it was time to go." She rolled her eyes. "Come look at this."

She plopped back in the seat and turned the screen so he could see it better. He hardly recognized the website, even though the address in the browser said it was the Emporium's.

She'd added photos from this evening already, showing families thrilled with their finds, him grinning at a customer, and the updated Santa photos. Along the sidebar, she had announcements about everything coming soon, from the scavenger hunt to story time with Santa to extra activities in the new year.

"Looks great. How did you do all this?"

"Tonight's pictures help." She leaned back and tucked a piece of hair behind her ear. "I couldn't have asked for better models. The kids' facial expressions … perfect."

"What do you mean?" He rested his hip against his desk and folded his arms.

"Look at this one." She pulled up a photo of the girl whose face had lit up when her mom had bought her the doll. "Pure joy."

"I don't get it." He tapped his fingers on his biceps. "I haven't seen happiness like that in a long time. Most days it's just kids throwing fits about not getting what they want—not the elation you captured. Was it just because it was something special tonight? Or that she actually got what she wanted?"

"The circumstances might have helped, but I don't think so. I think you simply haven't been looking for moments like this. You're too distracted by the other. And by the bottom line." She twisted her lips to the side.

"What?"

"You've lost the joy." She motioned toward the store. "You work in an environment that ought to be fun and playful and happy. But when I first met you, you were the opposite. You focused on numbers and making things neat and organized. Kids aren't like that."

He huffed out a chuckle. "You mean like Mark's decorating the other day?"

"Exactly like that." She laughed too. "Kids don't care if it looks perfect. They're more concerned with how fun it is. And that's why I'm trying to add some whimsy in here."

They were both silent for several minutes while she loaded her laptop back in her bag and gathered a few other things. Maybe she was right. He'd been so concerned with the business end of the store that he hadn't remembered why his grandfather had opened it in the first place. Nick had no idea how to ignore the bottom line and look at things differently.

Trudy snapped her fingers. "I know what we need to do."

He couldn't stop the groan that escaped. "It's already three hours past closing time. Can't we just go home tonight?"

"Not tonight, silly." She waved off that idea. "Let's see. The scavenger hunt starts Friday morning, so I have to paint Thursday night no matter what. Might be better if I start on at least a few of them tomorrow night. But we should still have time to pull this off before I paint a couple animals."

"Are you going to let me know what you're talking about?" He ran a hand through his hair and remembered her smoothing it down earlier. It had taken all his willpower not to catch her hand in his and kiss it for such a sweet gesture.

"Playing." She bounced out of her chair and wandered back into the mostly dark store.

"Playing?" He shut the light off in the office and followed her. "Playing what?"

"You need to remember how to play." She spun around and faced him so quickly he almost ran into her, something that grew more appealing the longer they spent time together.

"I think I know how to play, Trudy." He shook his head. "Isn't the saying that men never grow up?"

"I think you did, though." She studied him, her head tilted and a slight frown between her brows. "I think you grew up too much and forgot how to find the fun in life."

"This isn't *Peter Pan*." He huffed. "We're supposed to grow up."

"Yes, but not so much that we never do anything lighthearted." She gave a quick nod as if settling something in her brain. "No. Tomorrow night, we play."

His heart skipped a beat. "Trudy?"

"What, Nick?" She was already halfway down the aisle.

"What if I say 'no'?" He half-jogged to catch up with her.

She propped a hand on her hip. "Don't you want to have fun?"

He was reaching the point where he'd do almost anything she asked if only it let him spend more time with her. But this seemed ridiculous. "Wouldn't it be a better use of your time to hang signs and paint animals?"

"I'm finishing the signs and the walls in the extra room tomorrow during store hours." She cut her eyes sideways at him. "Besides, I think this might be even more important."

His heart skittered again. Did she mean he was more important than her job? Or was she including him as part of the job since he was the manager? Why was he so worried about her wanting to play? He groaned again as he followed her out into the parking lot. How did he get into this mess?

Chapter Fifteen

"What exactly did you mean by 'play'?" Nick's words made Trudy snicker.

"Are you worried?" She ran her hands down the edges of shelves as they walked the store late Wednesday evening.

"Should I be?"

The waver in his voice made her giggle. She was probably enjoying this too much, truth be told, but he made it so easy. She grabbed his hand and pulled him toward the back of the store.

"How about catch?"

"Catch?" He planted his feet and folded his hands across his chest again.

"Sure." She wiggled a ball free from the big bin and tossed it at him. "Didn't you ever play catch growing up?"

"Didn't everyone?" He hugged the blue orb to his torso and rolled his eyes. "How is this supposed to remind me of the 'wonder of childhood'?"

"I suppose you were more into competitive things, weren't you?" She tapped a finger against her lips.

"You mean you don't actually have a plan of action for this?" He replaced the ball. "I'm shocked. You, always so full of ideas."

"Want to race?" She dashed toward the bikes and went down the row until she found one the right size. She was already draping a leg over it when he caught up with her.

"What are you doing?"

"Racing you around the store. You better hurry, or I'll get a head start." She put her feet on the pedals and pushed away, her legs getting a feel for it again. It had been a while since she'd ridden a bike.

"You've got to be kidding."

"I'm going to win." She shot over her shoulder as she pedaled a little farther.

"Okay, okay." He pulled out a blue ten-speed and quickly mounted. "Let's get this over with."

"As you wish." She leaned forward. "Go!"

Her head start didn't last long.

His legs and bike were both longer, so he caught up quickly. "You didn't say what the course was."

"The perimeter. Twice." She lifted her bottom from the seat and pushed harder with her legs, trying to pick up speed. The book corner was ahead, so she slowed just enough to make the turn without collapsing on her side. Who knew the saying about always remembering how to ride a bike was true? It came back to her as if it had only been days instead of years.

They stayed neck and neck down the side aisle between books and video games, but as they neared the front, he pressed a bit harder and grabbed the lead on the office corner. She narrowed her eyes and gave it her all to catch up.

The cash registers flew by. The dolls all held their bright blue eyes open wide at the spectacle dashing through the store. One more corner and they'd be on the second lap. He was gaining even more. *Ugh!*

As they neared the book corner again, he misjudged his speed and wiped out, taking out a giant stuffed dinosaur with his bike.

"Ha!" She risked pumping her arm in the air as she passed him.

"It's not over yet!"

Trudy didn't dare look over her shoulder to see how quickly he regained his seat. The odds weren't stacked in her favor, but she was determined to give it her all. She might want him to remember how fun life could be, but she didn't have to let him win.

She made it past the registers and around the third corner before he showed up in her peripheral vision. Leaning forward, she pushed with all the energy left in her body, dreading how her legs would feel the next day. The last corner was close, and then they'd be back to the sporting goods. He came even with her just as they reached the bike racks, his breath coming hard.

"Tied." He huffed, as he leaned over the handlebars. "And I ought to scold you for not even grabbing a helmet. Not to mention the risk of putting a scuff mark on the floor with these tires. Or hurting the bikes."

"So much for teaching you to have fun." She rolled her eyes as she returned her ride to its slot. "Besides, I'm not the one who wrecked."

A laugh shot from his lips. "Touché."

"Should we go check on poor Dino?"

He followed her back toward the book corner and helped straighten several large stuffed animals who had been knocked on their sides. She put her hands on her hips and turned in a slow circle. There had to be something else that would help him remember how to be happy.

"That really didn't give you any joy?" She narrowed her eyes and then noticed the game section.

"I mean, it was okay, I guess. Probably would have been better if I hadn't wiped out." He limped on his right leg as he walked beside her.

"Did you actually get hurt?"

"It's so bad I should probably go home and ice it." He stuck out his lower lip.

"Oh, please." She pushed his arm and then continued on to the cards. Perfect. A brand-new deck beckoned to her.

He wagged a finger her way. "I can't sell those if you open them."

"Good grief. I'll pay you for them. They're only a dollar." She pulled him back toward the book section and the comfy beanbags. "Come on."

"What now?" He stretched his long legs out and leaned forward as she shuffled.

"Slap Jack."

"What?"

"The card game. You know? Where you slap the Jacks and try to win all the cards." She started dealing, tossing cards into piles in front of each of them.

"I know what it is. I'm trying to figure out why you're doing this." He leaned forward and straightened his hand.

"What's more fun than trying to win cards from someone else?" She lifted an eyebrow. "Should I start, or do you want to?"

"You're seriously going to make me do this?"

"Would you rather play War?" She glanced up just in time to see the look of horror cross his face.

"War takes forever. You said you wanted to paint some tonight too."

"Good point. Slap Jack it is." She readied herself to lay down a card. "Fair warning. I play fast. Do you need a refresher on the rules?"

"The rules are to slap a Jack before anyone else does when it gets laid down." He rolled his eyes. "It's not the hardest game in the world."

"Depends on who you're playing." She winked.

"Fine. Go." He lifted an eyebrow at how quickly she set down her first card. Then he caught up with her speed and was moving as quickly as she was. Their hands both went down hard about fifteen cards in, but she won that stack.

"Ready for more?" She asked, as she shuffled those into her hand.

"Bring it." He set down his first card and she quickly followed. They went fast, both quiet as they focused on staying alert.

"Ha!" She won the second slap too.

"You haven't won yet. There are four Jacks. I still have a few cards." He sounded more into it now, and that set her heart fluttering. Must be the adrenaline of the game.

They carried on, and he won the next slap.

"Okay. Okay. I'll give you that one." She nodded but leaned forward even more as they continued.

Cards piled up higher than she expected as they waited for another Jack. Where was it? They shouldn't have that many left to go through. There.

She won again. "Ha."

"Best two out of three?" He cocked an eyebrow.

She stifled a giggle trying to escape and shuffled the cards. The second round went faster, and he surprised her by winning.

"Okay. Winner round." She shuffled carefully. "Ready?"

"Do it."

Again, they raced through the cards until only a few were left. He ran out of cards before another Jack was laid and sat watching like a hawk as she set down one after another. She wasn't about to tell him she'd secretly hidden all of the Jacks on the bottom of her hand. No need to give away the secret her sister had taught her years before.

She won the next slap and all the cards. "Ha!"

"Good for you." He leaned back. "You owe me a dollar plus tax."

"Oh, good grief." Trudy stood and stretched her back. "All that, and you're still only thinking about the bottom line. I don't know what else to do for you, Mr. Huffypants. It's like you don't want to let yourself have fun. You're too worried about perfection or something."

Why was he watching her like that? Was she making him mad? Maybe that's what she needed to do. Maybe that would get through his thick brain.

"I mean, you spend all your time here, but you don't appreciate any of it. That's why your store has fallen apart. That's why your precious numbers aren't working out." She stomped her foot. "Your focus is on the wrong things."

He lifted an eyebrow. "Oh, really?"

"Yes. Really." She tossed down the last few cards in her hand, revealing that they were all Jacks.

He took one look at those cards and then glanced back up at her with a look she couldn't discern at all. "You cheated?"

"Does it matter?" She braced her feet a little wider apart. "Something tells me even if you had won, it wouldn't have changed anything."

He shook his head and planted his feet. What was he going to do? Was he angry? Over a game?

Before she could move or react or even take a breath, he shot up to his full height and pressed his lips to hers. She froze, then melted.

Nick's arms wrapped around her waist and pulled her in closer. Her hands slid up his shoulders and around his back. It was like a spring had wound tight inside her over the last week and now bounced up and down in her tummy, setting off more in her heart, her head. Every inch of her came alive. Trudy lifted up on her tiptoes and got even closer.

A low groan escaped before he pulled back. Once more she couldn't read his expression, but it didn't look happy. Had that been an accident? Accidental kisses weren't possible, were they? Everything in her wanted to believe he'd meant to kiss her.

What had he done? Nick dashed his hand through his hair and stepped back. Should he apologize? Should he go back and kiss her again? She'd definitely responded in a positive way. Yet now she looked a bit lost and uncertain.

"I—"

"Well—"

They both started to talk at the same time and then grew silent once more. Awkward. He grabbed the back of his neck and cleared his throat. He didn't even know where that had come from. One moment he'd been growing more and more upset with the haranguing she was giving him and the next, he'd figured the only way to shut her up was to give her mouth something else to do. Granted, kissing her wasn't the most ethical way to occupy her mouth, but it had been ... amazing.

"Man," he whispered.

She let out a soft laugh. "You can say that again."

"Should I apologize?" He was afraid to meet her eyes.

"Do you feel like you need to?" She moved into his view despite his lowered head.

"No?" His voice gave the word an upward lift, uncertainty coming through.

She quickly pressed her lips to his and then stepped back again. "That was the best kiss I've ever had."

His breath came out in a whoosh. She was okay with it. Not sorry. Not upset.

He still didn't know exactly where it left them, but at least some of the awkwardness had lifted. The playing cards were now scattered everywhere. He nudged several with his toe.

"Guess we have a whole other card game to play now." She laughed.

"What's that?"

"Fifty-two Pick Up."

He laughed and knelt down on the floor beside her, gathering up the pieces and stacking them straight once more. "Did you really cheat?"

"Bad habit." She worried her bottom lip, making him want to kiss it again. "My sister taught me that trick when I was in elementary school. I kept losing to some mean kids at recess and complained to her. She winked and taught me always to shuffle the Jacks to the bottom of the deck. That, and hours of practice."

"I never pictured you as a card shark." He handed her what he'd picked up.

"What can I say? I'm a woman of many talents." She set the pack aside and glanced at him. "I guess I better get busy painting. Are you going to stay, or do you trust me to lock up when I'm done?"

"I trust you." He reached out and tucked a strand of her silky hair behind her ear. "But I'm staying."

"And to think every other night over the past two weeks you've complained about having to stay late." She smiled and ducked her head.

"Maybe you really did remind me a little about how to have fun." He pulled her into his arms. "Or at least how to find more joy in life."

"Really?" She wrapped her arms around his waist.

"I don't promise to like Christmas much more, but maybe I'll notice the kids who are happy instead of always focusing on the selfish brats." He laughed.

"Did you really not like riding bikes and playing cards with me?" She gazed up, a small furrow between her brows.

"Somehow I can picture myself riding bikes and playing cards with you over and over and over again if I get to kiss you afterward." He couldn't even believe the words coming out of his mouth. Had she really changed him so much?

Her mouth dropped open in surprise. "My, but you move fast."

"Not really." He pressed a kiss to her temple. "I've wanted to kiss you for days now."

"So, you really were—Sunday—before Mark ..."

"You were just so cute standing there, looking caught between frustration and tears. You had a streak of flour across your forehead. And it was like you were a magnet or something."

"I'm not sure I'm okay with you always wanting to kiss me when I'm frustrated." She pushed away a little. "That's not very romantic."

"How about when you smooth down my hair?" He whispered the words directly in her ear, pulling her back into his arms. "Or when I see the intense focus you have on whatever masterpiece you're creating, be it a whimsical floor or a yellow wall or a website?"

"Goodness." She blinked several times. "How's a girl supposed to get any work done when she knows everything she does makes someone want to kiss her?"

He laughed. "How did we get here?"

"I have no idea. I didn't even like you two weeks ago." She wrinkled her nose. "Nerds aren't usually my type."

"Nerds?" He pushed up his glasses. "I'm not a nerd."

"*Mm*. Plaid shirts, glasses, messy hair, nose stuck in spreadsheets." She ticked the points off on her fingers.

"And did you call me Mr. Huffypants earlier?" He narrowed his eyes.

She pinched her lips together. "Did I? Everything from earlier is a bit fuzzy."

"Mm-hmm. Well, klutzes aren't usually my type."

One corner of her lip went up. "I told you. It's only when you're around."

"I'll just have to work to keep you off balance. Gives me an excuse to catch you when you fall."

She shook her head and stepped back, tripping over a bean bag. Unfortunately, he went down with her. They ended up in a tangled knot. Laughter exploded from her, and he couldn't help joining in despite the ache growing in his hip where he'd hit the floor twice this evening.

"Oh, man. We're a mess." She pushed up and straightened

the area. "I better get a few creatures painted, or I'm going to be here all night."

"I guess." He motioned toward the rest of the store even though he wasn't in a hurry to end their time together. "Where are you starting?"

She grabbed her supplies from the office, then lowered herself to the floor near the vehicles. He sat next to her as she penciled in a tiny mouse driving a car on the bottom shelf.

"You could go do something else, you know." She grinned up at him for a moment before adding some gray paint to her creation. "A few days ago, you swore you were too busy to do anything I wanted to do. Surely there's something calling you to work on instead of making me nervous."

"Nothing I can think of." He crossed one ankle over the other and laid his head back.

"You're crazy."

"Yeah, well ..." He might be crazy, but he was the happiest he could remember in a while. This whirlwind of a girl had crashed into his heart and splintered it wide open. Maybe he'd have his head on straighter if he'd gotten more sleep over the last two weeks.

On the other hand, maybe this was better. Could he convince her to stay in Temple instead of moving back to Austin after the holidays? He wasn't sure he could stand her being an hour away.

Chapter Sixteen

"Hey, Katt. What's up?" Trudy set her phone on speaker as she drove to the Emporium from the flooring store she'd just visited.

"Did Mark watch any television the other day?" Katt's voice was hard to read, but Trudy had a good idea her sister was angry.

"He watched a few minutes of a Christmas special while we cleaned up a flour explosion." Trudy rolled her eyes. She didn't always agree with her sister's parenting rules.

"And now he can quote the whole thing?" Katt's voice screeched a bit at the end of the question. "Verbatim?"

"Katt, we turned it on for less than half an hour. No more." Trudy pulled into a parking spot and killed her engine. "And I don't think he sat in front of the TV that whole time, either. He was too eager to come back to the kitchen."

How would things have ended differently Sunday if Mark hadn't come back in the kitchen when he had? Would Nick have kissed her then instead of waiting until last night? How would he act around her today? Had it been a fluke, or was there really something going on between them?

"Earth to Trudy." Katt's voice brought her back to reality.

"Sorry. I'm driving and got distracted for a minute." At least that was the story Trudy was going with. "I don't know what else to tell you. He didn't watch much television, so if he knows the whole thing, either he has a photographic memory or he's seen it somewhere else. But it wasn't Sunday. Besides, it was Nick's idea."

"Nick, huh? Tell me more about Nick."

"You mean about him using the TV to distract your son?" Trudy glanced at her watch and sighed. If she could carry everything in and hold the phone, too, she'd get out and get to work.

"No. I mean about how you and he are spending an awful lot of time together." Katt's voice was no longer angry. More sing-songy, in an annoying older sister way.

"I don't know if you noticed or not, but we work together." Trudy was grateful her sister hadn't called via Facetime. Otherwise her cheeks might give her away. "Hey, have you talked to Mom much lately?"

"You mean, besides all the times we've been together this week going through boxes?" Katt huffed. "You were supposed to be helping too."

"Well, blame that one on Mom. She's the one who practically insisted I take this job at the Emporium." Trudy tapped her fingers on the steering wheel. "But, seriously, has Mom mentioned Paul any?"

"Some, I guess. Why?"

"A car that looked like his was pulling away from the house when I got home last night, but Mom was already shut in her bedroom so I couldn't ask her." Trudy frowned. "And she left a note that she was running early errands this morning. I can't imagine why she needed to go to the store at six-thirty."

"I think you're reading too much into it." Katt's voice was muffled for a moment as she talked to Mark in the background. "Besides, so what if Paul's car was leaving when you got home last night? They're adults who like to spend time with each other."

Trudy pressed her lips together. "You don't think it's more than that?"

"If it is, good for them. You're not the only one allowed to have a romantic interest, you know."

"Romantic interest?" Trudy spluttered. "What are you talking about?"

"Oh, please, Baby Sister. I saw the way you and Nick were practically attached at the hip the other night." Katt barked out a loud laugh. "You're not fooling me at all. Maybe Mom feels like she can finally move on now that she won't have to worry about you as much."

"Worry about me?" Trudy resisted the urge to hang up on her sister. "What's that supposed to mean?"

"It means *you're* the one who isn't moving on after Daddy's death. Don't get me wrong. We all miss him. But he's gone, Trudy. Nothing will bring him back or change that." Katt sighed. "But it's hard for us to let go and start any new traditions when you're still clinging to the past as if that will bring him back. Mom and I are always afraid if we suggest doing anything that might've been on one of those stupid lists of yours, you'll melt down completely and make us all miserable."

"The lists weren't stupid," she lashed out. "You're just jealous because Dad did them with *me*."

"Yes." Katt's agreement shocked Trudy. "Yes, I am jealous. You got to do all those things, just the two of you. There. I said it. Are you happy now?"

"That's ironic." Trudy rested her forehead on the steering wheel.

"Why's that?"

"We started them the year you got your tonsils out because I was jealous of you."

"Jealous of me?" Katt made a scoffing noise. "Why? My sore

throats? Because I had to have surgery? What on earth was there to be jealous of?"

"Because you were always getting more attention for those things." Trudy picked up the phone and turned off the speaker, holding the device to her ear.

"Well, honey, I'd trade it all to have gotten thirteen years of special time with Daddy. But nothing can change it now." Katt was silent for a minute. "Listen, Mom's really happy right now. Please don't ruin it by being too stubborn to let go of the past."

Katt hung up before Trudy could reply. That had been one of the worst conversations they'd had in a while. A growl worked its way up through her throat but came out more a moan. It wasn't as if Katt hadn't had her special activities with Dad too. How could she and Mom want to move on as if Dad had never been a part of their lives? He wasn't replaceable!

Trudy slammed out of her door and tugged the hatch up on the back of her SUV. Maybe lugging carpet squares would release some of the emotions roiling inside her.

She struggled to get the door open with a basket of rugs in her hands and the wind pushing against her. The basket fell to the ground, and she just left it there for the moment. She lodged her foot in the crack and then leaned over to pick up the load when the door pushed open more. Nick took the heavy carpets from her and waited until she was in before letting the door slam behind them.

"Good morning." His eyes searched her face, and she hoped the dark hallway covered any leftover traces of the conversation with her sister. She wasn't ready to explain any of it. Especially since part of it had included him.

"Hi." She pointed toward the activity room. "Let's get these in so Santa can do story time on Saturday."

"Right. And I have something to talk to you about when you get a minute."

"Um, okay." Her spirits lifted some at the sight of the happy area. Colorful polka dots were scattered over the yellow walls, adding a splash of color and breaking up the monotony. One wall was lined with chairs for any parents who might want to join their children. Several folding tables were tucked into other areas for when they were needed. A second big wingback chair had been located in the storeroom and was in a corner ready for Paul to use. And now she had three baskets of these carpet squares to scatter over the floor so little bodies could sit on them. Perfect.

"I didn't realize you were going to do the polka dots, but I like them." Nick stepped in behind her. "Where do you want these?"

"Let's store them here by the door so people can grab them as they come in." She nodded back toward the parking lot. "I've got two more baskets. Three different stores offered up fifteen a piece. I don't think we'd have room for many more than that anyway, so it's perfect."

"Sounds good. If you'll hold the door for me, I'll bring them in."

"Sure."

Each time Nick passed her with another basket, his eyes sought out hers. What was he looking for? She locked her car and let the door shut again as he brought in the last ones. He set them down and smiled.

"This room is ready now, right?"

"As ready as I can get it." She glanced around once more and gave a nod.

"It's great, Trudy. Thanks for convincing us it needed to happen." Nick ran a finger down her cheek, and her heart gave a rebellious leap.

"That's my job, right?"

Something was bothering Trudy, but Nick wasn't certain what. Was she worried how he'd act today after their kiss last night? Or had something else happened?

He caught her arm before she could escape the room. "You going to let me in?"

"In?" She quirked her brow. "I thought we were already in."

He tapped a finger against her forehead. "In here. What's going on?"

"What do you mean?" She wouldn't meet his gaze, which only confirmed his suspicions.

"Are you upset about last night?"

"I got three animals painted. How can I be upset about that?" She shot him a grin, but it didn't reach her eyes.

"Trudy." He placed a hand on each side of her face and leaned in to kiss her, something he'd been wanting to do since he backed off the night before.

At first, she was stiff. Then she joined him, her lips warm and inviting under his. They parted at the same time, but he wasn't ready to let her go yet. He pulled her tight against him and buried his head in her hair, wanting to take away whatever ate at her inside but knowing he couldn't.

"I probably shouldn't have done that, but I couldn't resist."

"I know, I know." She tilted her head up to smile at him. "You always want to kiss me when I'm frustrated."

"Were you frustrated with me?" He rubbed his hand up and down the back of her jacket.

"No." She sighed. "Katt called just before I got here. She had several bones to pick with me, evidently, including you letting Mark watch that stupid Christmas special on Sunday."

"Really? That's ridiculous. He was in there maybe ten minutes."

"According to her, he can now quote the whole thing. I told Katt he must have seen more of it another time then, because I know for sure he didn't watch the whole thing on Sunday."

He laughed as red crept into her cheeks. "Did you tell her

why?"

"No." She averted her gaze, toward the window on the other side of the room. "Then we got into a disagreement about Paul."

"Paul? Uncle Paul?" Nick leaned back a bit to have a better view of her face. "Why were you talking about my uncle?"

"Well, I'm pretty sure it was his car I saw leaving my mom's house when I got home last night." She moved from his embrace, and he missed her instantly.

"Okay." Nick crossed his arms. "And this upset you?"

"Yes. He's been spending a lot of time with my mom and I think they might be more than just friends." She rubbed at a spot in the middle of her forehead.

She wasn't ready. This explained part of why she'd been so upset on Sunday too. It hadn't been spending more time with him. Or even making cookies, although that hadn't helped. Trudy was upset at the idea of her mom dating someone new.

"Sorry." She glanced over at him. "I know he's your uncle and you love him and everything, but ..." She spread her hands out in a helpless gesture.

"Hey." He reached over and grabbed them, twining their fingers together. "Do you know for sure that anything's going on?"

She shook her head.

"Okay then. Until you know for certain, don't let it eat you up inside. We've got a scavenger hunt to get ready for, after all. That paper cutter you brought is calling your name, asking you to cut all those cards apart." He winked. "Annnd I might have found a magician."

"What?" She followed him out of the activity room and through the store. "I thought you were against the magician idea."

"A friend of mine from college dabbled in it. Found him on social media." He purposely led her the long way around so they wouldn't walk directly past Paul. No need to stir up her emotions again. "I reached out to him, and he still does a few tricks. He said if I can hook him up with a few things at cost, he can do the show for free. We're talking January."

"Really?" She bounced on her toes in front of his desk as he showed her the screen shot his friend had sent.

"Think you can work up the ads and posts to let people know it's coming?"

"Definitely." She peered up at him and shook her head. "Are you sure you're the same guy who kept running me over when I first came here?"

"Nope." He dashed his fingers through his hair. "I have no idea who that other guy was, but if I find him, I'll kick him out."

Her laughter made his heart sing. There was the girl he'd grown to care for. The ray of sunshine with a bright idealistic attitude about almost everything. Apparently, her optimism ran short of his Uncle Paul. Ironic, considering his uncle had been the one who insisted on hiring her, making everything possible.

She plopped down in her chair and opened her laptop, skimming the piece of paper where he'd scribbled down the details. Her fingers soon flew over the keys as if she couldn't write fast enough. Maybe she was afraid he'd change his mind again. He shook his head and glanced through numbers for the week.

Something was working. Either the nearness of Christmas or everything Trudy had done online, in their ads, on social media, and by word of mouth. No matter what it was, the figures added up nicely. He'd even had to rush-delivery order a few more toys they'd sold out of. They should be delivered this afternoon—just in time for the scavenger hunt madness and countdown to Christmas chaos.

"Hey. Didn't you say you needed to tell me something?" Her voice pulled him from his math.

"Oh. I just wanted to run an idea by you." He held up a finger. "Hang on."

He pulled up the information he'd discovered last night while he was still wound up from that kiss. He glanced at her, took a deep breath, and flipped the screen so she could see it. Her eyes morphed from curious to surprised to shaded in a matter of seconds.

"Might be fun." He came around to her side and squatted beside her to look at it together. "You mentioned you never got to attend five years ago. And they're going to be in Austin next week."

Trans-Siberian Orchestra pictures filled the screen along with details of the upcoming concert. It had seemed like such a great idea. Went right along with his plan to do something with those lists he'd stolen pictures of the other day. Yet here she was looking blue again.

"Trudy?" He touched her arm, tried to turn her around to face him, but she was stronger than he assumed given her petite frame. "Think about it, maybe?"

She gave one shake of her head. "No, Nick. I can't. Not yet. Maybe not ever." A pause. "Thank you for wanting to do this for me, though."

He slowly rose to his feet. He'd obviously blown it. What had seemed a good idea at midnight last night didn't go as well in the light of day.

"They're probably already sold out anyway. Those tickets go fast." She clicked several things on her screen as if she hadn't just given him one last hope. "It took us years to get tickets back when my dad ... Anyway, thanks, but no thanks."

But her tone in those two lines had lifted his spirits more than she might ever know. A wistfulness tinged the edges, as if she wished what she said wasn't true. And he was more determined than ever to make this happen. Something inside him said it might be the key to healing the rest of her heart and allowing her to move on. He'd just have to be sneaky.

She was right. Everything he'd read told him these events closed quickly. But if Uncle Paul could work a Christmas miracle for the store, surely there were other areas where such magic could work too. Right?

W ait. Was that for real? Trudy gawked as she pulled
into the Emporium's parking lot Friday morning. A
line of people waited to get in, and every parking
spot was full, including a few unpainted spaces. She barely
squeezed her SUV past a couple of cars in the fire lane. As soon
as she cut her engine, she performed a little happy dance,
stomping her feet and pumping her fists.

"Yes, yes, yes!"

It was one week until Christmas Eve, and this store was
finally as busy as she'd expected it to be the first time she came.
Then, she'd had over half the lot to choose from and almost no
line to see the big guy. As of this morning, schools were out on
Christmas break, so that could explain part of it, but she'd prefer
to think it was her scavenger hunt—the one that had kept her
here until three a.m. finishing all the paintings. All this for a
chance to win a fifty percent off coupon next week? She'd take it.

Trudy hurried inside and down the hall, only to halt at the
back of the store. Families meandered everywhere, looking high
and low, working together and squealing when they discovered
another of the fifteen animals. It took all her self-control to not
let her eyes dart to where her mouse drove across the bottom of

the shelf as she moved past. She didn't want to spoil the fun of finding it for the little girl in the red dress fervently studying every inch as she walked by.

Trudy passed the bicycles, where a family of toads rode in tandem toward the ball bin, and she booked it down the side aisles toward the office to drop her stuff. With this many people in here, it was sure to be all-hands-on-deck, and she was anxious to make sure things were going as well as they appeared.

"There you are." Nick caught her arms right before she ran into him coming out of the office.

"Sorry." She brushed a strand of hair out of her eyes. "I guess the late nights finally caught up with me, and I slept through my alarm this morning."

"It's okay." He waved a stack of papers in excitement. "Can you believe this?"

"We've got to be at capacity, right? The parking lot had overflowed into the alleyway when I pulled up." She glanced over her shoulder at the line ten deep waiting to check out. "Nick, this is amazing."

He followed her gaze, paused a moment, then pulled her back into the office and squeezed her tight. "I can't even wrap my mind around this. I've called in all our afternoon workers, as well as Dad and Uncle Andy. I asked them to bring anyone else from the family who is available. You're a genius, Trudy."

"I'm not a genius, but I'm glad my idea worked. I never imagined this." She shook her head. "If this happens Saturday with the Santa story time, we may have to offer a second session or something. I wonder if we should order more cookies."

"Let's cross that bridge when we get to it. For now, how good are you at wrapping presents? That station has the biggest back-up." He noticed what was in his hands. "Or you can go make some more scavenger hunt forms."

"How can we possibly be out already? We made two hundred to start with."

"You said it yourself. We're probably pushing the limits of

fire safety right now." He dashed a hand through his hair and rocked on his heels. "Several families are letting each child do it, so that makes the forms go a bit faster. I'm glad we limited it to under eighteen, or we might have to make a thousand."

"A thousand, really?" She reached up on tiptoes and pressed a kiss to his cheek. "You go copy and cut those. I'll go help wrap gifts."

"Oh. Here." He grabbed a cup off the desk. "Coffee."

"You're the best." She took a sip and smiled at the peppermint flavor. She'd either won him over to her favorite, or he got it simply for her. She wouldn't complain either way.

"I might remind you of that next time we have a slow moment to talk." He winked.

No time to explore that statement further. She scurried out of the office. Flirtations were fun, but they wouldn't help shorten lines of waiting customers. Time to get busy.

"Hi." Trudy dashed behind the counter swarming with tissue paper. "I've been sent to help."

"Oh, hallelujah!" A girl, maybe mid-twenties, glanced up from trying to wrap a basketball, pieces of tape clinging to various parts of her maroon sweater. "When Nick sent out the distress call to the whole family, I didn't realize what I was in for. I'm Nick's cousin Michelle, in town for Christmas."

"Trudy." Trudy grabbed the edge of the paper that kept slipping from Michelle's grasp and held it in place until they could secure it. "Let's get this done."

The girl gave her a thankful grin, and then they both looked out to help the next customer in line. If Trudy had considered the queue for the cash registers crazy, this one blew her mind. A glance to the left showed the line to see Santa wound through all three rows of cordoned path for the first time this season. And someone stood at the door, making sure a family left before another was allowed in.

"I think half of Temple is here." Trudy tied a bow around a neatly wrapped doll set.

"Probably half of Temple and surrounding towns too." Michelle worked on a stack of books. "How far did the ad run?"

"I ran it in a forty-mile radius." Trudy shook her head. "But I didn't really expect people to drive that far."

"Oh, my. Look." Michelle froze in the middle of covering a building set, her gaze fixed on the door.

A local news anchor, Ann Powers, stood there, microphone in hand, a camera crew at her shoulder. She pointed and spoke to the older gentleman at the door, who Trudy guessed might be Uncle Andy. He pointed at Nick, near the registers, and then back to her. She'd never dreamed of attracting this much notice. Maybe they'd have to make a thousand copies of those cards after all.

Nick froze as Ms. Powers approached him. Was he in shock? He glanced over his shoulder at her, his eyes wide. Trudy giggled and finished wrapping three sets of air dart guns.

"I don't think Nick expected any of this."

"Did you?" Michelle quickly covered a grimace as the next person in line rolled up with a cart full of toys of various shapes and sizes.

"Honestly?" Trudy stared around at the chaos again. "No."

She hated to abandon Michelle, but she had at least helped knock out five or six people before Nick motioned her to join him. Andy and Paul and his dad, James, also ended up in the activity room, and Trudy was glad they'd finished setting it up the day before. The anchor arranged a few things and then did a quick question and answer session with the older gentlemen, asking about the history of the store. Paul begged off, needing to get back to the kids waiting to see Santa.

Next up, Nick and Trudy were put in the spotlight. Trudy willed her hands to not fidget as the camera zeroed in on her. She also fought down the urge to reach up and smooth Nick's flyaway hair, where he'd been dashing his hands through it. Too late now.

"We're doing a segment on various businesses around town

that, despite having been around for a while, are bringing new life to Temple. Several people suggested Russo's Toy Emporium. Can you tell us a little bit about what inspired your changes and what we can expect to see coming up in this beautiful room?"

Ms. Powers thrust the microphone toward the middle of them as if unsure which family member would know the answer.

"As you saw a minute ago, we have a personal connection with Santa here at the Emporium." Nick let out a chuckle. "He happened to know the mother of this gem of a lady, Trudy, who developed all the great ideas you've seen out in the store. We've added better lighting, more signs to help shoppers find products, and even pops of color to brighten up the floors.

"In addition, Trudy painted all fifteen of the surprise animals around the store, which are part of our scavenger hunt going on right now. Those will stick around to make our place more fun for years to come. She helped give some new life to this room, as well, where we plan to have activities take place, beginning this weekend."

"And what kind of activities are you talking about?" The anchor prompted.

"Story time with Santa will be Saturday at ten. We'll have cookies and coloring pages." Nick smiled at Trudy. "In January, I've lined up a magician to come in and teach magic tricks. And we're considering painting sessions and building times, possibly other activities down the road."

"That sounds amazing." Ann Powers nodded her head. "Where did the inspiration come for all of this?"

Nick nudged Trudy, indicating she should answer this one. What could she say? She wasn't even sure what had inspired all these ideas.

"From the first moment I entered the store a few weeks ago, when I brought my nephew in to see Santa, I knew there was hidden potential here." Trudy couldn't keep from grinning. "It practically ran me over."

Laughter shook Nick's shoulders, but he somehow kept it quiet.

"When my mom talked me into taking the position to help revitalize the store a bit, I wanted one thing. This store needed to say *fun* every time you turned a corner. The colors, the brightness, the animals. A toy store should be played with as much as the toys it sells. I mean, if a toy store isn't a fun place to visit, what is?"

"I can definitely say you've accomplished what you set out to do." The woman turned and stared directly into the camera. "If you want a closer look at these changes, or a chance to find all fifteen animal paintings scattered throughout, come on down to Russos' Toy Emporium.

"To be entered in the contest for a chance to win a fifty-percent-off coupon—a perfect prize right before Christmas—make sure you complete the scavenger hunt by Monday at seven. Santa will be reading stories tomorrow morning. And it sounds like many other fun times are coming in the new year. I have a feeling I'll be back with my niece before next weekend."

Nick reached over and squeezed Trudy's fingers as soon as the camera light flickered off. Part of him wondered if today were only a dream, but her skin was warm beneath his hand, and the return squeeze she offered was strong. He almost didn't want her to leave him and go back to wrapping presents, but Michelle would kill him if he didn't return her assistant.

"We're going to wander around just a little to get some footage of the store itself, as well as the crazy crowd out there." Ms. Powers wrapped up a cord. "I'll do my best to get this aired tonight. Otherwise, it will be too late for the Santa story time bit that's happening tomorrow."

"I can't thank you enough." Nick shook her extended hand.

"This whole morning has far exceeded expectations, but gaining the interest of the local news station is amazing."

"You're very welcome." She leaned closer. "Seriously I'll probably be back with my niece. She wasn't very impressed with the Santa her mom took her to the other day. And she's wanting a new set of art supplies for Christmas."

"We definitely have those in stock right now." Nick nodded. "And she might be interested in the painting sessions we'll offer next year."

Ms. Powers clicked her bag closed. "What all will be involved with that?"

"We haven't worked out all the details, but we're hoping to bring in an instructor who can walk the kids through how to do a painting, sort of like the places a lot of adults attend. The cost will be the supplies, and then anyone who takes the class will get to take their painting and leftover supplies home with them."

"This room is perfect for it."

"It is." Nick examined the happy walls. "When Trudy first threw the idea at me, I couldn't picture it. But now I can't believe I almost tried to talk her out of this."

"She's brought a breath of fresh air to this place, huh?"

"In more ways than one." Nick nodded and led the way out to the chaos of his store.

"If you haven't already lined someone up for the painting instructor, I might have a name to give you. Here's my card. Give me a call when it's not quite so crazy, and I'll look up the information." She rummaged in her bag and handed him a slightly creased white card.

Nick stuck the information in his front pocket and barely restrained himself from doing a celebratory jig. One step closer to making Trudy's dream come true. He couldn't wait to tell her.

As the afternoon dragged on, the traffic flow slowed somewhat but was still higher than normal a half an hour before closing. Trudy had taken over the gift wrap station and sent Michelle home sometime mid-afternoon. She'd piled her hair up on top of her head in a messy bun, and it made her look younger. When she caught him looking at her, she shot a saucy grin his way.

A sudden realization hit him that they had no reason to stay late tonight. She planned to finish setting up for Santa's story time in the morning. But everything else was done. He needed to check and make sure he didn't need to place another rush order for a few items that had sold well today. Other than that, he'd be able to head home at a normal hour. The thought would have elated him two weeks before, but now a sense of loss settled about his shoulders.

Granted, he could ask her to join him for dinner or something later, but would she be interested? After all, she was supposed to be spending time with her mom, too, and she hadn't done much of that in the last week. But on the other hand, she'd been the one to kiss his cheek that morning, so maybe she'd be amenable to the idea?

He shook his head as he turned the sign on the front door to *CLOSED*. He was overthinking this. Even if they didn't spend the evening together, it would give him more time to work on the idea that had popped in his head late last night while he watched her paint. Obviously, she was rubbing off on him with all these midnight revelations. He went through the motions of thanking all the workers who had put so many extra hours on the clock today.

Trudy waved at him with a new stack of scavenger hunt cards. "I think we're up to six hundred now. If we get another day or two like this, we might hit your goal of a thousand after all."

He ran a hand through his hair and let out a deep breath. "I'm not sure my feet can take it."

"I bet they'd survive." She motioned around the store. "Did you sell out of anything? I think I wrapped at least five bicycle helmets and fifteen baby dolls. And don't get me started on remote control cars."

"I'm going to go check. I think that's all we have to do tonight, right? You didn't have anything else on your to-do list?"

"Nope." She stretched her arms out in front of her, fingers interlocked. "I'm done, believe it or not."

"I'm not sure I want to believe it." He took a step toward her and then backed up again as Paul walked up.

"Trudy McNamara, you are worth much more than I paid you." He held out his hand to her, and she hesitated only a moment before accepting it. "Today has been a real-life Christmas miracle. Even better than the old days when my dad first started having Santa visits at the store. You, my dear, are a jewel." He leaned closer and glanced at Nick while he turned his voice down to a stage whisper. "And make sure my nephew treats you as such."

"Oh." Her cheeks grew pink. "I, um ..."

"I will see you both in the morning." Paul saluted them and slipped out the door.

"I guess I'd better go check inventory." Nick shifted his weight, still uncertain about asking her to spend more time with him.

"Sounds good." She tucked a stray strand behind her ear. "I guess I'll see you bright and early tomorrow."

"Right." He fidgeted. "Unless .... You wanna go grab a bite to eat before you head home?"

"Oh." She ducked her head. "Um, not tonight, Nick. It's not that I don't want to spend more time with you, but I'm really beat."

"I understand. I gave up before you last night. When did you leave?"

"Three, I think." She pinched her lips together. "I may see if Mom wants to hang out this evening. I've sort of been neglecting her, as Katt reminded me yesterday."

"Right." If he kept repeating the same things, he'd sound like a broken record. "Let me walk you out to your car, at least."

She nodded and grabbed her things from the office. He let

his fingers graze the small of her back, wanting even that small connection as long as he could get it. He held her car door while she stowed her bag. The brisk December wind whipped around them and made her jacket flap.

He ran a finger down her cheek. "See you tomorrow?"

"Yes. I'll be here."

"Trudy, thank you." He cupped her shoulders with each hand.

"For what?" Her blue eyes widened.

"For everything you've done for the store. Uncle Paul was right to hire you. I'm sorry I fought against it for so long." He pulled her closer. "You really are a miracle worker."

She willingly offered her lips to him as he leaned to press a kiss to them. The wind faded to the background as he let himself get wrapped up in her for several long moments. Her eyes sparkled as she backed away and got in her car.

"You keep doing things like that, and I'm not going to want to go back to Austin in the new year."

"Challenge accepted." He winked before shutting her door.

Was she really still considering returning to the capital? Hadn't the store proved that there was work to be done right here in Temple? She didn't have to be in the big city. Away from him.

If being apart for this one evening was rough, her being in Austin would be much, much worse. Time to put his plan into action. And hope what had sounded like a good idea in the middle of the night worked as well in the light of day.

Chapter Eighteen

Trudy's Friday night had not gone the way she'd
envisioned when she left the store for Mom's house.
Instead of being welcomed by her Mom and dinner, a
note on the counter informed her Mom had gone to something
at Mark's preschool. Nothing in the fridge sounded good, so she
settled for a bag of popcorn and some cider as her meal.

Out of curiosity she'd watched the news broadcast and been
duly impressed by the small segment on the Emporium. Even
having been there in the midst of it, seeing that crowd on screen
struck her with awe. And made her wonder why she hadn't
agreed to spend more time with Nick after work.

Now it was Saturday morning, and they would host the Santa
story time in only a few hours. She had an easier time getting
into the parking lot, but there were still more cars than there
had been in the days before. She parked and took a deep breath.
After yesterday's success, her nerves shouldn't be this geared up.

"Good morning." Trudy found Nick in the activity room.
"What are you doing?"

"Making sure everything is set up." He glanced up from the
tray of cookies in his hands.

"I thought all we had left was the food. Did I forget

something?" It was entirely possible, as crazy as things had been the last few days, but she didn't think anything had been left out.

"No." He grinned. "I'm just being overly cautious, I guess."

"I understand." She shifted the strap on her shoulder. "I woke up with this sense of doom hanging over me but no idea why."

"Everything is going to be great." He squeezed her shoulders and steered her toward the office. "Uncle Paul's ready, and we have more family coming in around nine to help with the extra customers."

"Okay, okay. I believe you." She laughed and set her bag in the chair that had become hers over the last few weeks.

"Did you have a good evening last night?" He leaned against the doorway, so there was no way she could sneak around him and not have to answer the question.

"Not my best, actually." She gave a half shrug. "Mom was gone to some function at Mark's preschool and didn't get back until I was about to crash. Nothing on TV except some news report of a toy store being revitalized."

"Oh, man. Sounds horribly boring. Who cares about toy stores?" The crinkles at the edges of his eyes told her he followed her tease. "Sorry you didn't get to spend time with your mom, though. I know you wanted to."

"Maybe tonight." She did a little drum roll on the desk. "For now, we've got cookies to set up."

"Right. I'll leave you to that. I'm expecting a delivery truck this morning with a few more things we're low on." He glanced at his watch and then at his computer screen over her shoulder before quickly returning his gaze to her.

"Okay." She wouldn't remark on how weird that sequence had been. Maybe he was just distracted by all the extra work she'd brought to his store. He'd already had too much before she started. "I guess I'll catch back up with you in a bit, then."

"Sounds good." He inched farther into the office as she

walked out. If she didn't know any better, she'd think he was hiding something.

Just over an hour until she'd start letting people enter the activity room and find a seat. They'd agreed yesterday that if they had more than fifty kids wanting to attend, they would divide it into two sessions an hour apart. She located the rest of the treats in the kitchenette and quickly got them situated with napkins and plates on the table in the back of the room. The tree Nick had borrowed from his aunt glowed in the corner. Santa's chair was ready with three different holiday stories.

She headed toward Santa's area in the middle of the store. Paul sat with two girls on his knee and a boy staring him down from two feet away. The mom was trying to coax the boy to get closer to the others so she could take their picture, but he was having none of it. Paul leaned over and held his hand next to his mouth.

"If you come stand where your mommy wants you to, I have a surprise waiting to say thank you." His stage whisper carried to where Trudy stood at the edge of the doll aisle.

The boy's arms uncrossed an inch. "What is it?"

"It won't be a surprise if I tell you, but it's really yummy." Paul winked.

The boy rocked on his heels a moment before he stepped a foot closer to the chair. It wasn't as close as his mommy had requested, but she obviously decided it would work because she feverishly snapped several shots and mouthed a *thank you*. Paul caught Trudy's eye before waving her nearer.

"This is my elf." Paul pointed to Trudy. "She has some treats waiting for the kids who come have story time with me this morning, but I think there might be enough extra that these good children could have one now. What do you think, Miss Elf?"

"Oh, um, yes." Trudy nodded, realizing that was the surprise he had promised. "Why don't you follow me?"

"She doesn't look like an elf." The boy tilted his head as he studied her. "Where's her pointy ears?"

"I have to hide them when I'm not at the North Pole." Trudy had no idea where the explanation came from, but it seemed to placate the stubborn fellow.

"Thank you so much." The mother squeezed Trudy's hand as her children munched down their treats. "The girls always believe with no problem, but Silas here has decided he might not like Santa after all."

Trudy widened her eyes as she gave a glance at all the kids. "You know what kids who don't believe in Santa get on Christmas morning?"

Three heads shook slowly, their expressions curious.

"Underwear and socks." Trudy nodded as if it were the most solemn news she could bestow. "Only children who believe in Santa get fun things in their stockings."

"Underwear!" The smallest girl burst into giggles, but the boy scowled.

"He needs new socks anyway." The mom whispered to Trudy. "This might be just what I needed. Thanks for that too."

Trudy hid her laughter behind a hand as the mom led her children back out to the store once more. Fifteen minutes until time to start letting people in. Was Nick unloading a truck? She hadn't seen him walk by or heard any deliveries.

A glance in the stock room showed only a few teenage workers. Up front, the office door was closed. Had something happened? Nick usually kept it open since they'd shared it.

She knocked on the door. No response. A twist of the knob, and it opened easily. She peeked through the crack before going all the way in. Nick sat, his eyes focused on his computer screen, earphones in, one finger hovering over something on his phone. What in the world?

He jumped when she tapped him on the shoulder, spinning around so quickly one of his earpieces fell out. She grabbed it up and placed it in her own ear, curious as to what had him so enthralled. A Christmas song blared through the tiny speaker, and she lifted an eyebrow.

"What are you doing?"

"Any minute now, they're supposed to be giving a clue. If I'm the fifteenth caller and get the answer right, I could win tickets." He avoided her gaze, and she narrowed her eyes.

"Tickets?"

He pointed to a small sidebar on the screen, which showed the radio station's web page.

"TSO?" Her knees wobbled a bit. He was trying to win tickets to the concert for her. That explained the funny way he'd acted earlier. It was supposed to be a surprise.

"I know you said you didn't want to go." He held up his hands as if to ask her to let him explain. "But something inside me just couldn't let it go that easily. You were right of course. They were sold out. But then I heard this contest announced as I drove in this morning." He shrugged.

Part of her wanted to hit him for not listening to her two days before. The other part of her melted a little at the knowledge that he was going to such extremes to try and make her happy. Not that he knew everything about that failed concert five years before. Maybe she should tell him now. Before she could make up her mind, the song ended and Nick froze as if moving or even breathing would hinder him from hearing what they were about to say.

"Okay, Jingle Belles and Jingle Boys." The radio announcer's voice was much too cheery for anyone in real life. "Here's the moment you've been waiting for. The clue is, 'This is why the alphabet is shorter at Christmas.' If you can be the fifteenth caller and give me the right answer, you will win two tickets to the sold-out TSO concert happening in Austin Tuesday night." He repeated the riddle and gave the phone number, but Nick had already had the digits programmed into his phone and was hitting dial as the announcer switched over to another song.

"Do you know the answer?" Trudy frowned.

"It's easy. Noel." Nick tapped his fingers as he waited for something to happen on the other end of the phone.

"Noel?"

"Yeah. The alphabet is shorter because there's no *L*." This time Nick separated the word into its syllables so she could hear the answer.

"Ah."

"Okay, thanks." Nick talked into his phone.

"Were you the wrong number?" She couldn't believe how much she now hoped he won.

"Caller seventeen. They'll give the fifteenth caller a chance, then go down the line until they get a right answer." He dashed his hand through his hair.

Her heart sped up. He was only two callers away from winning tickets. Could this really happen? When had she started thinking this was a good idea?

Classical instrumental music hummed from Nick's phone clashing with the song playing on the air, so he pulled the earphone out where he listened to only one melody. When Trudy had first realized what he was doing, he feared she would throttle him. Now, however, she seemed almost suspended in time as she watched him with every fiber of her being. It amped up the nerves already haywire in his body. Did she think this might be a good idea after all?

Trudy pressed the earphone to her ear. "They're talking to number fifteen now."

Nick waited, not daring to draw even the slightest breath. Trudy's eyes locked with his, and she almost vibrated as they waited to see what would happen. And then her whole being slumped and she pulled the earbud from her head and handed it back.

"Hello?" It took Nick a moment to realize the greeting came from his phone. "Are you still there?"

"Yes. I'm still here." At least in body if not heart. Because Trudy's defeated posture on the other side of the office told him what the intern on the phone was about to say.

"Thanks so much for holding and for your participation in our contest. Unfortunately, our fifteenth caller did have the correct answer, so you didn't win this time."

"Thank you anyway."

"We'll do this again in three hours." The chipper voice reminded him before hanging up.

Nick set his device down and let out a sigh. This was supposed to be the perfect plan. He was certain when the radio announced the contest everything would fall into place. Now he wasn't so sure.

"There's another chance in three hours." He stood behind Trudy and touched her shoulder. "Want me to keep trying?"

She shook her head. "I don't know, Nick. I don't know what I want."

A rap on the door had them both straightening and stepping a little farther apart. Paul stuck his head in and glanced between the two of them. Trudy turned away and rubbed a hand over her face.

"You guys ready for this thing?" Paul motioned with his head back toward the store. "We've got people asking where they need to go."

"Oh." Trudy smoothed out her sweater and glanced at Nick once again, most traces of disappointment and angst gone from her eyes. "I actually came in here to remind you it was almost time to start seating people."

"Right. Let's do it." He grabbed a device off the desk to help him keep track of how many were going in and followed her out of the office.

She picked up a handset from the closest register and pressed the button to make an announcement over the speaker system.

"Story time with Santa will begin in ten minutes. If you would like to participate, please make your way toward the back of the store and form a line. We will begin seating people in a few moments."

Just like that, her professional persona was on. Unless he studied her closely. There. Her hand shook just a tad as she hung up the receiver. Her eyes blinked a few extra times as she glanced around for her next step.

When she'd said she had a bad feeling about today, he assumed she meant something would go wrong with the activity, but maybe it had been about his ridiculous plan instead. Had he only made things worse by trying to win tickets? Was he simply exacerbating a problem?

He squared his shoulder and followed her for moral support. And in three hours he'd be right back where he'd been a few minutes ago, but this time, two seconds faster so he could be the first one to answer instead of the third. Because he didn't want to make things worse. He wanted to make her happy.

Chapter Nineteen

"**M**om?" Trudy almost dropped the stack of scavenger hunt entries she carried. "What are you doing here?"

"Well, we didn't get to spend any time together last night. And Katt needed me to watch Mark, so we decided to take you to lunch." Mom pointed to her nephew studying a display of radio-controlled cars.

"Katt is going to take advantage of you with you being so close now." Trudy shifted her load. Was lunch the real reason her mom was here, or did it have something to do with Paul? Trudy pushed that worry aside and accepted the reason given. "Okay, sure. Let me grab my jacket."

No sign of Nick as she set the cards on her desk and grabbed her coat. He'd disappeared in the middle of story time—a delivery. Fifteen minutes until the next radio clue. Would he really try again? Did she want him to? She pushed those thoughts aside. Time to live in the present, and that meant focusing on Mom and Mark.

"Hey, Mark-o." She ruffled his blond hair. "Where are we going to eat?"

Of course he wanted to go somewhere he could get a toy

with his nuggets. Out they headed into the cool day. Clouds hung overhead, threatening to drop their burdens any minute. One week until Christmas, and traffic matched the hectic atmosphere. Trudy longed for a few moments of quiet but didn't expect to find them before the new year.

As they searched for a parking spot at McDonald's, the radio station caught her attention. It was the same one Nick had called earlier. And they were about to talk to caller number fifteen. She reminded herself to breathe normally as the voice on the air replied with the correct answer to whatever silly riddle they'd given this time.

A female. Not Nick. Had he tried, or had he listened to her when she told him not to? Wasn't that what she wanted?

Even if he won the tickets, would her heart let her attend? Or would the guilt crush her until she wouldn't be able to draw a breath?

"Coming?"

Trudy glanced up and realized her mom and Mark were already out and waiting on her. She joined them and forced herself to focus on Mark's chatter and Mom's plans for Christmas dinner next week. She evidently nodded in all the right places because her mom didn't question her attention.

Mom pulled up to the front of Russos' an hour after they'd left. "You have a full afternoon ahead of you?"

"Shouldn't be too bad. Mostly just checking answers on scavenger hunt cards." Trudy glanced at the doors. What else waited for her inside? A giant raindrop splattered on the windshield. "I better get in."

"See you tonight."

Mom didn't have plans? That was unexpected, considering how much time Trudy assumed she'd been spending with Paul. Trudy rushed through the front doors just before the heavens opened. She stared back out at the downpour and let out a breath that fogged the glass.

No sign of Nick in the office when she dropped off her

things. Maybe he was still working on that delivery. Paul—rather, Santa—was back in his usual seat, but the crowds had thinned some with the lousy weather. He grinned at her, but she just offered a half-hearted wave in return.

A feminine laugh reverberated down the hallway as Trudy neared the back of the store. Strange. Maybe one of Nick's cousins was helping him.

Lights shone in the activity room. Hadn't she turned them off when the morning session finished? She stuck her head in the doorway and froze.

A blonde hovered close to Nick, her hand on his arm, giggling about whatever story he told. Who was she? Her light coloring didn't match the rest of the Russo family. Not to mention the flirty way she leaned in proved she was no relation.

"Oh!" The girl started as she caught Trudy's glare.

Nick turned, his laughter freezing when he spotted her. "Trudy! You're back."

"I just went to lunch with Mom and Mark. I would've told you before I left, but I guess you were still unloading that delivery."

"Probably." Nick walked over, his eyes trying to convey something she couldn't begin to make out. "I want you to meet Jessi."

"Hi." The blonde stuck her hand out, and Trudy took it for a second before dropping it again.

"Jessi is an artist who has agreed to come in and do a paint session for us next year." Nick frowned a bit, as if trying to figure out what was going on with Trudy.

"Oh. That's great." Trudy tried to smile, but it didn't feel authentic.

"Nick wasn't expecting me." Jessi touched his arm again. "I'm good friends with Ann Powers, the reporter who came yesterday. Anyway, she sent me over, knowing you were looking for someone. Nick was kind enough to drop everything and give me a tour." She couldn't keep her hands off Nick's arm. Not that

Trudy had any claim to that arm, but shouldn't those kisses count for something? She'd thought them sincere at the time.

"A tour of this room?" That wouldn't have taken long. Not long enough for Jessi to be so comfortable around Nick. Hadn't he given her the same prickly attitude he'd greeted Trudy with three weeks before?

"Oh, the whole store." Jessi let out that grating giggle again. "But we've been in here a while, figuring out how to set things up. And talking about how many supplies he'll need to have for each child."

"So, you've been here a while?" Trudy couldn't help but glance at her watch.

Nick's eyes widened, and he peered at his own timepiece. "Oh, man!"

Did that mean what Trudy thought it meant? He hadn't even tried to be caller fifteen back when the radio was giving away more tickets. He had been too busy letting this bimbo fawn all over him.

"What's wrong?" Jessi glanced between them as if just realizing they might be more than simply coworkers.

"Nothing." Trudy shook her head. "It was nice to meet you. I'll get the details from Nick later and work up an ad for the art session."

"Great!" And the perkiness was back. Was she truly so dense?

"If you don't need me for anything in particular this afternoon, I think I'll head out early." Trudy didn't even meet Nick's brown eyes.

"Trudy, wait!"

She refused to give in and turn around as she walked back through the store. She should be happy. He was making her dream happen. So, why did it hurt so much?

"Trudy." Nick closed the office door as he rushed in behind her. He didn't know how, but he had to find a way to make this right.

"Did you need something?" She dramatically straightened the scavenger hunt cards. "I can work on these at Mom's house if you need them before Monday."

He caught her hands between his own. "Stop for a minute and let me apologize, please."

"You don't owe me anything." She shook her head, her brown tresses waving like a curtain to shield the sides of her face.

"I wasn't expecting her. Ann Powers told me she knew someone yesterday. She asked me to call and set up a time to meet. I hadn't even had a chance to think about it again, then out of the blue, Jessi walked in this afternoon." He crooked a finger under Trudy's chin, tilting her head so he could see her eyes. "And I have half a mind to tell her I'll find someone else, anyway."

"What?" Trudy finally met his gaze. "Why would you do that? Isn't having an artist show up volunteering for my crazy idea perfect?"

"Not if she's going to paw all over me the whole time she's here. I can let her know I'll keep her in mind, but I'll check out some other options." He took a step closer. "She's definitely not my type."

"You didn't look too unhappy with her when I interrupted." Trudy's voice sounded petulant, and a look crossed her face that he would swear was probably embarrassment at her jealousy.

"I was telling her about you. How you came in like a tornado and insisted on changing that room around so we could have painting sessions and other activities. And about how Uncle Paul tricked us into attending a couple's session." He shook his head. "I was smiling because I was thinking about *you*."

Trudy pressed her lips together. Was she holding her tongue or thinking?

"I was literally sitting down to listen for the next clue when she appeared in my doorway, not taking 'No' for an answer. I assumed she just wanted to see the room and set up possible dates or something and that it wouldn't take that long. Instead, she ended up getting the guided tour and wanted to talk more details than I even knew we needed." Nick drew an *X* over his heart. "I promise at the next chance I will be right there listening and calling in, trying to win those tickets."

"Oh, Nick." Trudy turned her head to the side. "Why don't you just give up? I told you this wasn't a good idea, and everything seems stacked against it. Take it as a sign. This isn't meant to happen."

"But you want it to." He whispered the words and smiled when she jerked her attention back to him, her mouth slightly parted.

"It doesn't matter. It's too late." She pulled away once more, leaving him missing the warmth of her fingers immediately. "And I really do think I'll head to Mom's house. It's been a long couple of weeks."

"It's pouring outside. At least wait until it lets up some."

"From the look of the radar earlier, that might not happen for hours."

He raised his eyebrows. "And?"

A knock interrupted whatever answer Trudy might have given. Jessi poked her head in. Nick stifled a groan and forced a smile on his face as he turned toward her.

"I wrote down the information we talked about as well as some dates. And my phone number is here." Had she added emphasis to that particular fact for a reason? He hoped not. "Call me to set it all up."

"Sure, Jessi. Thanks for coming by this afternoon." He took the paper and stepped back again.

Jessi cut her eyes between him and Trudy, a glower forming as she eyed Trudy. "Okay, then. I'll wait for your call."

"It may be after the holidays." Nick wanted to give himself a little leeway. "It's pretty crazy right now, you know."

"Oh, sure." Jessi adjusted her purse strap. "Until then."

She finally backed out and walked toward the door but not before it gave Trudy enough time to gather her own things as well. He sighed when he saw how ready she was to go. So much for convincing her to spend more time with him today.

"I'll see you Monday." Trudy said it in a tone that brooked no argument.

"That's a long time from now. Won't I see you at worship services tomorrow?"

"It's less than forty-eight hours." She rolled her eyes. "And even if Mom goes there again, I'll probably go somewhere else. I can't ... handle the stress of ... that situation again."

"You mean sitting so close to me." He stepped closer.

Her lips twitched as if fighting a smirk. "Mom and Paul. I just ... I can't focus on God if I'm thinking about them and how close they're sitting to each other."

"Fair enough." He tucked a strand of her soft hair behind her ear. "But I'll miss you. We could hang out tomorrow afternoon."

"I think I need some time. Time to decompress and think and reevaluate some things." She ducked her head once more. "Maybe even spend some time with Mom."

"Sure. I get it." He couldn't push her. Something told him that would only drive her farther away. "Okay, Monday unless you let me know you want to get together before then."

"Just can't give up, can you?" Her mouth turned up in a semi-smile.

"Can't blame a guy for trying." He pressed a kiss to her temple. "And I won't quit trying on the other thing either."

Trudy took a deep breath. "I'll see you Monday, Nick."

She headed out, her bag flung over her shoulder, a hooded jacket shielding her from a few drops of rain. He leaned against the desk edge, breathing in the bit of her scent that remained in the room. This day had not gone as planned.

He had to make sure the rest of it went better. A quick glance at his watch showed he had two hours until the next chance to win tickets. He set an alarm and determined nothing would keep him from it this time. This was too important.

Only two more chances today, and after that he had no plan. Possibly drive down to Austin and see if any hawkers were trying to sell tickets last minute outside the venue, but more often than not, those weren't authentic. Definitely a higher risk than trying to be the fifteenth caller.

If he couldn't get tickets to this concert, it would put a major kink in his plans. This was supposed to be the crown jewel of his ideas. He needed a Christmas miracle, and quickly. Or a better plan. And who had time to think of something like that?

But two hours later he was caller thirteen.

And three hours after that, sitting at his kitchen table, he didn't even make it in the top twenty.

Nick hung up and let his forehead rest against the wood in front of him.

So much for Christmas miracles. What now?

Chapter Twenty

T aking time to be away from Nick had sounded like a great idea when Trudy first suggested it. The reality of it, however, wasn't so hot. She laid back in her bed late Sunday afternoon, pretending to nap so she could avoid week two of making Christmas goodies in the kitchen. Her mom was in charge today, and that was exactly how Trudy wanted it. If she were feeling more productive, she might get up and try to unpack a few more boxes, but the urge was nowhere to be found.

Nick hadn't won the tickets. She'd somehow found a way to listen each time. And she had to admit she was disappointed. Especially since one of his chances yesterday was blown by spending time with that handsy artist girl.

The now-familiar nudge of jealousy raised its head and growled inside her. When had things developed to the point that she would have a problem with him talking to another woman? Especially one that would make her dreams become reality.

When she came up here with her mom, the plan had been to stay a month tops. Had that changed? Just because of a guy?

Her phone chimed, and she picked it up to read the text.

Hey girl. I miss you like crazy. When are you
coming back?

It was Caitlyn, her Austin friend and roommate.

Not sure.

Trudy typed her reply carefully.

Things are sort of up in the air right now.

Please tell me you're not going to end up
staying there?

I need your artistic vibes to help me with my
new business!

Trudy rolled her eyes at the rapid-fire response. Caitlyn loved
to surround herself with creative people since she didn't have an
inch of imagination in her own body. And Trudy enjoyed being
part of Caitlyn's entourage of designers. But none of the little
jobs Caitlyn had lined up for Trudy were half as satisfying as
seeing the line outside Russos' door yesterday. She wanted to do
more work like that—something with meaning and depth and
personality.

Austin had a personality, and she would always love it, but
Temple had a fun side too. And it had Nick. The kind of guy she
might be able to picture forever with someday.

After all, he'd already helped her do two or three things she'd
never dreamed she'd be able to enjoy again. They'd decorated the
Christmas tree ... one she hadn't been sure she could stand to
even put up. And it had been magical instead of sad.

They'd made Christmas cookies. Granted, their almost-kiss
had distracted her from some of the grief. As well as Mark's
chatter and messiness. But still ... she'd made it through.

He'd even somehow convinced her heart to accept that it

167

might be okay to go to the TSO concert. Dad's last item ... She let out a sigh. Not that it would happen, but at least she'd accepted that she'd be okay if it did.

In the five years since Dad's heart attack, no one else had helped her work through her fear of enjoying Christmas again without the man who had made it so special. Her family had grumbled some but had accepted that she wasn't ready yet. And her friends just rolled with it when she declined any holiday invitations. They didn't even question why.

Not Nick.

Nick called her a tornado, but he had managed some upheaval in her life too. She scrolled through her phone's photos, stopping on the one of their painted reindeer. He had been so appalled to find out it was a couple's session. But his reindeer was almost cuter than hers. She spread her fingers across the screen to zoom in.

A short laugh escaped her lips. Their deer were kissing. Somehow, they'd held their canvases close enough for the animals to touch noses under the mistletoe. Had the signs been there all along?

Her phone dinged again. She hesitated to pick it up. She really didn't want any more pushing from Caitlyn. After the holidays was soon enough to make a final decision about that.

> Put on something warm and meet me out
> front in half an hour.

Nick's words brought a frown to her forehead. Hadn't she told him she'd see him Monday and not before? On the other hand, considering how many of her thoughts he occupied, she was basically spending tonight with him anyway.

A second text came through.

> Please.

She shook her head but got up and pulled on a thick sweater

over her long-sleeved T-shirt. Corduroys, boots, and a hat should keep her warm enough no matter what he had planned, even in December. She stepped out of her room and followed the sound of her nephew's giggles to the kitchen.

The table was covered with waxed paper sheets full of white-chocolate-covered pretzels stuck together to look like snowflakes and chocolate-covered pretzels arranged like reindeer, complete with red noses. Mark's mouth showed signs of having taste-tested more than a few of the treats. She ruffled his hair and snitched a goodie for herself.

"Aunt Tootie!" Mark put his little fists on his hips and scowled. "Those are for later."

"Hey, hun." Her mom stepped in from the laundry room. "You going somewhere?"

"Evidently." Trudy finished chewing her bite. "Nick said to dress warm and he'd pick me up but didn't say where we're going."

"Oh, fun." Her mom snatched the spatula out of Mark's hand before he could lick it ... again. "I think we're going to meet up with Katt and Brian for some dinner in a bit. Then, who knows?"

"Tell them I said, 'Hi.'"

"Mark, why don't you go in the bathroom and wash your hands, okay?" Her mom helped him down from his ladder and patted his bottom to get him going in the right direction. "He probably won't eat much dinner, but spoiling is what Nanas are supposed to do, right?"

Trudy rolled her eyes. "Sure."

Her mom surprised her by grabbing her hands. "I'm glad you're going out tonight. I've been worried about you. You seemed so down yesterday."

"I think I'm just worn out. I've put in a lot of hours this week to get everything done before Christmas, you know." It wasn't the complete truth, but it wasn't a lie either.

"I know. Believe it or not, I know more than you think I do. Like how little you sleep at night." Her mom tucked one of her strands of hair back under her hat where it had fallen over her cheek.

"Am I too loud?"

"No. I'm usually up too."

"You are?" How had Trudy not known this? She never heard any noise from her mom's room.

"It's lonely." Mom's eyes glistened with moisture. "After sleeping beside someone for over twenty years, it's hard to be alone again."

Trudy wrapped her arms around her mom and squeezed tight. "Mom. You could have come in and crashed with me. We might not have slept any more, but at least you wouldn't have been alone."

Her mom laughed and shook her head. "No, it's okay. But thanks for the offer."

The doorbell rang and Trudy jumped. "Oh! I was supposed to meet him. Oops."

"Go on, then." Her mom gave her a little push just as Mark walked in from the other direction, his sleeves wet up to his elbows. "Have a good time."

Trudy opened the door and then stilled, unsure what to expect. Nick stood there, every hair in place, a small pot of poinsettias in his hand. He gave a little grin and held out the flowers.

"Hi."

"Hi." She grabbed the container before he dropped it and set it on the table next to the door.

"I take it by your outfit that you got my text?" His eyes took in her sweater and boots with a look of appreciation.

"I did. Where are we headed?" She grabbed her purse. "Do I need anything else?"

"I don't think so." He twined his fingers through hers and walked her out to his car. "I'm glad you're coming with me."

She was, too, though she wasn't sure she should let him know. No need to give him too big an ego. She slid into her seat as he held the door. Her eyes followed him around the front of the vehicle and in.

"What?" He brushed at his pullover as if she'd seen a piece of lint or something.

"I don't think I've ever seen your hair so ... *not* messy." She tilted her head and studied it. Was it damp or actually gelled into place? For her?

"Oh." He started to reach for it, and then stopped himself, as if self-conscious. "Yeah. Bad habit of mine."

"I know. But it's endearing." She reached over and ran her fingers through it. Damp. Good. That meant it could take back its normal persona soon instead of having to fight through hair product to be natural.

He caught her hand and brought it down to his lips to press a kiss in her palm. "I missed you today."

"Has it even been twenty-four hours since you saw me last?" She laughed, although she understood what he meant.

"Almost thirty-six."

"Really? That long?"

He grinned as if he knew exactly how much of a sap he was being. She giggled in return. It was like being in high school all over again.

"So, are we actually going somewhere?" She finally broke the silence.

"Oh. Yes." He started the engine and pulled away from the curb. "Let's go."

Still no word on where they were headed. Was he trying to drive her crazy?

This was probably one of the craziest things Nick had ever done. But there was no going back now. Everything was arranged and waiting for their arrival. Would she like this surprise? He hoped so. Otherwise, he had no back-up plan.

As they drove down the farm lane half an hour outside of town, she scanned the horizon. "You're not kidnapping me or bringing me somewhere to murder me or anything, right?"

"Why would I do that?"

"I don't know. It's just very isolated out here, so I wasn't sure what your plans are." She shot him a teasing grin.

"Nothing so nefarious, I assure you." He squeezed her fingers and turned into his cousin's drive. "We're almost there."

"People actually live out here?" She leaned forward and stared at the house all covered in Christmas lights.

"Yes." He laughed. "My cousin Trey and his family own this land. He married into it. His wife's family had the ranch, and they all live nearby, I think."

"Wow." She studied the area as he parked near a barn. "I read about places like this in novels, but I've never been on a real ranch before."

"Well, now you have." He helped her out of the car just as Trey came out of the barn leading two horses.

"We're not riding those, are we?" She took a step back.

"Nope." Nick chuckled. "Keep watching."

Behind the horses was a sleek and shiny red sleigh. The team's harnesses jingled as they shook their heads and stomped their feet, waiting to go. Trudy's mouth hung open as she took it all in.

"A sleigh? But don't you have to have snow for a sleigh?" She reached out and touched the side.

"Not this one. It's a Texas sleigh. It has rollers on the bottom." Trey winked. "Hop on up and give it a try."

Nick grabbed the opportunity to put his hands at her waist as she hiked her knee to get into the vehicle. She settled onto the leather seat, her eyes still wide. Nick sat beside her and wrapped a thick blanket around their legs.

Trey handed him the reins. "You remember how to do this, don't you? It's been a few years."

"Like riding a bicycle, right?" Nick smirked, remembering

racing Trudy around the store the week before. "Yes. I remember."

"Have fun then. I'll listen for the bells so I'll know when you're coming back, but if I don't come out, just bang on the back door."

"Thanks, Trey." Nick saluted him, then let the reins lightly slap the backs of the horses.

Trey walked over to a nearby control panel as they jingled past and flipped a few switches. All around them, trees lit up with thousands and thousands of light strands. Trudy gasped and peered every which way, mouth agape.

"Trey's in-laws started doing the lights about ten years ago. One of their other grandchildren was diagnosed with leukemia, and Christmas is her favorite holiday. They strung all the lights, over four acres that year, for her. Then as people asked to drive through, they put a little box for donations and collected quite a bit to help pay for her treatments.

"They've continued it ever since even though she's been in remission for over five years now. They donate it to the local children's hospital for other kids going through similar situations." Nick waved his hand around. "I think they're up to almost seven acres of lighted paths now. It takes them over a month to set up every year."

"Wow." Trudy flopped back against the bench beside him. "But how are we the only ones out here tonight?"

"Trey never has it open on Sundays. I pulled some major cousin favors to be able to bring you."

She snuggled into his side. "This is beautiful."

"Ever done anything like this before?" He relaxed a bit, allowing the horses to pick their own speed as they sauntered down the lane.

"No. I mean, I've seen lights before. There's a huge area down in Zilker park we'd walk through every year. But never in a sleigh." She leaned her head on his shoulder.

Good. So far his plan was going perfectly. He relished the feel of her hand wrapped around his arm as they made their lazy way by a pond that reflected the lights and made them look twice as bright. Above the path, stars had been hung, and more dangled from nearby trees. Other areas had little figurines lit up, and some were even animated, throwing snowballs or waving. She seemed to take it all in like a child.

"This is so magical," she breathed as they made their way across the back of the display in a wide loop so they could return. "Almost too good to be real."

"Christmas is supposed to be magical, right?" He nudged her with his shoulder.

She let out a deep breath. "It used to be."

"I don't think it's Christmas that's lost its magic." He kept his voice low, calm. Anything to keep her listening and not get her hackles raised.

She didn't reply, but she didn't pull away either.

"Sometimes when you step away from something for a while and then come back, you can see the magic again with fresh eyes. Sort of like you did for me with the store." He pressed a kiss to her head. "I don't know how I would have acted Friday morning with all that chaos if you hadn't helped me remember to start looking for the fun and not only the bad moments. Granted, the weight of worrying about numbers and trying to keep the store from going under didn't help, but you were right. I was too focused on those things and forgot the real reasons behind why my grandfather opened the store in the first place.

"I think maybe you're doing the same thing with Christmas. You've let yourself be so focused on what you *don't* have any more that you're missing the good things still around."

Had he gone too far? She had stiffened though she still snuggled close. He tugged on the reins and stopped the horses in the middle of the area. The wind blew the branches, making the lights twinkle and shimmer. He lifted her face so he could see her expression and found tears on her cheeks.

"I wasn't trying to make you cry." He pulled her into a hug.

"No." She shook her head in his shoulder. "No. It wasn't you. I was just thinking earlier that you're the first person who's tried to help me through my grief instead of either ignoring it or pushing too hard."

He held her. He'd hold her as long as she needed him to.

She pulled back and swiped at her cheeks. "Thank you."

"For what?"

"For helping me remember that there's still magic to be enjoyed even if it's different."

"You're welcome." He urged the horses to move again. "There's more where this came from."

"Oh, really? You've got more cousins with acres of lights and a sleigh?"

"Ha!" He shook his head. "No. But there's more magic."

"Now I'm intrigued." She leaned her head on his shoulder.

"Good." That was exactly where he wanted her. Though he still wasn't sure how he could find tickets to that concert in two days. At least this had gone well.

Maybe they'd go get hot chocolates on the way back to her mom's house. With peppermint. She was rubbing off on him for sure. But he couldn't complain. There couldn't possibly be anything out there that could ruin this perfect evening.

Chapter
Twenty-One

"How did you know this was exactly what I needed?" Trudy relished the warmth blowing from Nick's car vents as he drove her back to Mom's. Her belly was full of the best chicken pot pie she'd ever eaten, thanks to Nick's cousin's wife. And her hands were snugged around a warm cup of peppermint hot chocolate.

"Lucky guess." Nick shot her a grin.

"Oh, dear. Now you're going to be full of yourself." She shook her head and chuckled. "Of course, this also means all the other dates you plan have to live up to the caliber of this one."

Nick snapped his fingers. "I hadn't considered that." He paused. "Other dates, huh?"

"Unless you prefer someone like Jessi …"

"Ugh." Nick shook his head. "Too soon to make a joke like that."

Trudy frowned. Paul's car sat in her mom's driveway like it belonged there. "She said she was meeting Katt and Brian."

"Maybe her plans changed." Nick shrugged.

Trudy didn't even wait for him to come around and open her door. Once and for all, she wanted to know exactly what was going on. Her feet ate up the damp grass of her mom's front yard and took the porch steps two at a time. She pushed the front door open with so much force, it banged against the wall and almost hit her as it rebounded.

They weren't in the living room or dining area.

No sounds came from the back of the house either.

She paused before the corner that led to the kitchen, suddenly not sure she wanted to see what might be on the other side.

Her heart thudded in her ears as she took one step. Two. And came face-to-face with her current biggest fear.

"Mom?" Somehow, she squeezed the word past the lump in her throat.

Paul and her mom jerked apart where they'd been locking lips in the same spot Nick had almost kissed her a week before. No. She pushed that disturbing thought aside. There was no comparison.

"Trudy." Her mom pressed her fingers to her lips and leaned against the counter as if the world weren't crumbling to pieces all around them. "I didn't hear you come in."

"Did you lie to me?" Trudy couldn't control the pitch of her voice, her emotions making it shrill. "You said you were meeting Katt."

"And I did." Mom tugged at her sweater hem. "I met them for dinner and dropped off Mark."

"And Paul just happened to run into you and wanted to come over for a make-out session?"

"Now wait just a minute." Paul straightened from where he leaned against the table.

"No." Trudy held up her hand. "No. I don't even want to know."

She spun on her heel and almost rammed into Nick, who had stopped right behind her.

"Trudy!" Her mom called after her.

She wouldn't listen. Not now. She couldn't.

Kissing!

They had been kissing.

She assumed something had been going on but hadn't let herself fathom that it had become so out of hand. How could her mother let her lips touch those of a man not her dad? And one with a fluffy white beard? That just seemed to make it worse for some reason.

"Trudy, wait up." Nick caught her halfway across the yard. "Where are you going?"

"I don't know." She slammed her fists against her thighs. "I can't stay here. I can't face this right now."

"Come on." Nick cupped her upper arm and led her to his car. He waved at the house, and she noticed her mom standing in the doorway, her arms clasped around her middle. Trudy quickly glanced away. Her perfect evening had lost its charm faster than gifts unwrapped on Christmas morning.

She dashed the heels of her palms against her cheeks, swiping at the moisture there. What was wrong with everyone lately? First Mom got the brilliant idea to leave the house and city she'd lived in for over twenty years, pack everything up and move up here to be close to her grandbaby. Then she pushed Trudy into a new job she hadn't even wanted. And now she was moving on to Paul? It was too much. Too fast. Too soon.

If only there were a way to go back and undo some of this. Not the date Nick had taken her on, necessarily, but the rest of it. Her heart was shattered.

And Christmas? It would be ruined forever. And it was all her fault. *I'm so sorry, Daddy.* She brushed away a tear.

"Where are we going?" She finally spoke ten minutes after Nick had pulled away from the house. She'd been too overwhelmed before.

"I didn't really have a destination in mind. Let's just drive awhile." He tapped his fingers against the steering wheel in rhythm with the Christmas music she hadn't even been aware was playing. "If the confectionary were still open, I'd go get you some chocolate, but it's too late."

"No. That's okay." Chocolate wouldn't fix this.

The Christmas lights on the houses they passed mocked her with their cheery glow. This was the season for joy and giving and love and family. Not making a new family and moving on from the one you had.

She studied her hands instead. They were almost exactly like her mom's, though, so that didn't help much either. New tactic. She glanced at the man beside her who drove along, his eyes on the road, giving her the space she needed, not demanding anything.

"Thank you." She wasn't sure what all she meant by it—just that if he hadn't given her this escape, time to think things through and calm down, she might still be throwing a fit in her mom's yard. She took a wavery breath. How could she go back there? She couldn't face it again.

"I Saw Mama Kissing Santa Claus" came on the radio, and Nick had the good sense to switch the station before the first line finished, although she could have sworn his lips twitched as though he were swallowing a laugh. Surely not. Such an awful song. Who wrote such drivel?

Not ten minutes later, the same song came on the other station, albeit a country version instead of pop. Trudy groaned and turned the music off. Nick burst out laughing this time, no holding back.

"You think that's funny, huh?" Trudy shot him a scowl.

"I'm sorry. But you have to see at least some of the humor in it." He barely got the words out between chuckles.

"I don't." She crossed her arms over her chest. "I suppose you think the whole situation is funny."

"No." Nick coughed as his laughter continued to shake his shoulders. "No. I'm sorry. What you're going through is not funny."

"I mean, what if you walked in on one of your parents kissing someone else?" She flopped her hands in the air and slapped them against her lap. "Would you be able to giggle at that? You were out on this perfect date, thinking nothing could ruin the evening, and *bam!*"

"It was a perfect night." He reached over and squeezed her fingers. "This doesn't have to ruin that."

She sighed. "Doesn't it?"

"Trudy, don't let your feelings about them ruin what's between us. We had a good time."

"No. You're right. We did." She hung her head. "I just feel taken advantage of. Mom knew I was going out with you and chose to ... do that. And she didn't even look guilty about it."

"Last time I checked, adults are allowed to make decisions, like who to date and whether or not they should kiss while doing so." Nick's nonchalant tone set her teeth on edge.

"So, you don't see the problem with her dating your uncle? Aren't you even a little upset that he's moving on from your aunt?" Trudy turned to face him more fully.

"Look, I loved Aunt Addie to pieces. But she's been gone several years now. And nothing I can do will change that." He tried to grab her hand again, but she pulled away.

"Addie was a very special lady. Paul loved her for more than twenty years. She was the one who helped decorate that tree in the store every year after Grandma passed. But I know he's lonely. So, if he finds some happiness with your mom, I won't stand in their way."

"I suppose you probably helped them set it up in the first place." Trudy pressed her fingers to a spot in her forehead that throbbed to a rhythm somewhere around a Native American war chant. "I'm an idiot. How did I not notice this earlier?"

"What?" He glanced at her, a lost expression on his face.

"This whole thing was a setup!"

Was Nick dating a lunatic? He must be. There was no way Trudy could honestly believe what she was saying right now. Sure, she had the right to be upset, but this went beyond that. What was driving her preposterous thought-process?

"No, seriously." Trudy slapped her hands together. "Paul and Mom were talking together before they came over and basically forced me to take the position at the store. They knew it would require late nights. Maybe they even hoped you and I would ... well, start dating or something. This would be perfect for them. Give them oodles of opportunities to spend time together without me around to get in the way."

"Trudy. If you want, we're only a few blocks from the store now. I'll show you the numbers. The situation needed someone of your caliber and expertise to turn things around. And as to us dating, I doubt it even crossed their minds until the last week. Let's be honest. We butted heads more often than not at first." The fact that he was having to explain all this to her raised his ire. So much for not letting it ruin their evening.

"But you could have brought in anyone. Why me? Because it was in their best interest." Trudy pushed the point again. "Maybe that's the real reason Mom moved up here in the first place. Not for Katt and Mark. She knew your uncle lived here and wanted to get together with him again."

Her theories made his head spin. "Again?"

"Evidently they dated in college before she met my dad." Trudy closed her eyes. "Mom showed us a stack of letters from Paul that she'd kept all these years. Seriously. I'm an idiot."

"If you believe all this craziness you're spouting right now, I'm liable to agree with you." He said it just loud enough for her to hear, but he'd reached his limit. Uncle Paul didn't have a mean bone in his body and would never formulate a plan like that if he knew it would upset Trudy so much. Not to mention the fact that it was ridiculous and far-fetched.

"Oh, well that's a fine thing for the man I'm dating to say." Her arms crossed again. "And to think I was considering giving up Austin to move here and give us a chance."

"You're going to let your frustration with your mom ruin

181

what's going on between us?" He definitely wasn't keeping his voice down now. No way.

"It's more than frustration! She's betraying my dad." Trudy's voice broke at the end.

"She can't betray someone who isn't here anymore." Nick tried to keep his voice level. After all, her grief was real. But she was being extreme. "Trudy, your dad's been gone five years now."

"You don't think I know that? I miss him every day. I can't go twenty-four hours without thinking of him at least once, and usually multiple times. But especially now. At Christmastime."

"I know you two had a special bond at Christmas, but that doesn't mean this time can't be just as good. You still have people who love you and care about you and want to do fun things with you."

"No! I can't let *anyone* else do activities like my Dad did." She covered her face so that he could barely make out the next words. "Because I don't want to lose them too."

He jerked the vehicle into a nearby parking lot. "What did you just say?"

She shook her head, her shoulders shaking with silent sobs.

"Trudy, do you think your dad died because of the activities you did together each year?" He tentatively reached out and placed a hand on her shoulder.

"No. Just that stupid concert." She choked the words out. "It killed him. *I* killed him."

Nick's own heart skipped a beat. She couldn't truly believe that, could she? Why would she jump to such a conclusion?

"That's not possible. You said you didn't even make it to the concert." Nick tried to keep his voice steady and calm, as if he were dealing with a wild animal. In some ways, it felt like it.

She lowered her hands. "He wouldn't have been in the car at that time of day if he hadn't left work early. He left early to come home and get me so we could head to the concert. He had his heart attack while he was driving to get me. Don't you see? He was stressed and in a hurry because of *me*."

"Trudy." Nick's chest tightened. "He could've been driving somewhere else at that time if you hadn't planned to go to the concert. Wasn't it Christmas Eve? Not everyone works that day."

"He'd gone in to finish up a few last things before the end of the year." Her eyes were glassy and stared into the distance. "And he'd snagged some extra hours to be able to get Mom a big gift she'd been wanting."

"See? Not your fault. Not anyone's fault."

Trudy shook her head. "Can you please take me back now? I just want to be alone."

"Trudy."

"No, Nick. I can't handle any more tonight. Obviously, no one in the world understands what I've done. I need to be alone."

With a sigh, he turned the car around, directing it back toward her mom's house. He sent up a silent prayer that his uncle had the good sense to leave while he'd been trying to help Trudy cool off. Better to face her again when her head was on straight. Or straighter, as the case may be.

He parked by the curb once more, grateful the driveway was empty of the familiar Honda. "We're here."

She put her hand on the door handle to go, but he stilled her with a touch to her wrist. "Trudy, please don't fight with your mom tonight. Give this all time to settle some and face it after you've had more time to think."

Trudy pressed her lips together. Her mom had done the same thing earlier, and Nick wondered if she'd learned it from her. She tugged a little as if unwilling to stay any longer.

"See you in the morning?" All his dreams of kissing her goodnight had evaporated the moment he'd seen his uncle doing the same with Ms. Connie. If they wanted to continue dating women in the same family, some boundaries might need to be set. Of course, that was a big assumption, after Trudy's rants about being used so her mom could start dating behind her back.

"I—" Trudy glanced at the house and then back to him again.

"I'll bring those scavenger hunt forms back sometime tomorrow morning." She blinked several times as if trying to remove tears. "Only a few of them had any wrong answers."

"Great. I'd love for you to help me wrap it up tomorrow evening and do the drawing. We need to set up the ad for the painting session too." He didn't want to let her go. Not after everything that had happened in the last hour. But he couldn't make her stay either.

"Sure. Of course." She nodded. "I'll see you tomorrow."

She slipped from his car and made her way across the lawn much more slowly than she had earlier. Her steps dragged this time instead of rushing in to a fire. Had she known what she would find earlier? Would she have to talk to her mom when she went in tonight, when her head was still so confused and hurt?

All the momentum he'd gained with the sleigh ride earlier completely unraveled with that one moment in her mom's kitchen. How he wished he could find other ways to help, but there was only so much she'd let him do. Until she was willing to let go of her self-imposed guilt, she could never process her grief. Her life would be frozen, unable to move forward.

On the porch, she glanced over her shoulder as if wishing for his support but unwilling to ask for it. She slipped in the house and flipped off the porch light. He released his breath and prayed she had a quiet rest of the evening.

She'd said she would come to the store tomorrow, so he had until then to work out some sort of plan. Could anything help? He wasn't a counselor or psychologist. He didn't know how to help someone work through guilt and grief. He'd just continue to be there and offer any support she'd be willing to accept and hope that was enough.

Now that he'd found Trudy, the idea of her leaving was more depressing than the idea of having to close the store. Surely, he could have both, right? It didn't have to be one or the other?

Chapter
Twenty-Two

T he aroma of coffee lured Trudy's eyes open the next morning despite her best efforts to keep them closed. Cinnamon mixed with the smell ... and bacon. *Mm*. She pulled the pillow from over her head and stretched.

Her eyes were puffy and swollen, crusty around the edges. She rubbed at them and grimaced. No amount of makeup would hide those circles. How had they grown so bad?

The night before came flooding back. All of it. Every. Last. Moment. She groaned and flopped back on the bed. How could she possibly face anyone today? Maybe she'd just hide in here instead.

But the scents wafting under the door from the kitchen pulled a growl from her tummy. She beat her pillow with a fist and sat up. She'd have to face people again sometime. Might as well get it over with.

Hair up in a messy bun, she splashed cold water on her face and got dressed. She didn't even care that she wasn't pulling on something necessarily attractive. Nick had already seen her at her worst. Skinny jeans and a boyfriend sweater weren't going to change his mind if last night hadn't. And something told her from the way he'd watched her all the way into the house that his feelings hadn't wavered one inch despite her insane outbursts and ranting and raving.

Somehow, she'd made it all the way back to her room without seeing her mom. She didn't know if Mom had been hiding behind her own door or something else, but she counted it a favor from God and went on to bed. Not that she'd slept much.

Mom pulled a pan of cinnamon rolls from the oven as Trudy entered. "Good timing."

"The smells wouldn't let me stay in bed any longer." Trudy grabbed a mug.

"You're already later than normal." Her mom dolloped icing on each doughy circle. "I almost wondered if you'd somehow snuck out earlier without me knowing."

Trudy stirred in creamer and took a long sip. "No way."

"I'm glad you're still here." Mom handed her a plate. "We need to talk."

"I hate those words."

"You and me both, but after last night ..."

Trudy sighed and perched on the edge of a chair, biting into a piece of bacon. Here it came. Mom was either going to apologize or kick her out. Considering this was her favorite breakfast, maybe it was the first?

"I loved your daddy very much." Her mom sat in the chair across from her as she delivered the line that promised an apology to follow. "And I miss him like crazy."

Trudy struggled to swallow her coffee around the lump in her throat. "Me too."

"I know you do, honey. But you miss him differently than I do." Her mom reached over and squeezed her hand. "I miss the companionship. When your dad passed, I lost my best friend, the one who understood almost everything about me, who liked the same kinds of music, who wasn't afraid to hash out an argument from Bible class or talk politics with me because eventually we always saw eye to eye. We had the same sense of humor and the same favorite burger place. He was the one I went to whenever I didn't know how to deal with something you girls were going through. And there's no one else out there who can replace him."

"But you're trying anyway." Trudy unrolled her cinnamon roll inch by inch, refusing to meet her mom's eyes.

"I'm lonely, Trudy." Her mom sat back again and let her hands fall in her lap. "I don't know how else to explain it. I'm lonely. Katt understands a little better now that she's married. She misses Brian when he has to go on a business trip for a week or so. But even she doesn't have the history with Brian that I had with your father. Over twenty years."

"Of course Katt understands. Katt's always been perfect. It's why you wanted to move up here, right? So you could be closer to the one who understood you better?" Trudy pushed away from the table, her breakfast mostly uneaten despite her earlier hunger pains.

"You're not listening to what I'm saying." Mom stood too. "Neither of you understands or knows what I'm going through. And I don't ever want you to have to understand it. But I want you to at least consider my feelings and not just your own."

"I am considering your feelings. I helped you pack up the house that you and Dad bought together when I was a baby. I watched strangers walking through it, complaining about some decorating aspect or older appliance that hadn't bothered us a bit. I had to drive away and leave it behind when it sold so you could move up here. All I've ever known is Austin, but I helped you do this anyway because it was what you wanted. Do you think this was the way I wanted to end my year?"

"Are you even hearing yourself?" Her mom shook her head, tears welling in her eyes. "No, Trudy. You're still thinking about how *you* feel in all of this. Not me. Because that wasn't easy for me either. But neither was staying there with a memory around every corner, reminders of what I was missing. It's why I wan— need to get rid of some of this stuff. I can't stay tied down by the past anymore. *I'm* not dead."

"I never said you were dead." Trudy was working extra hard to keep from yelling. Mom never responded well to raised voices. "But you're not acting like my mom anymore. I walked in on a couple behaving much more like teenagers last night than a woman nearing sixty."

"I'm only fifty-six, thank you very much." Her mom crossed her arms and leveled her with a stare that would have wilted her in middle school. "And I suppose you and Nick are behaving like complete grownups and haven't had any fun?"

Trudy pushed the memory of riding bicycles through the store last week out of her head. "Nick and I have nothing to do with your actions. Except that I notice you keep seeing Paul only when I'm occupied somewhere else. You never talked to me about it. One minute you were catching up with an old friend, and the next I'm noticing his car driving away as I get home late at night or hear about you guys going out to eat or walk in on you kissing in the kitchen. You went zero to sixty, Mom."

"It was fast." Her mom nodded. "But at the same time, it wasn't. Paul lost Addie four years ago. I lost your dad five. We're both in similar situations in life, with grown children and no one to talk to in the evenings. I went to dinner with him that first time with no intention of it going any further, but we enjoyed each other's company so much that we decided to meet up again. And again. And even though our relationship didn't work out in college, we're in a different place now. We want to see where this might go."

"It's like I'm the only one who wants to hold on to Dad's memory." Trudy's tears overflowed and ran down her cheeks. "And I just can't be okay with this right now."

She walked away before her mom had a chance to come back with any response. Trudy didn't want logic or explanations. She wanted what she couldn't have anymore, and that was for things to go back to the way they'd been before.

She washed her face one more time, grabbed her things, and headed out. Maybe coming up with an ad for the painting sessions and organizing the scavenger hunt entries would help keep her mind occupied on other things. Assuming Nick let her in the door of the store. Had he reconsidered things after dropping her off last night? She hadn't been reasonable.

But he hadn't been very understanding either. Laughing at that stupid Christmas song. *Ugh*. And now the tune was in her head again.

Nick glanced out the doors again. Still no sign of Trudy. Maybe she was avoiding the store because Uncle Paul was here? No. She said she'd be in sometime this morning to drop off those scavenger hunt forms. It wasn't even eleven yet. Still morning, technically.

He turned and met Uncle Paul's gaze. They hadn't talked this morning either. He honestly didn't know what to say. He wasn't opposed to his uncle dating again, was even rather happy for him. But it upset Trudy so much. How could any of this possibly work out? Would she break things off with Nick simply due to whom he was related? She hadn't seemed that fickle when he first met her, but that was also before her mom started dating again. He pushed his fingers through his hair and let out a deep breath.

Focus.

Only four and a half shopping days until Christmas now. Time to buckle down and make sure they got through the week. Customer traffic was still up with all the publicity and changes, and he hoped it continued even after the scavenger hunt concluded at day's end. The winner would be announced in the morning so they could come in and claim their coupon.

He double-checked that there were plenty of forms still available near the front door. There were. All the employees were performing their jobs well. The line waiting for Santa was almost ten families long, but the other queues were only two or three deep. The lights on the tree behind Uncle Paul twinkled and sparkled on the peppermint ornaments, bringing Nick's thoughts right back to Trudy.

He shook his head and walked toward the office. There was plenty he could do besides standing here daydreaming. Wasn't daydreaming what had caused Trudy to collide with him that first visit to the Emporium? And there she was in his thoughts again. Seemed like there would be no escaping her whether she was here or not.

As he walked past one of the registers, the conversation the customer was having with the clerk caught his attention. "I normally don't pay this much for a toy, but I couldn't find any in the online swap shops I'm a member of."

"Oh? What's that?" The clerk was a girl in her late teens.

"Groups on social media where you can resell things." The customer handed over her credit card. "I think I'm in about five or six different ones."

"Is it just for toys?" The clerk asked.

"No, honey. Clothes, lawn equipment, cars, furniture, anything. I even see people selling concert tickets on there." The woman shook her head and accepted her bag. "You just never know."

"I may have to check those out. I still need to get my mom something for Christmas."

Nick didn't stick around to find out what his worker wanted to buy. One line of that conversation repeated itself over and over in his head, and he had to see if it would work for what he needed. What was the chance he could join a group and find exactly what he'd been trying to get his hands on for a week? He didn't care to do the math.

No time anyway. The concert was tomorrow night, and if he still wanted to go, he needed to act fast. He logged on to the only social media site he used and started looking up local groups. After joining several and searching for concert tickets, he finally found a promising post in the third group.

"Great seats, awesome price, you can't find these anywhere but here."

The picture of the tickets appeared legitimate, though Nick might argue with their definition of "awesome price." Even online he'd been able to see the tickets originally sold for one-third the price of what these were listed. Still ...

He pressed the button that let him send a message to the seller. "Would you be willing to come down some on the price?"

A shuffle at the door drew his attention as Trudy walked in. She was dressed more casually today than she had been over the last few weeks, but it suited her. She moved her sunglasses to the top of her head, and he winced at the dark circles around her eyes. Should he get up? Say something? She hadn't even acknowledged his presence yet.

"Here's the stack of scavenger hunt forms from last week. I paperclipped the ones with wrong answers here at the back by themselves." She dropped the cards on his desk, her voice completely professional, no sign of anything personal between them at all.

"Thanks, Trudy." He reached for her hand, but she pulled back. He swallowed his disappointment. "I'm glad you're here."

Her eyes refused to meet his. "Are you?"

"I am. I've been watching for you all morning. Spent a great part of last night wondering how you were doing, wishing I could help. Praying." He stood and came around to her side of the desk. "And counting the hours until I could see you again."

"Nick ..."

"What?" He ducked his head to meet her gaze, where it was focused somewhere around the floor. "I thought you wanted me to be more fun and enjoy life."

Her lips twitched with what he hoped was a smile fighting to break through. "Okay, but don't go too far with it. There's enjoying life, and then there's just plain sappy."

"Right. Got it." He saluted her. "Did you get a chance to talk to your mom?"

She huffed out a sigh. "My life is in a bit of a shambles right now. I'm trying to decide if I should maybe move back to Austin like I meant to. My roommate has been texting me almost nonstop for two days, begging me to come sooner than planned. That would give my mom room to do whatever it is she's doing right now. Midlife crisis? And I wouldn't have to see ... it."

"Please don't. Not until after Christmas at least." He tugged her fingers. "It would break your mom's heart."

"That would only be fair since she's doing a great job of breaking mine." Trudy rubbed her forehead.

"I doubt she means to."

"Doesn't mean it won't happen." Trudy clenched her lips. "I don't know. I promised I'd work here today to help finish the hunt and work up the advertising for the paint sessions next year. So, let's get busy and knock this all out. I can't think of any other unfinished projects, can you?"

He could think of one, but she obviously wasn't in the mood to be open to ideas right now. It could stay in his back pocket for another time. Instead, he dug through a stack on his desk until he found all the notes from Jessi.

Trudy wrinkled her nose as she took the page gingerly between her fingers. "Thanks."

"It won't bite you." He laughed.

"I don't know about that." She set it beside her laptop. "I saw the girl who wrote it. Something tells me if she had figured out half of what our relationship was that day, her claws would have come out in full force."

"What if she came today? Would the same be true?" He held his breath as he waited for her answer. Where exactly did she see them standing, relationship-wise? Were they as close as the other day when her jealousy had flared so cutely, or were they closer to when they first started working together?

"Does she really expect you to do all this?" Trudy ran her finger down the list, either ignoring his question or already too focused on her job. Something told him it was the first.

"All what?" He peeked over her shoulder.

"Buy all these special supplies? That's going to make the classes cost much more than I originally planned. Actually, they'd cost more than that one we did, and we're adults." She circled the supply list, which included professional brushes, high-end acrylics, and fancy smocks. "I could probably get my mom to make smocks for a fraction of that, and we could just keep them here at the store. And if you got multi-packs of cheaper paints, the kids wouldn't know the difference. They don't care how much they cost as long as they're the right color. Not to mention we could get good paintbrushes for less than this too."

"I'll send her an email with what we're willing to do and see if she's still okay with teaching the class. She might back out though. She was pretty adamant the other day that her plan would only work this way." He frowned as he read through the list for the first time. He'd been too distracted before now to even give it a cursory glance.

"Sure she wasn't simply trying to impress you?" Trudy shot him a glance that was almost flirty. Between the twinkle in her eyes and her unconsciously including herself in future store plans a moment before, his heart lifted a bit.

"If she was, she failed. I know nothing about paint brands or canvases or brushes. If it were up to me, I'd probably just order the kind most kids use at school." He shrugged.

She let out a small laugh. "That would work just as well and be at least five times cheaper. Which would make the moms happy too."

"Sounds good to me. I'll send her an email now. No need to work up ads if she's just going to back out." He sat at his computer and noticed he'd gotten a message back from the seller he'd contacted earlier.

"Sorry. I can't go down any more on these tickets."

He let out a sigh. If he bought these, it would use up a big chunk of the money he'd been saving to replace his home laptop. But on the other hand, it would let him do something for Trudy that no one else had been able to do. Maybe even help her work past some of this grief she clung to. Was it worth it?

"What's wrong?" She glanced over at him, and he turned the screen a bit to make sure she couldn't see it. "What are you doing? I thought you were emailing Jessi."

"I was just replying to a message first." He moved the cursor to the reply spot. "It's too close to Christmas to ask questions."

"Nick Russo, don't you dare!" Trudy stood behind him before he could hit *send* to agree to the outrageous price. "That person is totally ripping you off. Especially since I already told you to quit trying to buy me tickets to this concert."

"But, Trudy—"

"No." She reached over and deleted his message. "Tell him that price is insane and get out of this deal."

"But I want to take you—"

"I won't go with you if you spend that much money on it." She crossed her arms over her chest, and he could see the argument was over.

He typed, "Thanks, but no thanks." And sent it off to cyberspace before he could change his mind. Every inch of his heart squeezed tight at the realization that his Christmas miracle wouldn't happen. So much for winning Trudy over to staying in Temple or falling completely in love with Christmas again. The concert had been his last hope.

Chapter Twenty-Three

"You two do know the door is open to the office, right?"

Trudy spun around at the sound of Paul's voice. He leaned against the doorframe, one brow raised as he looked between her and Nick. Had their voices been raised? She didn't remember yelling. Though the exorbitant amount Nick was about to spend on something she'd told him time and again she didn't want would've been a good cause.

"Yes." Nick rose to his feet. "Sorry."

"Everything okay?" Paul didn't move.

"Aren't you seeing kids? The line was backed up pretty good earlier." Trudy just wanted to get through today and get out of here. Having Paul butt into her conversation with his nephew wasn't part of that equation.

"Things slowed down when it started raining again a few minutes ago. I took advantage of the lull to grab a short break." Paul adjusted his Santa hat. "When I saw customers looking toward the office and whatever you two were arguing about, I decided to come make sure there was nothing I could do to help."

"We're fine. It was just a misunderstanding." Nick closed the message screen on his computer.

"A lover's spat, huh?" Why wouldn't Paul just leave it alone? They were adults. They could work through their own problems by themselves.

"Not quite." Nick tossed a pencil on the desk.

Paul came all the way in the office and pulled the door closed. "Tell me you're not fighting over my relationship with Connie."

Trudy flinched at her mom's name. She'd been trying to pretend Paul was Santa instead of Mom's new boyfriend, but that question ruined the image. She crossed her arms and barely kept from stomping her foot. "This has nothing to do with you, believe it or not."

"Okay." Paul held up his hands. "I just wanted to make sure you weren't ruining your chances with my nephew over the misunderstanding between you and your mom."

"I think it's more than a misunderstanding, don't you?" Trudy narrowed her eyes. "More like a great, big, giant disaster."

"Look, Uncle Paul." Nick stepped forward, obviously afraid of what else might come out of Trudy's mouth.

He had a valid reason for concern as she wasn't happy at all right now.

"It honestly had to do with a plan I had been working on earlier this week. I was trying to find a way to take Trudy to the Trans-Siberian Orchestra concert, but they're all sold out. She was upset with the other options I was exploring."

"TSO? But why didn't you say something?" Paul pulled out his wallet. "I have tickets you can have."

"For tomorrow night?" Nick's mouth dropped open as he stared at his uncle. "Are you kidding me?"

"No, Thursday night."

"Thursday? But they're playing in Austin tomorrow." Nick dashed his fingers through his hair.

"Dallas, Nick." Paul held up the slips of paper. "They're in Dallas on Thursday."

Nick slapped his forehead. "Why didn't I think to check Dallas?"

Trudy barely refrained from laughing at his reaction. It was too much. Especially since it didn't matter. She was sticking to her earlier stance.

"Keep your tickets, Paul." She closed her laptop. "I'm sure my mom will enjoy going to the concert with you. If you're lucky, I'll be back in Austin by then and you won't even have to worry about sneaking out when I'm not around."

"Austin?" Nick caught her arm as she picked up her bag. "I thought we agreed you should at least stay until after the holidays."

"And I thought I told you a few weeks ago that I don't really celebrate Christmas anymore." She pulled her sleeve from his grasp. "If Mom wants to celebrate with all the bells and whistles this year, that's her prerogative, but it doesn't mean I have to participate. I'm not ready. I'm still grieving, not that anyone cares."

"Grief." Paul's voice reminded her that she wasn't alone in here with Nick as usual. If she were a cat, her hackles would have risen at his persistence in butting in.

"Yes, grief. Don't you grieve your wife? Or is that only something kids do? On second thought, maybe only second kids? Katt never seemed to grieve much." She rubbed the spot on her forehead that was quickly becoming a constant ache.

"For one thing, everyone grieves differently." Paul held up a finger. "For another thing, yes. Your mom and I have both grieved our lost spouses. So, please don't act like we don't simply because we're moving on."

"Moving on? Moving on?" She was repeating herself. This was never a good sign. "How do you move on from a lifetime commitment? Your life isn't over yet."

"No. My life isn't over yet. And that's something I've been remembering more since I started seeing your mom. But the commitment to Addie was until death do us part, and her life

197

here is done. I can't change that, much as I'd like to. Same thing for your mom. Connie would love to bring Derek back, but it will never happen. His life was cut short too. That doesn't mean we don't miss them like crazy. But it also doesn't mean we have to stop living just because they did."

Trudy shook her head, tears welling in the corners of her eyes.

"I've discovered something about grief through the years, first losing my parents and now my wife. It's not something you do for a little while and then stop. You don't 'get over' it." Paul pursed his lips as if trying to figure out how to say what he wanted to convey in the best way.

"It's something you live with for the rest of your life because that person will always be absent from you until we meet again on the other side of judgment. But, it is something you can learn to live with. Because you are still living. And the loved ones we lost wouldn't want us to quit simply because they're no longer here. Especially since, as Christians, we have the hope of seeing them again someday."

Moisture ran over onto her cheeks. She didn't want to hear what he was saying even though it rang with truth. She wasn't ready to accept it as fact. Wasn't ready to accept him.

"Here. Take the tickets." He held them out to her.

She slapped them away, and they fluttered to the ground. "I don't want your tickets. You can't buy your way into my affections. And I don't want you trying to replace my dad."

"Trudy!" Nick followed her as she pushed past Paul and out through the store.

Several customers shot her curious glances as she stormed past the toys. She forced her feet to slow down. No need to ruin business.

"Trudy." Nick held his hand against the back door before she had a chance to pull it open. "Please stop and talk to me for a minute."

"I suppose you want to accept those blasted tickets and force me to go to the concert Thursday night?" She leaned her head against the door, her hands fisted, her heart pounding in her ears. Why wouldn't he let her leave?

"Forget the stupid concert. Obviously, it was more important to me than you." He slapped his palm against the frame. "But I can't let you leave until you calm down. Talk to me."

"Right. Sorry." She swiped at her eyes. "I forgot I was supposed to be helping you with the scavenger hunt and the ads."

Nick dug his fingers so deeply into his hair she wondered how he didn't come away with a chunk of strands. "You are the most exasperating woman!"

"And that's supposed to get me to listen to you?" She punched him in the chest.

Nick barely hid the wince she caused with her abuse. Her voice echoed some on the linoleum in the hallway. This wasn't going to be any more private than the office with the door wide open. If he'd only shut it earlier, then Paul wouldn't have come in, and Trudy would still be in there, where he might have a better chance of convincing her to stay.

"Come here." He grabbed her hand and drug her into the kitchenette, kicking the door closed behind him.

She folded her arms across her chest and leaned back into the corner farthest from him. "Okay. You've got me trapped. Now what? You sneak in food and a pillow and keep me here until after Christmas?"

"Don't tempt me." He paced the tiny space, made smaller by the fact that he was maintaining a perimeter far enough from her where she couldn't hit him again. He rubbed the spot absentmindedly.

"Nick, be serious. What do you want from me? If you send me the information, I can put the ads together from anywhere."

She shifted the shoulder strap of her bag. "And if I have to, I can come back this evening to help finish up the scavenger hunt thing and put together the social media posts and stuff for it. But I can't really do anything else on it until we have all the entries. Why are you holding me here?"

"Because I couldn't stand it if you moved back to Austin." Nick grimaced as he pulled several strands out from running his fingers through his hair again.

"Why should I stay? I'm not happy here. For a short while I thought I might be, but I can't be here and watch my mom date someone else. And you and I can't stop fighting. I mean, it's how we started, so I don't know why it surprises me, but ..."

He ached to wipe away the tears once more dripping down her cheeks. "But we don't have to fight. If we could get past all this other stuff with your mom, maybe—"

"No." She shook her head. "I don't even think that's a possibility. I don't foresee a day when I can be okay with what my mom is doing."

"Then at least let me be with you through it." He dared to step close enough to cup her shoulders. "I think we could have a chance if you'd just let it happen."

Her messy bun flopped forward as she hung her head. "It's not that easy."

"Who told you love was supposed to be easy?" He grabbed her chin and lifted her face so he could see it again.

"Nick." A sob choked her, and she didn't say anything else.

"Trudy, please. Please don't go back to Austin yet." He wrapped her in his arms though she stayed stiff and unyielding. She let him hold her for a few minutes but then pushed roughly away.

"Send me the information for the ads once you hear back from Jessi. And let me know if you need help with the social media posts for the scavenger hunt winner." Trudy paused in the doorway. "I don't know where I'll be, but I'll have my phone and laptop with me."

Nick collapsed against the counter. Letting her walk away so broken and downcast had to be the hardest thing he'd ever done. But she didn't want to stay. And he couldn't force her to let him help. That wasn't the way things worked.

He sighed and headed back to the office. Might as well send that email to Jessi. Maybe it would get him out of ever having to see her again if she didn't agree to the cheaper supplies. Then maybe he could talk another girl he'd discovered was an amazing artist into staying to be the instructor instead. Would that be enough to keep her in the area?

Would a mural?

Uncle Paul looked up from where he sat in what had been Trudy's chair, his shoulders slumped. He was the saddest-looking Santa Nick had ever seen. Nick squeezed his shoulder and moved to sit behind his own desk.

"She's gone, then?" Paul glanced back out the door.

"For now." Nick tapped his fingers against the keys of his keyboard, not actually pushing any letters yet.

"Connie's going to be heartbroken if our relationship drives her daughter to move farther away again. She was hoping Trudy might stay in this area." Paul shook his head. "Maybe we should back off for a while. Give Trudy more time ..."

"You deserve happiness too." Nick pushed away from the computer again. "I know you've missed Aunt Addie, but you've been happier the past couple of weeks than I've seen you in a while."

"But I don't want to do it to the detriment of Connie's relationship with Trudy. That's something I can't live with." Paul shook his head. "Trudy's still too deep in the grief process. It's taking her longer than some of us to accept her dad's loss."

"This time of year is especially hard for her. She used to do this bucket list thing with her dad each Christmas where they came up with three or four ideas for the two of them to do together each holiday season. The concert never got crossed off their last list. It was the same night he passed." Nick mussed his hair even more than normal. It probably stuck out every which direction now, but he didn't care. "She blames herself for his death because he was driving to pick her up."

"No wonder me offering the tickets set her off. The man 'replacing her dad' in her mom's life offering her access to attend an event she didn't get to attend with her dad." Paul beat his fist lightly against the arm rest. "Of all the stupid things I could have done."

"You didn't know." Nick pulled up the pictures of the lists on his phone. "I snuck these photos the other day. I got the idea of maybe doing things with her that she'd never done with her dad, starting a list for just the two of us. I figured I could use the painting session. And last night was almost perfect—"

"Until you walked in on us kissing." At least Paul's face was carrying a bit of a blush now.

"Yes." Nick smirked. "Not the best way to end a date. But before that, we went out to Trey's house and rode the sleigh around through the lights. And ate Becca's pot pie. And had hot chocolate. I probably would've gotten a nice kiss goodnight if we hadn't walked in on yours."

"Sorry about that. Well, not about the kiss, per se, but about the timing." Paul tapped his fingers against the desk and frowned a bit. "Does she know you're trying to make a new list of things for her to do?"

"No. I was going to write it out and give it to her at the concert, but that fell through. I need to come up with something to replace it." Nick accepted his phone back.

Paul shook his finger in the air. "I might have just the thing."

"Hey." Nick's dad tapped on the doorway. "Did you know there are kids waiting to see Santa out here?"

"Hey, Dad. Where'd you come from?"

"Just wanted to see how things were going. And Mom wants to know if she can put you down for having a plus one at Christmas dinner." His dad wiggled his eyebrows.

"Maybe." Nick shot a glance at Uncle Paul. "We're working on it."

"We?" His dad asked.

"I'll look up that information at lunch." Paul stood up. "Better get out and take care of those children. We might want to give Connie a head's up too. We may need all hands on deck to keep Trudy from leaving town before we can pull this off."

"What's going on?" Nick's dad stared between the two of them.

"It's a long story." But hopefully they could pull off a happy ending.

Chapter
Twenty-Four

Three days. Trudy's keys had been missing for sixty-six hours. Possibly a few minutes more. She'd run into the house hoping to pack up her things, but when she went to grab her car keys to load a box or two, they weren't in her purse. Her suspicions ran high.

Mom had to have hidden them. It was the only reasonable explanation. Trudy had been over just about every square inch of the house trying to find them. But she'd never know for sure, since she was avoiding her mom—not the easiest thing in the world to do when stuck in the same house with no way to escape.

She let her head fall back and bang against the wall. She was twenty-three years old. Her mom shouldn't have the right to take away her car keys anymore.

If she had her guesses, someone had put her up to it. And she'd lay odds on that someone being a lanky guy with hair that usually stuck up in all directions. That certain someone who didn't think she should move back to Austin.

Trudy had considered Nick more reasonable than that, but she must be wrong. Because here she sat, stuck in a town she no longer wanted to be in, in a house with a woman she refused to talk to, and no way to go anywhere else.

> Update?

Caitlyn's text was only the latest of a steady stream. She texted at least four times a day.

> Still stuck. WWIII may be impending.

> Let me go hide in the bunker first.

Caitlyn's dry sense of humor brought a grin to Trudy's lips for the first time in days.

How had she reached this point? Moving her mom up here was supposed to be simple. Bring the boxes, unpack, return to Austin. Period.

Instead, here she sat, four weeks into this "move" and no end in sight. She'd even taken advantage of some of the enforced house arrest to go through a few more cartons of her dad's things and reorganize them into keep and toss piles. Nick had sent the information for the scavenger hunt winner so she could post those social media announcements. That had taken her a whopping ten minutes. But no word on the Jessi situation. Was he still working on that? What did she care? As soon as her keys showed up, she was out of here.

It was Thursday. Had her mom left for the concert yet? If she had, Trudy could safely leave her room and rummage through the kitchen for something to munch on. She glanced at her watch. It should take them a couple hours to get there with traffic on I-35, so the coast might be clear, depending on what time the concert started. Did she care enough to check online and find out?

Her tummy grumbled, complaining again about how unscheduled her eating habits had become in the last few days. The risk was worth it. She was too hungry to wait longer.

Rounding the corner to the kitchen, she smacked face-first into her mom's back. "Mom!"

"Trudy, you about gave me a heart attack." Her mom put a hand to her chest. She wore a sweatshirt and old paint-splattered blue jeans, her greying hair thrown back into a ponytail. Not what Trudy would have worn to go on a date.

"I expected you to be gone by now." Had Trudy misread her watch?

"Gone?" Mom frowned.

"The concert. Paul has tickets."

"He never invited me to a concert, but even if he had, I probably would have turned him down. That was more your dad's thing than mine." Her mom turned back to what she'd been doing, tying a ribbon around a perfectly wrapped Christmas gift.

"Never invited you?" Had Trudy misunderstood? But she'd told Paul to take her mom, and he hadn't denied it. "I'm sort of losing my mind the last couple of days since my keys disappeared. It is Thursday, right?"

"All day long. Two days to Christmas." Her mom set the present aside. "Got all your packages wrapped?"

This was surreal. Didn't Mom hear her say her keys were missing? She was behaving like things were normal, when she knew perfectly well that everything was insane right now. How did she keep up the façade?

"I just came in for something to munch on." Trudy pointed to the pantry.

"Sure, honey. I noticed you missed lunch. Would you rather I fix you something more substantial?" Her mom set the scissors down.

"No. I was just going to make some popcorn and maybe go work on more boxes."

"Okay. I appreciate it. It's going a bit slower than I expected, but of course, we lost a bit of time while you were working at the store. Are you done there now, or did Nick need you to come back and wrap anything else up?" Mom tore off a piece of tape and made a loop to stick a bow onto another box.

"Done, I think. I might do one or two more ads, but he should be able to handle it now." Trudy blinked a few times as she opened the cellophane and popped the bag in the microwave.

"I think it all turned out lovely. It was a nice place to begin with, but you brought out the best features and livened them up again." Her mom continued to talk as if this were the most normal occurrence in the world. Maybe a week ago it had been. But now? "Oh. I just remembered I have a few more things stashed in my closet. Need anything else, Trudy?"

"No." Trudy took a deep breath as her mom disappeared through the doorway. Maybe she'd been hypnotized or something. Was this a dream?

Another minute passed, and her popcorn was done, if slightly scorched. The smell would linger all night, but it was too late to undo it now. She held the bag by the corners so as not to burn her fingertips and padded down the hallway. As she neared her mom's room, Trudy heard Mom's voice and paused outside the door.

"Oh, Derek. What am I going to do?"

Trudy peeked around just enough to see Mom sitting on the floor beside the bed, a picture frame in her hands. It must be the photo of her and Dad's wedding day, the one that lived on her nightstand. Mom pressed her forehead against the glass, and her body shuddered with a sob.

"I'm so lost. You were always the one who understood Trudy better, knew what she needed. She and I have never seen eye to eye, but it's gotten so much worse since you left. Like she's going through life without a compass.

"I thought we'd raised her to rely on God and be strong enough to make it without us, but now I wonder if we failed her somehow. How can I help her move on? I wish you were here to talk it through with me. You always had a way of helping me see things from a different perspective. Without you, I seem to be bungling things."

Trudy leaned against the hallway wall outside her mom's door and squeezed her eyes closed. Tomorrow would be five years. Five years since that fatal accident. Five years without him. While she'd assumed her mom had lied when she said she missed Dad, apparently Trudy was wrong. Tears squeezed past her lids and forced trails down her cheeks.

Was she really that hard to live with? That uncooperative or hardheaded? If so, why was Mom keeping her captive here? Why did she want her near her instead of letting her move out and live life somewhere else?

And wasn't she relying on God? Just because she wasn't ready to leave her dad totally in the past? Even Job got to mourn his family when they died. Did missing Dad mean she wasn't strong enough in her faith?

She straightened quickly and dashed past the door, hoping her mom didn't notice the smell of burnt popcorn lingering where she'd been. No need to add eavesdropping to the list of reasons her mom didn't know how to be around her.

And how much longer would she keep Trudy's keys? Until after they "celebrated" Christmas? Well, if they expected her to willingly participate simply because she was here, they had another thing coming. She was not in a celebratory mood. And she didn't foresee that changing any time soon.

Nick closed the spreadsheet he'd been studying. Numbers were better than he could have imagined them a month ago. They had less than twenty-four hours until they'd close two days for Christmas. Then only a month left in the fiscal year. The totals wouldn't change much between now and then, but they were enough right now, so he wasn't worried. Not anymore. Not about the Emporium anyway.

No, the girl who had helped save his family's store was who held most of his concerns at this juncture. Was she furious with him? Did she even have an inkling it was his idea to do whatever was necessary to keep her here? Something told him it wouldn't take her long to reach that conclusion.

An email notification popped up on his computer. Jessi had replied. He braced himself as he opened the screen.

> Nick, I'm sure you don't understand, not being an artist yourself, but using cheap supplies as children is only going to ruin their love for art now so that they never explore it down the road. If you're not willing to use the brands I have listed, I don't think I can be the instructor for your store. I take my work too seriously to have someone else come in and undermine my goal of raising a whole generation of future artists.

He rolled his eyes. It was no less than he expected. At least he didn't have to worry about her getting handsy with him again.

> Thank you for your reply, Jessi, as well as the time you took the other day to come tour the store. Unfortunately, at this time I don't think we can afford to buy those more expensive supplies and expect to have any customers take us up on the sessions. If things change down the road, I will let you know. Until then, I will be on the lookout for another artist to fill the spot.

He already had someone in mind, but he would never let Jessi know. He hadn't even brought the idea to Trudy yet. Hadn't contacted her at all except about the scavenger hunt winner since she ran out of the store into the rain on Monday, much as he had wanted to. She needed time. And he was working on Uncle Paul's plan too. It had to be perfect. Or at least as close as he could make it.

"I finally found the address I was looking for." Uncle Paul stuck his head in the office door at the end of the day. "Got something to write it down, or want me to text it to you?"

"You can text it. That way I can just copy and paste it into the map app. I'm thinking of taking her tomorrow."

"Probably a good idea. Connie says she's still avoiding her. She only accidentally ran into her this afternoon. Evidently, Trudy assumed I was taking Connie to the concert and that she'd be gone." Paul shook his head. "I feel like I messed this up before it even had a chance to start."

"You didn't know the background beforehand, though." Nick leaned back in his chair. "Why didn't you go?"

"The tickets were actually for Bruce and his girl. I hadn't told them yet. It was an early Christmas surprise, but I could have given them something else if you had wanted them." Paul shrugged as if giving away his son's Christmas present were no big deal. And to Paul, it wasn't—he always had ideas for people. That's why he was such a good Santa.

"Our numbers are up." Nick tapped a stack of reports. "Way up."

"Enough?" Paul stepped fully into the room.

Nick nodded.

"So, no matter what, all of this was worth it."

"I'm still hoping we'll get more out of it than simply saving a business though." Nick rose and stretched.

Paul grinned. "Like both of us getting a girl?"

"Exactly." Nick debated on putting his plans into action tonight instead of waiting, but something urged him to hold off until tomorrow. He missed Trudy like crazy, something that should probably seem strange, considering they'd only known each other a few weeks. But in those few weeks, they'd crammed a lot of hours of togetherness. Now the store seemed empty without her, no matter how many customers filled the aisles.

"You coming in tomorrow?" Nick shut down his computer and turned off the desk light.

"For a few hours. Then, of course, I'll have to head to the North Pole and prepare to deliver presents on the other side of the world." Paul touched the side of his nose in his signature Santa gesture.

"Of course." Nick winked. "Well, throw a little magic or luck or something on your sleigh for me. I have a feeling I'm going to need it."

"How about a whole lot of prayer? That's much better than luck and magic." Paul clasped his shoulder. "If she's the one, she's worth every effort you're putting into this. And eventually, she'll see how much you care not only about making your relationship work but also helping her out of the dark period she's let herself fall into."

"Thanks, Uncle Paul." Nick nodded. "I really like her."

"If she's anything like her mom, I understand why." Paul pulled on his heavier coat and a toboggan in place of his Santa hat. "I'll see you in the morning."

"Christmas Eve."

"And you said we couldn't keep the store open this long." Paul laughed. "Onward and upward!"

Nick watched Paul's taillights recede into the parade of traffic on the road in front of their store. This time of year, cars were everywhere, with last-minute shoppers, people going out to look at lights and eat, and others driving in for the holidays. He turned carefully out of the parking lot and headed for home.

Time to finish up his plans. And send up a few prayers of his own that they would work. He just couldn't stand the idea of Christmas or any time after it without a certain petite brunette in his life.

W hat was that noise? Trudy frowned, listening again. Was it singing? She eased up from the position she'd been in on the floor, going through yet another of the boxes stacked in her room. The path was opened up to four feet wide now.

Pushing some more stacks out of the way, she pulled the blinds aside and peeked through the window. Nick stood, bundled against the cold, misty rain, his hands over his heart. Singing "Blue Christmas."

She closed her eyes and backed up before he saw her. She hadn't talked to him since Monday, but there he was on the lawn, crooning about being blue without her. She peeked one more time and shook her head. The neighbors would start thinking the people who had moved in this house were insane. She was liable to agree with them.

Trudy padded through the house, silent except for her. Mom had gone out with Katt, Brian, and Mark to look at lights. Trudy hadn't even fixed her hair today. She'd accepted the fact that she couldn't go anywhere until her mom gave her keys back, so she might as well make the most of her confinement. No time to change out of her sweatpants now. She had to get Nick inside before he drew a crowd.

She swung the front door open and leaned against the doorframe, arms crossed over her chest. "What are you doing?"

"Caroling." Nick sang the words to the tune of the song he'd been murdering, then went right on with the original lyrics.

"I wouldn't quit my day job if I were you." Trudy giggled when he scowled her way.

He held up his finger and added several flourishes to the end. She clapped more over him being done than for the performance's caliber. He bowed several times and then came onto the porch with her.

"It's cold out here." He brushed some moisture off his pea coat.

"Well, it is December twenty-fourth. Officially the second day of winter. Or is it the third?" She shivered in the breeze.

"I can never keep up." He pointed at the house. "Mind if I come in? I wanna talk to you."

She hesitated a moment, then opened the door wider. "Come on. Something tells me you're not going away again until you've had your say."

"I could sing a few more songs." He hooked his thumb over his shoulder and shrugged.

"No, no. That's quite all right. I think the neighbors might start complaining if I let you do that." She tugged him into the entryway and shut the door behind him. "You can't possibly sing that badly normally. I heard you in church a few weeks ago, and your voice was quite nice."

"I figured it would be more noticeable and make you want me to come in quicker if I botched it." He cut her a sideways glance. "Guess it worked, huh?"

"That's beyond ridiculous. I probably would have let you in if you'd sung normally too."

"Now she tells me." He rubbed his hands together and blew on them.

"Come on." She motioned toward the kitchen. "I'll make you some hot chocolate."

"I won't turn you down." He hung his coat on the hook by the door and followed her down the hallway. "Although I don't plan for us to stay here long."

"Oh? Did I miss a memo? I thought I wasn't allowed to leave." She poured some milk into a glass measuring cup to heat in the microwave.

"Really? I don't know why you'd think that." He kept his gaze anywhere but on her.

"Maybe because someone stole my keys Monday afternoon, and I haven't been able to find them since." She bumped him out of the way with her hip so she could get to the pantry. "Know anything about that?"

"I would never hide someone's keys."

She whacked him with a candy cane as she walked by again. "But you wouldn't mind having someone else do it, huh?"

"*Ow!*" He rubbed his arm. "Why are you blaming me? I haven't seen you since you left the store Monday morning."

"Aren't you the one who couldn't stand the idea of me leaving before Christmas?" She snapped the peppermint stick in half.

He rubbed his neck as if imagining her doing the same to him. She couldn't deny she'd had some temptations in that department the last few days. "I've been going a little stir crazy."

"You could have called. I would have come to your rescue." He moved closer and accepted the mug she pushed his way. She handed him a piece of candy cane, and he frowned.

"Use it to stir with. It gives a peppermint flavor to the hot chocolate."

His eyes met hers and crinkled at the edges as he smiled. "Thanks."

"You're welcome." She took a sip of her own beverage. "So, tell me why you needed to talk to me."

"Maybe *talk* is the wrong word." He licked his lips where some chocolate remained, and her rebellious heart sped up. "But

I do have something I want you to see, if you'll agree to come with me."

"I don't know, Nick." She played with the tiny piece of candy left floating in her drink. "Today's not a great day."

"Please." He set both their mugs back on the counter and pulled her to him. "You said I didn't want you to leave before Christmas. That's true. But it's more than that. I don't want you to leave ever. The store's empty without you running around, painting and bringing new life. I keep looking up from my computer and expecting you to send me a smirk and a new idea of some great plan you want to put into action. I can't imagine you not being there for good."

"Nick—"

"I know there's more going on in your life right now than just us. Where I want to take you, I think might help with some of that. But it's up to you. I won't force it, but I hope you'll trust me and come."

He held her so close she could feel his heartbeat under her fingertips. She rested her forehead on his shoulder and squeezed her eyes closed. She wanted to trust him, but he was right. Her hesitation was about more than simply how they'd left things on Monday.

Today was the anniversary of her dad's death. Five years ago this afternoon. And thoughts of him had haunted her all day, more than normal. Could she go out, let herself be distracted, maybe even have fun? On this blackest of days?

She started to shake her head, the grief too much.

"Please." His whisper cracked a little as it hit her ear, and something inside her broke too. She wasn't able to tell him, "No." She'd missed him too. And she was curious to see what was so important.

"Fine." She pushed back an inch. "But you have to let me change first."

"Why?" He grinned as his gaze moved up and down.

"Sweatpants would probably be warmer than some other things you could wear."

"Ha, ha." She moved from his embrace and pushed his mug into his hands. "Drink your cocoa, and I'll be out in a few minutes."

"Yes, ma'am." He schooled his features into a mostly submissive expression.

She rolled her eyes and dashed back down the hallway to see what clothes she had clean right now. With all the time she'd had lately, she should have done laundry, but the motivation had escaped her.

She found a red sweater and a pair of jeans that had been worn only once. Several brush strokes through her hair had it mostly snag free, enough to weave into a loose braid. A plaid scarf and some boots completed her outfit.

"Well, that was worth the wait." Nick's appreciative expression set sugar plum fairies dancing in her belly. She took another sip of her chocolate, fighting the temptation to ask where he was taking her. Something told her even if she asked, he wouldn't answer. He was the kind of guy who liked to pull surprises.

He ran a finger down her cheek and stepped close again. "Thank you."

"What?" She frowned.

"Thank you for trusting me." He motioned to her outfit. "For wanting to look nice for me."

"You think I put this on for you?" She smirked. "I got dressed for whoever else might see me wherever it is we're going."

"*Mm-hmm.*" He pulled her to him and pressed his lips to hers, silencing whatever comeback she might have been able to think up. She wouldn't have complained even if it were a possibility. His kisses were one of the things that had been on her brain all week. And this one was proving his earlier proclamations.

"Did I mention I missed you?" He breathed the words into her cheek as he cradled her close.

She was just as breathless as he was. "You might have said that a time or two."

After another couple minutes of standing there in each other's arms, he pushed away. "Want to take your hot chocolate with you?"

"Are we going on another sleigh ride?" She reached for a travel mug.

"No. But at least part of what we're doing is outside."

She was intrigued but still wouldn't ask. If he wanted to let her know, he would. She'd have to keep listening to the tiny voice inside her head that said she could trust him. That he'd never intentionally hurt her.

"Okay, let's go."

Jackets on, he walked her out to his car and made sure she was comfortable before going around to the driver's side. She studied the city as they drove toward the center of it. Where was he taking her? Would she regret coming?

"Why do you hate my uncle?" The question escaped Nick's lips before he realized he would ask it. Maybe he couldn't stand the silence in the car any longer. Maybe it was something he'd secretly wondered for weeks and it wouldn't stay unasked anymore. He honestly wasn't sure.

"What?"

"What do you have against Uncle Paul?" Nick stopped at a red light and glanced at her.

She collapsed back against the seat as if much of the air had been sucked from her chest. "Why do you think I have something against him?"

"You're so set against him dating your mom." He drove on as the light changed once more. "I figured it must be something about him that you couldn't stand."

"He's not my dad." Her voice was quiet. "It isn't really about him except that he's the one my mom chose to date."

"So, your mom could have chosen to date, say ... the Easter bunny—"

"Nick!"

"Sorry, sorry." He waved his hands in the air. "That's just what popped in my head first. Let's say a preacher or a doctor or—"

"*Anyone*, Nick. Anyone who's not my dad." Trudy rubbed her eyes. "Seeing her open to the possibility of falling in love with someone else ... it's killing me. Every day I turn around, expecting to bump into my dad in the kitchen, to have him ask what ideas I have for our bucket list this year, or smell his ever-present peppermint—"

"That's why you like peppermint so much." He snapped his fingers.

"Yes." She stared out the window though he wasn't sure she saw any of the scenery they passed. "I guess I didn't even realize how much of him I picked up. But yes. The peppermint is from him."

"It's definitely grown on me." Nick reached over and caught her hand in his. Now that they were almost to their destination, doubt was setting in. What if she hated him for this? What if she wasn't ready? Would never be ready?

No. He silenced those worries. Everything about this plan had fallen perfectly into place and seemed like a great idea. He saw the signs up ahead and pulled into the parking lot.

"You're taking me to a church?" Trudy leaned forward in her seat and studied their surroundings.

"Sort of." He followed the arrows around to the back, where there was a courtyard with a huge pine tree in the middle. A few others milled around, touching various ornaments on the tree lit only by white lights. "They call it an angel tree."

"Like where you adopt a child and shop for Christmas presents?" Trudy frowned at him. "Wouldn't that need to be done earlier?"

"Let me explain." He parked the car and grabbed her hands.

"This isn't that kind of tree. Instead, every year this congregation lights up this tree and offers wooden ornaments in the shape of an angel. Whoever is mourning or grieving a loss can come and write the name of their loved one on the angel. Then various members of the church take turns praying for the families of those listed on the tree."

Her hands trembled within his, but she didn't pull away. She stared at the tree in silence, tears trickling down her cheeks. Maybe this had been a bad idea after all.

"So, you want me to write my dad's name on an ornament and hang it up there?" Her voice wavered.

"I decided to bring you and see if you wanted to." He waved in the direction. "I think it started out being for people who'd lost loved ones that year, but I figure since you didn't get to do it five years ago, maybe it would be okay to do it this year instead. What do you think?"

"Okay." She pressed her fingertips against her mouth as if she couldn't believe she'd agreed to this plan. But his heart leaped in his chest. Steps one and two were going well. Time to send up some more prayers that steps three and four would go as smoothly.

She gripped his fingers so tightly he couldn't tell if they were cold or if the blood flow was cut off. But he wasn't about to take his hand away from hers. Instead, he gave her a squeeze and walked a couple inches closer.

"Merry Christmas." A woman in a green hat sat at a table on the edge of the parking lot. "Are you here to hang up an angel?"

"Yes, please." Nick answered.

"Of course." The woman beamed and pulled out a basket of wooden ornaments someone had carved into the shapes of winged people. "We have several people due to arrive and start praying in the next half hour, so this is good timing."

"Thank you." He accepted the ornament and a marker and steered Trudy gently over to a bench on the other side of the tree.

"What do I do?" She whispered, the Sharpie trembling in her hand.

He studied the ones already hanging and noticed no one stuck to a real formula. "Looks like whatever you want to." He pointed out several. "That one just has the name. One over there has dates written on it. Down here is one with a little story of what happened. And it looks like several have scriptures."

She uncapped the pen, then stopped. "I'm not sure I can."

"This isn't saying you're never going to think of him again. This is a way to memorialize him and also allow others to pray for you, so you have the strength to get through this hard time." He put his arm around her shoulders.

She sat still several more minutes. Was she frozen? Could she honestly not do this? Finally, her fingers pushed the marker across the wood in a neat, precise calligraphy.

"Derek John McNamara, the best Daddy a girl could ever want. Christmas will never be the same." Half the words were on the front and half on the back, but it expressed what Nick had learned about her dad perfectly.

"Ready to hang it up?" He helped her to her feet and stepped over to the tree.

What must have been hundreds of other ornaments already dangled from limbs, lit by the white Christmas lights strung through all the branches. So many people missing loved ones this holiday season. Did this help them? Would it help Trudy?

She pressed a kiss to the wood and then reached up to an empty spot to add her dad to the mix. His heart skipped a beat as she slumped into herself. But then, as if in slow motion, she straightened and stared up at the angel she'd just hung, tears streaming down her cheeks.

It wasn't the way he'd pictured spending Christmas Eve three weeks ago, but he couldn't imagine anywhere he'd rather be right now than here, supporting Trudy through this moment. Especially since he'd have to pass her on to someone else momentarily.

" I 'm so proud of you, honey."

"Mom?" Trudy spun from Nick's arms and found her mom standing right behind her. "Where did you come from?"

"Nick told me the plan to bring you here, and I wanted to come too." She opened her arms, and Trudy hesitated only a moment before stepping into the embrace. "You needed to be the one who wrote and hung the ornament."

"Because you've moved on and I haven't?" Trudy's question was muffled in her mom's coat sleeve.

"Not entirely. I still have many moments when I wonder if I'll ever be able to move on with my life, to turn around and not expect to see him sitting in his favorite chair or asking what dinner will be. Wishing I could talk to him about the problems going on in your life." Her mom ran a hand over her hair, smoothing it down. "You don't have to go through all this alone, you know."

"It felt like I was the only one still wishing he was here." Trudy leaned back and peered at her mom. "Katt is living her own life with Brian and Mark. And you ... you are dating again. But I couldn't seem to find my place without him."

"What about now? Have you found it now?" Her mom tilted her head and glanced behind Trudy, to where Nick must still be standing.

Trudy pressed her lips together, thinking. This had been the happiest Christmas she'd had in five years—mostly thanks to Nick. No one else had drawn her out and encouraged her to do holiday activities since her dad passed away. But Nick had. A smile tugged at the corner of her lips. "Maybe."

"I hope so." Her mom squeezed again. "I'd love to have both my girls here close to me."

"So much so that you'd hide my keys?" Trudy raised an eyebrow.

"It was the first thing I could think of." Her mom shrugged. "When Nick said he needed help keeping you in town until he could pull off this plan, I panicked. After all, you're a grown woman. I can't force you to do something or not do something. But when I saw your keys just lying there on the table in the entryway, it was one of the easiest ways to keep you from leaving."

"Where are they?"

"In the freezer," her mom gave a sheepish grin. "Behind the broccoli."

Trudy shook her head. "The freezer. I think the only other place I didn't check was the toilet tank."

A man approached, bundled up against the weather. He offered a gloved hand and shook both of theirs. "I'm Tom, one of the members here. I'll be praying for all the families of the names on these ornaments tonight. Is there anything specific you want mentioned?"

Trudy's throat tightened. People had prayed for their family around the time of the accident, but how long had that lasted? When did people quit petitioning God for peace and comfort for those grieving? And was there anything else she needed?

"Thank you so much." Her mom pointed out their ornament.

"We're remembering my husband. We lost him to a heart attack and car accident five years ago tonight, but this is our first year in Temple, so we wanted to participate, if that's okay."

"That's fine." Tom nodded. "We're so sorry for your loss."

"Thank you. It makes this time of year a little harder for us. Derek loved Christmas more than anyone else I know. We haven't really figured out our traditions now that he's gone. And this is our first year in a house and town where we didn't live with him. We're trying to find the new rhythm in our life, to work to live without missing him so much." Her mom tightened her hold around Trudy's waist.

Tom nodded. "Would you like me to pray with you now?"

She and her mom bowed their heads. Nick had stepped away to another area somewhere, and she couldn't see him. He hadn't left, had he? Sure, she could catch a ride with her mom, but she'd wanted to talk to him again before they parted for the evening.

"Father God, we thank you for blessing these ladies' lives with Derek, their husband and father. Thank you for the memories you gave them of so many good years together. We ask your peace and comfort as they remember and miss him through this season he loved so much. And we ask your blessings and grace on them as they transition to living in a new place and living their lives without this man who meant so much to them."

Tom continued on, pulling on every one of Trudy's heart strings, coaxing more tears from her eyes. And yet, a peace settled around her shoulders more fully than she'd ever remembered it being there since Dad's death. She looked up as Tom finished his prayer, and the ornament waved in the wind as if bidding her farewell.

For some reason, she didn't have the heart heaviness she expected from such a gesture. Instead, her feet felt like they'd been released from the mud-like substance she'd been slogging through the last five years. She leaned into another hug with her mom.

"I'm sorry I've made your life so miserable the last few days."

"You were hurting." Her mom brushed some hair off Trudy's face. "I was moving too fast for you. And not talking things through as they happened. You were gone so much, I didn't get to ease you into the idea of Paul. Instead, it was more like I dumped a bucket of cold water over your head."

Trudy laughed. "That's a really good explanation for how it felt."

"He feels awful, by the way. Like this is all his fault."

Trudy shook her head. "I wasn't very nice to him the other day at the store."

"He and I have agreed to slow things down some, take our time with this. We both had great marriages the first time, so the fact we're even thinking about moving into another relationship caught us both off guard. We want to make sure we're not just looking for friendship, someone to talk to and spend time with. Not that those aren't good qualities, but marriage is a big commitment, and neither of us want to go through another loss anytime soon." Her mom kissed her fingers and reached up to touch the ornament. "We'll always miss our firsts."

"I'm sorry you've been so lonely, Mom. I haven't listened like I should have. Or just spent time with you."

"You were living your life. And that's exactly what I raised you to do. No apologies necessary." Her mom ran a finger over Trudy's cheek. "And I want you to keep living your life. Even at Christmas. Your dad would've been so sad to see you give up the joy of this season simply because he wasn't around to experience it with you."

Trudy ducked her head. "You're right."

"I know. I'm your mom. That's my job. And I enabled you to do it, too, so I'm just as guilty. I hoped after a year or so you'd be able to celebrate again. But you kept locking it away as if it wasn't Christmas without your dad."

"It's all my fault." Trudy shivered.

"What? Grief isn't something you're at fault for—"

Trudy shook her head. "No. The reason he's not here. It's all my fault."

Mom pulled her back over to the bench and turned to face her. 'What are you talking about?"

"He never would've died if we hadn't been going to that stupid concert."

"What? Your father died from a heart attack."

Trudy took a shuddering breath. "A heart attack that happened while he was driving home from work early. So he could take me to the concert. If we hadn't made those plans, he would've been at the office and someone could've helped him in time."

"Oh, honey." Mom wrapped her up tightly. "You don't know that. None of us know what would've happened if things had been different." She stroked her braid. "And your father was so excited to go to that concert. It was more his idea than yours that year, remember?"

Trudy could barely nod, Mom had her clasped so tightly.

"It was *not* your fault. It wasn't anyone's fault." Mom pulled back and grasped Trudy's face. "Okay?"

"But if he hadn't bought concert tickets, he would've been home that day. He was working extra hours to buy you that ring. The money for the tickets would have covered most of that ring, and he would've been home."

"Well, for one thing, I told him not to buy me that ring. So, that was his own stubborn fault." Mom raised an eyebrow. "I'd much rather have him. And for another thing, even if he had been at home, that doesn't mean we would have been able to get him help on time."

Trudy swallowed a lump of emotion. The truth of her Mom's words poked at her wall of grief and guilt, letting light shine through the holes left behind.

"But—"

"No, ma'am." Mom clasped Trudy's chin in her mittened fingers. "No more buts, if's, or might've-beens. They don't change a thing. And they never will. We all loved your father. And we all miss him. But that doesn't mean he would want us to hang on to him the way you have been. And he definitely wouldn't want you feeling guilty over his death. We can't change the past. All we can do is learn from it and let it help us grow. Got it?"

"I'll work on getting it." Trudy sniffled.

"I guess I'll have to take that." Mom gave a watery smile. "And maybe you can work on enjoying Christmas tomorrow too? Even without your dad?"

"I'm trying."

"I know. Just remember, Christmas happens with or without us. But it's more fun if we're together."

"I ruined five Christmases, didn't I?"

"No, honey. No. We just didn't celebrate them with as much gusto as normal. And Katt made sure Mark had more at their house than at ours since you weren't ready." Her mom gave her another hug. "But I think everyone will be relieved when you participate tomorrow morning."

"I think I'll be the most relieved of all." Trudy twisted her hands together. "I've missed it. Nick pulling me out and making me decorate a tree or ride a sleigh through twinkling lights, it reminded me how much fun it is this time of year."

"You rode a sleigh?"

"Yeah. That date was amazing—until I got home." She twisted her lips to the side.

"Oh." Her mom scanned the area. "Did Nick leave?"

"I hope not." Trudy glanced around the tree. "I think that's his car still over there. Mind if I abandon you?"

"Go on. I'm going to stay here a few more minutes, so you can come tag me if you need a ride home." Her mom pulled her coat closer and wiggled toward the center of the bench.

Trudy tossed *thank you*s to the girls sitting at the table and speed-walked through the parking lot. She tapped on the window of Nick's car and was pleased when he pushed it open for her to climb in the passenger side. The heat blowing from his vents was bliss after being out in the chilly mist.

"I was afraid you'd left." She rubbed her fingers together.

"Not yet. I wanted to make sure I didn't leave you stranded." He grinned. "Sounds like you don't like being stranded much."

"Would you like it if your keys disappeared for a week?"

"No." He shook his head. "I wouldn't."

"Okay, then."

"Are you glad you didn't go back to Austin, though?" Nick held his breath as he waited for the answer. Trudy obviously didn't hate him, considering she'd come over and climbed in his car. But that didn't mean she wanted to stay.

"I am. I've had a lot of time this week to think. And go through boxes of my dad's old stuff. And see how lonely and sad my mom is too. And ... and miss you."

"You missed me, huh?" His heart picked up a faster rhythm.

"Yes, though I'm still trying to figure out why." She laughed. "You aren't always the most pleasant person to be around, you know."

"I think I'm perfectly delightful." He brushed some imaginary lint off his shoulder and raised his nose in the air. "So, I have no idea what you're talking about."

"And humble too." She shot him a teasing grin.

"I'm so humble and fun to be around that I'm going to assume you'll say yes when I ask you to join my family tomorrow evening for dinner at my mom's." He couldn't meet her eyes. Much as he was playing up his ego, he honestly wasn't sure how she'd react.

"I'd love to."

His gaze jerked up to see if she was being honest. She beamed a smile at him and reached for his hands, twining her cold fingers through his. He lifted them to his lips and pressed a kiss to them.

"Really?" He gave a squeeze.

"Really. Unless you were still joking, in which case you don't have to feel obligated."

"I was serious. Am serious." He shook his head. "My mom's been bugging me for weeks, asking if I was bringing someone. I told Dad on Monday that I was still working on it but that I hoped so."

"You put a lot of hopes into having those hidden keys work to keep me around this week, didn't you?"

"I did."

"We always do our family Christmas in the morning and then eat a big meal at lunch. I may waddle home if I eat two big meals tomorrow." She laughed and rubbed her belly. "But I'm willing to try. I can't think of anyone I'd rather see on Christmas."

"I feel exactly the same way."

"That you want to see yourself on Christmas?" She nudged him with her shoulder.

"You know what I mean." He pressed a kiss to her lips, happier than he'd ever been in his entire life. "So, you're feeling better about the holiday?"

"Mom reminded me that Dad wouldn't have wanted me to quit celebrating and enjoying his favorite time of year simply because he's not here to do it with me. He wanted to instill the joy of the season in me so it would be there long after he was gone, even though he didn't know he'd go soon—much sooner than we wanted." She stared out the windshield. "And I haven't done that. I bottled it all up and set it aside, thinking it couldn't be the same, so it couldn't be as good. That it was my fault—I'd ruined Christmas. That's not true."

"Of course it's not true. How could you ruin Christmas?"

She shook her head. "All those stupid bucket lists we did each year. We kept trying to top the ones before. Maybe it got to be too much."

"So, you probably don't want this then. Now that I've worked so hard on it."

Nick rummaged through the console between them and extricated a slightly rumpled piece of paper. He smoothed it out and handed it to her. She frowned then her eyes skimmed the words.

"What's this?" She flipped it over and then back again.

"A new list." He pointed to the top line. "Things you had never done on your bucket lists before. Painting reindeer. Sleigh ride. Angel tree."

"How did you know I hadn't done any of these?" She stared at him warily.

"I might have seen your old lists on your dresser when you let me borrow a shirt a few weeks ago." He ran his hand through his hair. "And I might have taken pictures of them to make sure I didn't repeat anything."

She leaned back toward the door. "You did what?"

"Hear me out." He caught her hands before she could bolt on him again. "Please."

She clamped her lips together for a moment but then nodded. "I'm listening."

"I wanted to help you." He searched for the right words. Now was not the time to say something stupid. Not after she'd agreed to come for Christmas dinner. Not with one more item on the list he'd just handed her. Not to mention his other plans.

"You were so sad and lost. When I saw the stack of pages there, I don't know. Something inside me ... it was like a hand poking me and telling me these lists were the key to making your holidays better. After all, you made the holidays better for me. It was only right I return the favor."

"I made the holidays better for you?" She gave him a

skeptical look. "I was the one who kept fighting all things Christmas, remember?"

"For years now—since I took over managing the store—all Christmas has been to me is a final sales push to get through the end of the year. You were right. It was all about the numbers. This year I wasn't sure the store was even going to make it to the twenty-fifth. Then you came in. And everything about you made the store brighter. Your ideas. Your creativity. Your outlook on life. And I could suddenly remember that there was more to Christmas than numbers. There was joy and laughter and playfulness. And love."

"Love, huh?"

"Yes, love. I know we haven't known each other very long. Less than a month. But if you had gone to Austin, my Christmas would have been ruined. Having you here, no matter what else is under the tree, it's going to be perfect."

She grinned and ducked her head. "Even after all I put you through?"

"Yes. But please don't do that again." He poked her playfully in the arm. "I'm not sure my heart could handle it."

"I'll do my best." Her voice was just above a whisper, solemn. "After all, you have a big piece of my heart now too."

"Yeah?" He leaned forward to meet her eyes. "Best Christmas present ever."

She laughed and met him with a kiss.

"Better get you home soon. It is Christmas Eve after all. Santa won't come until all the children are in bed." He winked as he started the car.

"You think I've been good enough for Santa to fill my stocking?"

"I'd almost bet on it."

She was quiet most of the way back to Connie's house, but then suddenly lifted the list again and pointed to the bottom of it. "What's this last thing? I know we didn't make the concert, so what's this?"

"You'll have to wait until tomorrow for that. It's too late tonight." Out of the corner of his eye, he caught the pout she sent his way. "Besides, you said you didn't want to go to that concert."

"Not this year. Maybe Katt and I can go together next year."

"What about me?"

"What about you?" She nudged him with her elbow. "You didn't even know who TSO was until I told you."

"So? Doesn't mean I'm not interested in going." He pulled up to the curb in front of her mom's house.

"We'll see how good you are this next year." She winked.

"Oh, ho. *Now* who's playing Santa?" He crossed his arms.

"Nick, thank you." She reached over and pulled his hands into her own. "Thank you for helping this be the best Christmas in a long time. I couldn't have decorated that tree without you. It would have sat in my storage unit for eternity, never being enjoyed. And the lights with the sleigh. And tonight." She ducked her head before meeting his eyes once more. "You helped fill some spots in my heart that had been empty for a long time."

"I'm glad I'm the one who got to do those things with you." He pulled away and walked around to help her out. His hand at her waist, he walked her up to the front door. "Well, what have we here?"

"What?" She glanced up and saw the sprig of mistletoe he had spied a moment before. "Who put that there? Do you think Mom and Paul—"

"Don't even go there tonight." He playfully growled the words in her ear before pulling her to him for a goodnight kiss that left him aching for more. "You better get inside. I'll see you tomorrow afternoon."

"I'll look forward to it." She dropped one more kiss on his nose, having to stand on her tiptoes to reach. "Merry Christmas Eve."

His heart thudded in his ears as she closed the door behind

her. Now to get through Christmas with his family tomorrow. Then he could surprise her with that last list item. It wasn't a concert, per se. But maybe it would hold her over until next year. As long as Uncle Paul didn't ruin things when she saw him at dinner tomorrow.

Chapter Twenty-Seven

T rudy braced herself as the doorbell rang the next morning.

"Who could that be?" Her mom glanced up from her cup of coffee, her slipper-clad feet tucked under her on the couch. "Katt has a key."

"Probably Paul." Trudy refused to meet her mom's eyes but instead jumped up and headed to answer the door.

When she'd sent the text last night, she hadn't been sure if he'd come or not. After all, she'd really lit into him earlier in the week. But after everything else that had been talked through, Trudy needed to apologize to Paul face to face. And an invitation to Christmas brunch just might be the way to do it.

She turned the knob, and there he was, dressed in green today instead of the red she'd grown used to seeing him in. He had to be at least fifty pounds lighter than his padded suit made him look at the store. And his beard was trimmed a bit shorter, closer to his face than it had been. He offered a tentative smile.

"Merry Christmas, Trudy." He thrust a bag of wrapped packages at her.

"Merry Christmas, Paul. Come on in." She stepped back to allow him entrance. "I'm glad you came."

Paul studied her as if uncertain what he saw was real. "Are you?"

"I owe you an apology. Probably more than one." Trudy studied her fuzzy slippers, unsure how to say what needed to be said. "I wasn't ready to face my mom dating again. But that was no excuse for how I treated you these last few weeks."

"I forgive you." He squeezed her arm, and she finally met his gaze.

"Maybe you and I can get to know each other a little better this morning. Possibly even find a chance for me to explain some things more." She lifted a shoulder. "But if you don't want to talk about it—"

"I look forward to getting to know you better too." He cut her off before she could talk her way out of the offering. "Your text last night was probably the best Christmas present I'll get this year."

"Nick and my mom have been helping me see some things differently. Work through some of my grief that I hadn't dealt with." She swallowed. "I'm not promising I won't wince a little every time you and mom are affectionate, but ..."

"Thank you."

"Paul?" Her mom appeared at the end of the hall, no longer in her robe, but dressed in a red and green plaid sweater she'd had for as long as Trudy could remember. She and Katt referred to it as "Mom's Christmas outfit."

"Trudy invited me to brunch with you. If that's okay." He took her mom's offered hands and squeezed them.

Her mom gaped over at Trudy who remained in the doorway. "Of course. She didn't even let me know you might be coming."

"If there's not enough food—"

"Oh, no," Trudy and her mom said at the same time and then laughed.

"There's always more than enough." Her mom led him toward the kitchen. "Come on in. Katt's family will be here soon, too, and then the festivities will really get started. Trudy and I were just enjoying our coffee. Would you like a cup?"

"What's going on?" Katt's voice startled Trudy from where she'd been watching her mom and Paul walk into the kitchen. In her rush to apologize and make things right with Paul, she'd left the front door wide open, and her sister stood in it now with hands full of food, Mark running past her legs to get inside too.

"I invited Paul to brunch with us." Trudy took a casserole dish from her sister's hands.

"Talk about a Christmas miracle." Katt's mutter was loud enough to be heard, but Trudy didn't reply. In a lot of ways, it was true.

Brian came in a minute later, more gifts in his arms. "What did I miss?"

"Come on in, big brother." Trudy motioned toward the kitchen. "I think everyone's down there. I can put packages under the tree if you'll carry the casserole."

"Sure."

They swapped loads, and Trudy stepped into the quiet living room, grateful for a minute to herself before facing everyone once more. She carefully found spots for all the additional presents that had come that morning, making sure no bows were squished. As she stood once more to survey the glory of a tree bursting with joy, she noticed an ornament she hadn't seen on the tree before. She stepped to that side and fingered the rough wooden angel piece she'd written her dad's name on the night before. How had it ended up here?

"They told me last night that if I wanted to keep it, I could." Her mom appeared behind her. "They'll take them all down in a few days anyway. And we'd already been prayed over. I figured it meant more here than in a pile at that church building, possibly never to be seen again."

"I'm glad you brought it home." Trudy traced it once more before letting it nestle back among the branches. "It's sort of like he's still here with us, isn't it?"

"His spirit of fun and his love of this holiday will always be here with us as long as we remember them." Her mom squeezed her shoulders. "The cinnamon rolls are coming out in just a minute. Come help me set the table, and we'll eat."

"Sounds good."

The meal was glorious, with fruits and bacon and ham, hash brown casserole, the cinnamon rolls, and biscuits with jelly. Mark wavered between wanting to eat a few more bites and wishing to be under the tree, finding all the packages with his name on them. He'd learned how to spell it this last year and planned to make good use of the skill. The adults polished off their plates, topped off their coffee cups, and followed the four-year-old into the living room.

Packages that had taken weeks and months to purchase and wrap were opened in less than half an hour. Mark sat in the middle of a large stack of paper and tissue, running his new fire truck through the debris. The new clothes were stacked to the side, deemed less fun than the toys.

Paul patted his tummy and stretched. "It's a beautiful day outside, and I think after a meal like we had, I could do with a stretch of my legs. How about you, Trudy?"

She hesitated only a second, then nodded. "Let me grab my shoes."

Ignoring the curious looks Katt and Mom sent her way, she grabbed her tennis shoes and a light sweater. Although it was warmer out than it had been for the last several days, it hadn't quite hit sixty degrees yet, and the wind whipped the bare trees around with a fierceness that showed up only in December. She met Paul at the front door, and they set out together, taking a left at the sidewalk.

"You know I didn't want to upset you, right?" Paul was the first to break the silence.

"I do now." Trudy glanced up at the blue sky. "Though when I first figured out what was going on, my heart didn't want my head to think things through logically. I was still too deep in my grief, too stubborn to let go of what I could no longer hold. And too unrealistic to realize my mom was still grieving, too, though in a different way. I guess I'd always pictured her being alone once Dad was gone."

"I never planned to marry again when my Addie passed a few years ago." Paul tugged her arm to swerve her around a boy trying out a new bike. The boy wasn't paying a lick of attention to the world around him, just peddling to see how fast he could go.

"What changed?"

"Your mom walked into the Emporium. I recognized her right away." He sighed. "I had always wondered what happened to her. She was the girl I believed I'd marry at one point, when we were dating in college. Then we had several disagreements and grew apart instead of working through them. She met Derek, and I met Addie. Both great choices for us."

Trudy nodded. Her dad had been perfect for her mom—probably why she'd had such a hard time wrapping her head around someone else filling that role.

"But we're both in different places in life now. We've learned how to work out problems that arise. And we've both grown lonely over the last few years, wishing for someone to talk to in the evenings." Paul cut her a look. "Not that she didn't have you girls, and I didn't have my boys. It's just not the same."

"Especially when we're all totally wrapped up in our own lives." Trudy kicked an acorn down the sidewalk in front of them.

"Yes. Which is as it should be. But it doesn't help us out." Paul took another left at the corner. "When your mom and I got to talking, we discovered we had a lot more in common now than we did back when we dated the first time. Similar tastes in movies and music and food. Similar lifestyles. It was like she was a puzzle piece I was missing to make my life complete. We just forgot we had other people to consider besides ourselves this time. I'm talking about you and your sister, as well as my boys.

Since my sons live farther away, they don't even know about all this yet."

"Nick asked me last night why I didn't like you."

Paul's feet stumbled, but he righted himself quickly and leaned his head toward her as if to hear better.

"I don't *not* like you. It was more that you aren't my father. That was the part I didn't like."

"Connie has told me some about your special traditions and relationship with him."

"He was amazing." Trudy fiddled with the zipper pull of her cardigan. "But Nick has helped me see that I can still find joy in the season even without my dad here. Somewhere along the way, I forgot that there were other people to have fun with at Christmastime. Isn't that crazy?"

"It's easy to focus too much on one thing and forget to see the big picture. That's not hard to believe at all, but I'm glad Nick is helping you find that joy again." Paul nudged her lightly. "And that you've brought a smile back to his face too. I was worrying about that boy. Thought maybe I'd have to fire him."

"Oh! I'm glad you didn't do that." She shook her head. "He loves that store. And you're the one who started all this anyway."

"I am?"

"You're the one who forced us to work together and signed us up for that painting class that turned out to be for couples. Did you know that?"

"Did it?" His voice betrayed that he had known exactly what kind of session he'd registered them for.

"Aren't you the sneaky one?" Trudy grinned at him. "Should I tell your nephew?"

"What he doesn't know won't hurt him." Paul chuckled.

They were almost back to the house, and he paused on the last corner. "Trudy, I don't promise it will grow easier right away to see your mom and me together, but I'm more than grateful you're willing to give us a chance to see if this relationship can grow. If things do keep progressing the way they have, I promise to not try and replace your dad. But maybe you'll let me be a stepdad down the road?"

She swallowed the lump in her throat. "I think that would be an excellent compromise. Just make sure I have time to wrap my mind around it, okay?"

"Scout's honor."

"I better get you back in there. I think there were a few cinnamon rolls left, and if we don't hurry, Brian will eat them all."

"Lead the way." Paul motioned with his hand, and they headed back inside to the chaos of Christmas music, fire engine sirens, and laughter. And the last two cinnamon rolls.

"I was so glad you could join us, dear. I just wish Nick weren't carting you off again so quickly." Nick's mom squeezed Trudy's hand as he tried to steer her out the front door.

"I have no idea what this scheme of his is, but he promises me I'll like it. Thanks again for a delicious meal." Trudy resisted his tugging one more minute to hug his mom. How did women bond so quickly? They'd been together only for three hours and already felt comfortable enough to embrace? Nick would never understand the female race.

"Mom, I'll bring her back soon, but I have to time this just right." Nick widened his eyes at his mother.

"All right, all right." His mother made a shooing motion. "Go on, then. But I'm going to keep you to that promise."

Nick finally walked Trudy out and down to his car. "Thought we'd never escape."

"Well, you did sort of say we were doing Christmas evening with your family. And it's still evening." Trudy pointed to the starlit sky.

"I can't help it if this is one of the last chances we have to do this." He slid into his seat and buckled before pulling out and heading toward the other side of town. He really hoped his research was correct. If he missed this by even a minute, it would be an utter failure.

"Where are we going?" Trudy shifted her jean-clad legs and tossed her brown curls over her shoulder.

"To finish off the bucket list I gave you last night."

"So, this is the TSO clue?" She tapped a finger against her mouth. "Please tell me you didn't hire the whole orchestra to come down here and play just for me."

"Weren't you yelling at me a few days ago for trying to spend too much money on tickets?" He gave her a play frown. "I don't want to cause something like that to happen again. Although it thrills me to know you think the store is doing so well I could afford that."

She laughed, and he smiled in return.

"You're going to make me wait until we get to wherever we're going, aren't you?"

"Yep." He tapped his fingers along to the radio. "We'll be there in a few minutes."

Turning into the correct neighborhood, he slowly maneuvered the streets until he spotted the house that must be the one he was looking for. Almost every inch of their front yard, siding, roof, windows, even the garage, was covered in lights. For now, they flashed in a random pattern, but in a few minutes, they'd be able to roll down the window and listen to the show.

Trudy glanced at him and then at the house as he parked by the curb in front of it. "Do you know these people?"

"Nope."

"But we're parked at their house?"

"Yep." He glanced at his watch, then rolled down her window. "Ready?"

She shot him another skeptical look. "For what?"

The first loud notes of a popular TSO song blasted from speakers near the front door, and Trudy jumped before turning to take in what was happening with the lights across from them. Every note of the music was synchronized with the flashing bulbs to make it appear that the whole house and yard were rocking out and dancing to the tune. Trudy laughed and covered her mouth.

"Not quite as good as one of their concerts, but better than nothing, right?" He leaned over so he could see it better ... and be closer to her too.

"It's wonderful." She placed her hand on his cheek and leaned back until his chin rested on her shoulder.

Minutes later the show was over and the lights flashed in their random order once more. He rolled up the glass to stop the cool air from creeping in more. She sighed and sat back in her seat.

"How did you know when it would do that?" She redid her seatbelt as he started the engine.

"They posted about it on social media. I found it on one of those bargain groups I joined trying to find tickets. My searches caused ads for all sorts of things like this to start popping up in my feed. But when I saw this one, I knew it had to happen. Also, I have treats for us."

"Treats?" Trudy groaned and patted her tummy. "I don't think I could eat another thing today."

"Not even a peppermint hot chocolate truffle?" He shook the white bag he pulled from the console.

"Maybe just one."

"That's what I thought." He passed the bag to her. "You know, we need to get busy coming up with a list for next year. It's not easy thinking up new ideas you've never done before."

"Next year?" She licked her fingers. "Nick, we're not even done with this Christmas yet. And I have no idea where I'll even be this time next year."

"True." He nodded. "But you could be here. After all, the store still needs you."

"Needs me? You didn't even send me Jessi's information to

come up with those last few ads. What else could I do?"

"Well, I didn't send you Jessi's information because I told her we couldn't use her services." He glanced at her as he stopped at a red light and caught her shocked expression.

"What? What about the paint sessions?" Trudy shook the bag at him. "You better give me a good answer or I'm eating the last one of these truffles."

"The last one? There were four in there!" He reached for the bag, but she held it out of the way.

"Nick, answer me." She wagged her finger under his nose. "What about the paint sessions?"

"I had this idea we might use another artist I happen to know." He pressed a kiss to her finger.

"Who?"

"You."

Silence greeted that answer. He'd been afraid of that. This whole time, every instance she brought this subject up, she'd mentioned finding someone else to do it. He pulled into the store parking lot and around to the back.

"Why are we here?"

He snatched the bag out of her hand and glanced in. Three truffles remained. He glanced up to chide her for lying, but she wasn't looking at him.

"I want you to see something." He helped her out of the car and through the half-lit store to the front.

He pointed next to the front door where he'd installed a plaque yesterday.

"What?" She leaned forward and read the words, gaped at him, then back at the sign. "What is this?"

"It's a way to let everyone know the person who did the amazing art all over this store now. You deserve the credit for it. Those animals have been a huge hit, as well as the activity room. You saved this place for our family, Trudy. I wanted to make sure you were aware we were grateful."

"It was my job, Nick. I'm glad it worked out so well. But I

don't know the first thing about running a painting session. And I don't need this plaque letting others know who did the little pictures all over the store." She stepped back and shook her head.

"Well, I don't believe that first statement. Just the other day you told me exactly what supplies you'd need and the prices I'd expect to pay. And you probably even have ideas already of simple paintings you could teach the kids." He chucked her gently under the chin. "You don't give yourself enough credit."

She glanced away, blinking away ... tears?

"Hey." He pulled her closer. "Don't cry. It's a good thing."

"What if I mess up? I don't want to ruin all the hard work we've done here." Her words were muffled in his shoulder. "I almost ruined Christmas, so I know I'm capable of such a thing."

"You didn't almost ruin Christmas." He pressed his forehead to hers.

"Oh, yes I did."

He huffed out his exasperation. She was bound and determined to not believe him tonight. What could he do to get her to have faith in herself again? His eyes caught on the bicycle that stood in the returns section. Okay. Time for a change of tactics.

"How about this? Let's have another race."

She jerked at the sudden change of topic. "What?"

"A race. On bikes. Three times around the store." He cocked an eyebrow. "If I win, you stay and do at least one paint session. If you win, you don't have to do the paint session. But you can start arranging for someone to do a mural on the front wall."

Her breath hitched. "Nick, you're insane."

"Does that mean you're chicken?" He backed up, tugging her fingers along behind him.

"No." She leapt up and wrapped her arms around his neck. "It just means I better win." She pressed a kiss to his lips, stopping long before he was ready. With that, she let go and dashed toward the back of the store.

"Hey! You know I win no matter who comes in first in the race, right? Because both of those options have you staying in Temple." Nick spun on his heel to race after her.

"Who said I wasn't planning to stay in Temple anyway?" She tossed the words over her shoulder.

"Wait, what?" He tripped over the flat surface of the floor and almost didn't stop himself from face planting.

"You heard me." For having such short legs, she sure could move fast. She was already past the trucks and fashion dolls.

"What about Caitlyn?"

"I texted her yesterday that I would be sticking around here for a while. Paul even agreed to help me bring my stuff up in his truck."

"Paul?" He skidded to a stop at that news. "I didn't see you talk to Paul at dinner."

"I invited him to brunch with my family this morning." She leaned down to undo the chain holding the bike to the rack. "I assumed you knew."

"I didn't know." He caught her before she could move past him on the bicycle. "When did all this happen?"

"When I fell in love with you, silly." She kissed him on the nose and pushed away again, slinging her leg over the bike. "Now watch out. I'm determined that this time I'm going to beat you fair and square. A mural!"

Her laughter echoed through the empty store, filling his heart with joy he hadn't even known he was missing before she showed up. When he'd hoped for a Christmas miracle, he had no idea it would come in the form of a girl who ran him over every time she turned around, all because her mom had dated Santa. He shook himself out of his stupor and quickly mounted his own bike. He better kick it into gear fast. She was already almost to the book corner.

Not that he cared either way. She was staying.

Best Christmas present ever.

A Note from the Author

Hello, dear readers,

Let me tell you a story. Oh, wait. I just did that, didn't I?

Well, let me tell you the story BEHIND the story. You see, this book started with the title, believe it or not. How did I come up with a title like *Mama Dated Santa*?

I'm glad you asked.

Shortly after we moved to Tennessee a few years ago, we attended Breakfast with Santa. The man playing Santa was the dad of one of our friends, and he's a good one. Very merry and with a real beard. He heard our last name and asked if we were related to my husband's parents. Of course, we answered yes. He sent his greetings and condolences because we'd lost my mother-in-law a few months before.

When we passed on Santa's message, including his "real" name, my father-in-law laughed. Yes. They all went to college together. In fact, my mother-in-law had DATED the other guy before she started dating my father-in-law. I looked at my husband and said, "Your mom dated Santa!" As we told some other friends about it, one of them looked at me and said, "That would make a great book title." And it does, doesn't it?

Trudy and Nick came to life in my head, both with their own

personal vendettas against Christmas. And I knew they were going to have to help each other fall in love with Christmas again ... all while falling in love with each other, of course. And the cast of characters and setting fleshed itself out into what I think is one of my most delightful books yet. But I'm biased.

I hope you enjoyed hanging out at the Toy Emporium, riding a wagon through lights, and soaking up a bit of Texas-style Christmas.

If you did, I'd love it if you would take a moment to leave a review—it doesn't have to be long or fancy—on Amazon. Reviews help other readers decide if a book is worth trying or not. And please share with other reader friends too. Word-of-mouth is an author's best friend.

Thanks again for giving my story a try. I appreciate you!

Love,
Amy (*almost* married to Santa's son)

Discussion Questions

1. Trudy holds onto grief to the point it overshadows her memory of the joy of the season of Christmas. Have you ever focused so much on something you lost that you can't see the good things right in front of you?
2. Nick has let the business side of Russos' Toy Emporium take over his life. He can't see the joy in working at a toy store. Have you ever lost your passion for your job because of the "boring" parts?
3. The idea of her mom dating before or after her dad throws Trudy off. The idea of only one man or woman for everyone is a naïve one, but wouldn't it be nice? Have you ever been caught off-guard by the idea of someone else dating a person you know is/was happily married?
4. Katt and Trudy both had different relationships with their dad so Katt can't understand why Trudy can't move on. Have you ever had to deal with someone grieving differently than you?
5. Connie is a bit of a pack rat and has kept more memories and paraphernalia than her girls know what to do with. Have you ever helped go through years' of

"stuff?" What's something interesting you found from the past?

6. Nick struggles with the changes to the store, even though he knows it needs an uplift. What do you think holds him back? Does he like it more once it's done?

7. Trudy and Nick disagree about painting a mural on the front of the store. Murals are a huge trend in downtown areas right now, and quite a few cities encourage people to take photos of the interactive ones. Do you like walls painted with murals? Have you ever taken your picture with one?

8. Memories can be triggered by many senses. A sound, a smell, a taste. Trudy doesn't even realize her dad is the reason she loves peppermint hot chocolate so much until Nick points it out. What's a smell or taste that always triggers a memory with you?

9. The angel tree Nick takes Trudy to is based on one my home congregation does each year. We add the names of members or relatives or friends we've lost through the year and then pray for those missing them. I've included several loved ones on our tree over the last few years. Have you ever participated in something like this? Do you think it helps bring people peace?

10. Nick doesn't end up taking Trudy to the concert—at least not this year. Do you think they'll go to one in the future? Do you think it will help bring even more healing to her hurting heart to mark that last item off her bucket list?

11. Speaking of the bucket list, how many items mentioned in this book have you done with friend and loved ones over the holidays? Do you have your own personal list of must-do activities each year? Do you try to come up with new activities every year?

About the Author

Amy R Anguish grew up a preacher's kid, and in spite of having lived in seven different states that are all south of the Mason-Dixon line, she is not a football fan. Currently, she resides in Tennessee with her husband, daughter, and son, and usually a bossy cat or two. Amy has an English degree from Freed-Hardeman University that she intends to use to glorify God, and she wants her stories to show that while Christians face real struggles, it can still work out for good.

Follow her at http://abitofanguish.weebly.com or http://www.facebook.com/amyanguishauthor

Or https://twitter.com/amy_r_anguish

Learn more about her books at https://www.pinterest.com/msguish/my-books/

And check out the YouTube channel she does with two other

authors, Once Upon a Page (https://www.youtube.com/@
onceuponapage3326)

Also by Amy R. Anguish

Window of the Heart by Amy Anguish

The Stained-glass Legacy Series—Book Three

Lennox Malone may not believe in love, but she's determined to do the
best job she can as her friend Sara Beth's maid of honor. Problem is, the
man in charge of fixing up the chapel doesn't match her determination.
Fighting against preconceived notions, a past that catches up to her,
and an attraction she wants nothing to do with, this wedding is turning
into more than she can handle.

Ty Dunne might be laid back and easy-going, but he's determined to
make sure the chapel is ready for his cousin's wedding. Not only is it his
duty as best man, but he wants to preserve the family's history in the
building. If only he could live up to his family's other expectations—or

those of Lennox Malone, the fiery redhead he can't stop thinking about. Before he can go any further with her, though, he has to convince her that love is real and worth the risk.

Lennox has built her walls high and sturdy, but Ty is determined to find a way in—even if it's a window. Maybe the history of the chapel itself along with the romance of a wedding will help.

Get your copy here:

https://scrivenings.link/windowoftheheart

Destination: ~~Fun~~ Romance

Roadtrip Romance—Book One

It's not every day you bring a boyfriend back as a souvenir.

Katie Wilhite is ready to settle into her new job as a librarian now that college is through, but friends Bree and Skye want one more girls' trip, and when Bree insists this is her bachelorette fling, Katie agrees. What she didn't agree to was allowing fun and flighty Skye to dictate the itinerary or for her anxiety to kick in harder than ever … right in front of a cute guy.

Camden Malone had no idea when he agreed to be the voice of reason on his cousin Ryan's vacation that the trip wouldn't stay in New Orleans as planned. But when Ryan plots with Skye so that the guys can tag along with the girls all week, he isn't nearly as upset as he should be. Not with Katie's fiery temper and flashing eyes intriguing him more by the minute.

Can Katie relax enough to trust Camden and a possible future, or will she continue to push him away as only a vacation fling? And can Camden move past a rocky history of his own to be able to jump into a better future? For a trip that was supposed to be all about fun, there's a lot of romance going around.

Get your copy here:

https://scrivenings.link/destinationromance

Roadtrip for ~~One~~ Two

Roadtrip Romance—Book Two

Recovering from heartbreak is hard when

the ex-fiancé tags along ...

Dallas wasn't in the plans when Bree Henley set out to use the nonrefundable honeymoon tickets from her canceled wedding. Nor was running into ex-fiancé Nathan Hart. But their mutual friends and the weather have other ideas. A hurricane cancels their cruise and Bree decides to turn the disaster into a roadtrip for one, never imagining Nathan would object.

Nathan is furious when he uncovers the plot to get him back with Bree. But he can't just let her go roaming around the big city of Dallas alone. Though he knows calling off their wedding was the right thing to do, he still cares for Bree. And before he knows what hits him, he's volunteered to tag along. Suddenly, it's a trip for two.

Spending the week together might remind them of why they fell in love. But is it enough to overcome the obstacles standing in the way of "til death do us part"?

Get your copy here:

https://scrivenings.link/roadtripfortwo

Operation Find a ~~Job~~ Guy
Roadtrip Romance—Book Three

by Amy R. Anguish

She's set on saving her car ... and her heart.

Skye Jones has one goal for the summer—keep her father from taking away her convertible. That's the *only* reason she agrees to work at her sister's bridal shop in Boulder, Colorado, while she searches for a non-boring job. Why else would she have anything to do with weddings when she has no interest in marriage?

Benjamin Smith somehow ended up as a groomsman in two weddings over the summer, so he's spending a lot of time at Happily Ever After events. Falling for a blonde with no dreams of settling down wasn't in his five-year plan, yet the more he sees Skye, the more he wants to figure her out.

But all she sees him as is a boring attorney-her complete opposite.

Besides, romance is supposed to be for Skye's friends, not her. And she's in Colorado to get a job, not a guy. Right?

Get your copy here:

https://scrivenings.link/operationfindaguy

Love Delivered

A novella collection, including "Romance at Register Five"

by Amy R. Anguish

Mack McDonald isn't happy about the Grocerease app coming to his grocery store. But he's committed to the sixty-day trial period, and braces himself to lose money. Kaitlyn Daniels loves how the Grocerease app helps her make ends meet so she can assist her mom, the reason she moved to small Sassafras, AR. Mack and Kaitlyn struggle to overcome differing opinions on the perks of the app. But if they don't, it could keep them from something even better.

Get your copy here:

https://scrivenings.link/lovedelivered

No Place Like Home

Can love secure Adrian's wandering heart?

Roots are overrated, at least to someone like Adrian Stewart, preacher's kid, who has never lived anywhere longer than six years. That's why her job with MidUSLogIn Inc., is so perfect for her—lots of travel, and staying nowhere long enough to have it feel like home. But when work takes her to Memphis, closer to her family for the first time in years and in the same small office as Grayson Roberts, she starts to question her job, her lack of home, and even her memories of her rocky past with the church.

Gray is intrigued by Adrian from the moment he sees her, and he's determined to get to the bottom of why this girl, who loves old movies and hums when she works, won't go to church with him. As they grow closer, he wants more too, but how can he convince her to stay in Memphis when she doesn't believe in home—or God? Can he use his own broken past to break through hers?

Get your copy here:

https://scrivenings.link/noplacelikehome

Saving Grace

Michelle Wilson's one goal in life was to become a top journalist at the local paper back in her hometown of Cedar Springs, AR. But on the way to bringing that dream to reality, a life-changing wreck interrupts Michelle's plans and adds an orphaned baby into the mix. Now, she has tough decisions ahead—did God put her in that accident to save baby

Grace? And if so, why is it so hard to convince everyone else she should be the baby's new mommy?

Greg Marshall has been Michelle's best friend his whole life. He's thrilled she's moving back home, but not so sure about her sudden desire to be a single mom. His feelings for her have grown through the years, but she's never seemed to notice. Can he help Michelle with the adoption and grow their relationship at the same time?

Get your copy here:

https://scrivenings.link/savinggrace

Faith and Hope

Get your copy here:

https://scrivenings.link/faithandhope

An Unexpected Legacy

Get your copy here:

https://scrivenings.link/anunexpectedlegacy

Scrivenings
PRESS
Quench your thirst for story.
www.ScriveningsPress.com

Stay up-to-date on your favorite books and authors with our free e-newsletters.

ScriveningsPress.com

Reflecting on Christmas Past by Heather Greer

31 Daily Devotions

with Annual Reflection and Journaling Pages

Get your copy here:

https://scrivenings.link/reflectingonchristmaspast

Chiseled on the Heart

by Elaine Marie Cooper, Kelly Goshorn,

Cynthia Roemer, and Candace West

A Christmas Legacy Novella Collection

Get your copy here:

https://scrivenings.link/chiseledontheheart

Coming Soon

True Blue Christmas by Susan Page Davis

True Blue Mysteries—Book Five

Available 11/7/2023:

https://scrivenings.link/truebluechristmas

12 Days of Mandy Reno by Regina Rudd Merrick

RenoVations Inc., Book Two

Available 11/14/2023:

https://scrivenings.link/12daysofmandyreno

Scrivenings
PRESS
Quench your thirst for story.
www.ScriveningsPress.com

Stay up-to-date on your favorite books and authors with our free e-newsletters.

ScriveningsPress.com

www.ingramcontent.com/pod-product-compliance
Lightning Source LLC
Chambersburg PA
CBHW070632100726
47907CB00007B/1953